TELL ME A TALE

A Novel of the Old South

James McEachin

BERKLEY BOOKS, NEW YORK

TELL ME A TALE

A Berkley Book / published by arrangement with
Presidio Press

PRINTING HISTORY
Presidio Press edition published 1996
Berkley edition / March 1997

The Putnam Berkley World Wide Web site address is
http://www.berkley.com/berkley

ISBN: 0-425-15689-3

BERKLEY®
Berkley Books are published by The Berkley Publishing Group,
200 Madison Avenue, New York, New York 10016.
BERKLEY and the "B" design
are trademarks belonging to Berkley Publishing Corporation.

PRINTED IN THE UNITED STATES OF AMERICA

10 9 8 7 6 5 4 3 2 1

TELL ME A
TALE

one

THEY WERE DEEP IN THE uncharted back country, and when they first appeared on the horizon they looked like a couple of misplaced dots bobbing aimlessly on a sea of nothingness. And then, in the stillness of that day, late in the 1800s, the tired and head-hanging youngster led the pack-weary mule across a set of weedy railroad tracks. Together they plodded down the long and lonely road that would offer no help as it unfolded and stretched on with arrow-straight boredom. Later there was a change. Exactly as it had done the day before the late-afternoon sky swung low with another charcoal-gray chill. It thundered, and in an instant the thick November rains came, and the road, as had the roads before, became grudgingly slow—and though it did not yet bend or curve, it grew into an obstacle course. Every step now was a fight underfoot. The pebbles became more stubborn, and the rocks would not give way. The weeds, rather than yielding to the onslaught, grew in strength, reached out, and seemed to send double-edged slivers slashing at him and gouging at the mule.

North Carolina's roads had a way of becoming instantly

swampy under a good rain, and this one was no different. Indeed, it was worse. Years of neglect had eliminated the wash and crumbled the bridge to such an extent that up ahead, the old road ducked low, slipped under mire, and dared the travelers onward. But the youngster was unafraid and led the mule forward. At first he started to go where there was sure to be a bend, but the footing and slope appeared more troublesome, and so they continued on until the water became ankle-high and then knee-high and then waist-high. The trailing mule would go no farther. The youngster pulled and pleaded, but to no avail. The rain slashed down harder. Again the shrill voice reverberated in and around the long ears, and even went so far as to promise there would be a slope up ahead. But the mule would not budge and virtually hawed her response. Animal instinct told her that even if the waterline didn't get any higher, what little footing they had would not hold and getting to—let alone climbing—a slope would be impossible, and that no matter what this lost, derby-wearing, circus-looking, sunken-faced hanger-on said or did, nothing was going to change.

The youngster was right in one way. There was a slope. There was a bend.

The rain fell harder, and from the bend came a torrent of water that carried big knots of debris that knocked him down and would have done the same to the mule had her back not been saddled with three big, cumbersome packs, three kegs, and three smaller sacks. It was then that the youngster made the decision that he would free the mule of at least part of her burden, if he could only get to her. It was not that he would leave the packs or forget them. No. No, he could not do that. Never. Never in a million years. It was just that as a temporary measure he had to do something—something to make the mule's burden just a little easier. He would do that. He would take the mule upstream. But the animal became frozen in place. The youngster pulled and

pleaded, but the beast of burden would not budge. Wells of
tears mixed with the rain and flooded the young face and
every bone in his body was drenched. He stood there.
Something told him to do more than just stand there. But
that, too, had a price. Pulling desperately, he would slip,
slide, go down, and rise up again—and when he was unable
to pull, he'd hold on for a breather. Over and over he'd find
himself underwater, but the young hands would not let go
of the tether. Over and over and over again the mule
bucked and brayed, but still the hands hung on.

The sky swung lower and cracked with another booming
round of thunder, and before it was over, two sharp and
deadly wicked bolts of lightning shot through the clouds
and powered down to the nearby earth with a vengeance.
The mule bolted up savagely and shot her head around hysterically. The young body went up, over, and eventually
sunk to the bottom. But it would not remain there.

Through the mud it clawed, clutched, and struggled. *The
mule. He had to get back to the mule.* To the surface
bobbed the body, gasping and lurching. "Tessss!"

"Tessss . . ." He cried again, choking, and sputtering.
"I'm gonna let you go!"

Lightning did not favor them, because the moment he
called the mule's name, a streak that looked as if it lit up
the whole of North Carolina seared the skies and rooted itself in the base of a tree. It did not hit the mule, but one
would have thought it had. Big wads of saliva foamed and
cornered her mouth, and her body shook with rage. First the
forelegs, and then the hind legs became trapped. No matter
how hard she tried, she could not free herself. The youngster tried desperately to reach her, but he was stopped by
the elements.

The rain fell even harder, and then from the bend came
another torrent of water. The debris sent the youngster underwater again, but his concern was still for the mule.

Again he clawed from down under. Again he fought to reach the mule.

"Tessssss!!! Hold on, Tess; I'm Comin'! I'm Comin', Tess . . . Tessssss!!!!"

He had called out louder the last time because the mule was underwater.

Down went the youngster. He tried pulling on the hind legs, but that would not work. Up for air and down again, he tried tugging at the packs; up for air and down again, he clawed for the animal's head and tried to elevate it to the surface. Nothing worked. He tried and tried again. And then, at last, he came up. It was all over. Tess had been entombed.

Tess had been a good mule. Now she was gone. All he could do now was to go down and retrieve his hat and whatever sacks he could carry, and pray—oh, how he would pray that at least some of the bottles were not broken. Fortunately, he was right. Most of the bottles did survive. So did two of the kegs. And the water-protected envelope was intact. All was not lost. When he went down that last time, he did not have to check the contents of the three packs. They were unbreakable. They could survive whatever nature had to offer. Their kind had survived the ages. That in itself was a blessing.

Clarity of thought told him that everything he couldn't carry but would need later would be safe there under the water. Clarity of thought said too: Get there. Get to where you're going and do what you have to do—and after everything is over, find another mule and come back.

AFTERWARD, AS THE YOUNGSTER SAT contemplatively on the side of the road, exhausted, shivering, covered with the mushy red mud, just a few feet forward of where the bridge had been, he looked skyward at the big clouds. Clouds. He remembered clouds. Oh, how he remembered clouds. These were not the same. None could be. But favoring him now, they showed some mercy by receding and dispatching smaller drops of rain. They did not favor him entirely, because before withdrawing they sent notice that darkness was approaching. Darkness meant trouble. Here he was, muddied and bruised, soaking wet, not looking the way he wanted to look, tired, missing some items, severely behind schedule, and not even knowing if he was on the right road—and most important of all, if "they" would even be there. But what if they were not there? They had to be. What if they were there and had repented? God would not punish him in such a fashion. They were there, and they had not repented. He would push on.

Along with the sack, he would find a way to bring at least one of the kegs.

His mind went back. From the start, Tess had been a good companion, and not, as the man had said, just a good mule. She was almost—almost—as good as Bess, the mule he knew when he was, to quote another man "not much taller than a cricket's behind." Bess, too, had suffered a tragic end, an awful end. Man and mule deserved a better fate. He thought about it again; he thought about them again. . . . "A better fate." That's exactly what he meant. A better fate. Those three little words had been almost an anthem in his young life. But along with it was the word *deserving*. Not *deserve*—but *deserving*. How apt, he always thought. How appropriate. How belonging. How them. How deserving. "Deserving," he always concluded, belonged right up there with the Ten Commandments. Moses himself would have approved.

t w o

THE YOUNG MAN'S DESTINATION WAS Red Springs, North Carolina. He was going there with justice on his mind. He did not want to think of that other burg that was around there somewhere, but the new thought came and hit with such force that it slowed him. There was a similarity between Red Springs and Rennert that he had never thought of before. He had covered North Carolina like a blanket, missing only Charlotte for reasons he thought obvious. He had criss-crossed the state, going from Lumberton to Fayetteville, from Spartenburg to Greenville, from Ashville to Winston-Salem, from Greensboro to Durham, from Chapel Hill to Raleigh. He had been from inland to the coast—morning, noon, night, and day, he had trudged roads, led mules and ridden wagons, walked the railroads, and caught boxcars all the way to Philadelphia, Pennsylvania. He was now here.

He picked up the pace and tried to out-walk his thoughts. But it didn't work. It was not necessary for it to work. There could only be one place called home. The fire down below told him so.

With the hastened pace, Rennert stayed with him for a little while longer. So did unwanted thoughts of the warm and generous couple who had found him at death's door. He was shapeless then. He had no clear-cut plan of action; he had no burning objective. Even his mind, the one that showed such promise and had been admired and praised by his father and beloved uncle, had deserted him. It was the same mind that he had promised them that long ago night that he would develop and find a way to serve them. In truth, though, it was not so much that he or the mind had been deserted. He had been robbed, stripped of all things thought good. Everything he had ever known or had desired had been taken away. The deed had been so downright total and final in its ugliness, that it stained all his yesterdays, and would never push a good tomorrow on the horizon. He once loved life. But no more. He once loved nature. But no more. Once there was a time when he was so awed and overwhelmed by the sheer rightness and fullness of life, when there was so much goodness in the world, goodness with all that nature had to offer that the only way to grasp it was to lay in the greenery and soak it all in, bit by bit. Then he was able to enjoy the verdancy of all things that grew. He enjoyed the majesty of color. He enjoyed everything then, things that moved with abandon, things that crawled, insects, busy going nowhere but moving with a determination that defied the mind. He enjoyed things that flew, big-winged things that fluttered from flower to flower and things that chirped and buzzed from blossom to blossom. But no more. Even the clouds, surely numbered among his all-time favorites could no longer be enjoyed. In his formative years, almost as much as anything in the world, he had a particular love of clouds, for those big cushy clean things that appeared from nowhere and when they felt like it, used their puffed gentleness to calm a blinding sun. He loved how magically and wondrously they hung from the endless blue and toyed and tickled the imagination, and how they used unrushed grace and solemnity to glide over the land and, from afar, took time out to enrich the broad fields that came forth with their own magnificent bounty. Truly, it was the best God had to offer. And then one day, suddenly, end-of-the-world-like, it was all over. The sky became colorless, the fields were gone, and from that day to this day, the all-time favorites were but visible bodies of particles, suspended in an unwholesome air.

Metaphorically speaking, the couple tried to re-seed the field. They knew nothing about his imagination, but when they found the emaciated and lost child, they tried their best to nurse him back to good health. Physically they succeeded, but beyond that they did not know. They would never know. He did not stay with them long enough for them to know.

They were a wonderful pair, Indians they were—Cherokees, he believed—forward thinking and trying their best to make it in the white man's world. It was a cozy little shack that they built, deep in the woods of Rennert. But they were unable to work and they were being starved out. The youngster tried to ward off the thought, but he was unable to do so and wondered if they were still alive. He wondered, too, if they had ever forgiven him for not being able to stay with them. He was so young then, truly a child, and so very much different. God watched over him, and he survived. Often he would pray. At the start of this mission he prayed for guidance. The voice he heard in return was familiar and gave comfort. It was from his childhood. It was from the big black lady with the glistening skin.

"*Think*." She said it quietly.

The youngster was walking faster now. He had to think about where he was going and what he had to do. Thoughts of Rennert were fading. He had wondered if the couple had ever understood that had he been able he would have given them his heart, as they had given theirs to him. And then he thought about it. He could not have given them his heart.

He no longer had a heart to give. The last thought came. He thought about how he had been pushed into silence at the time, and didn't know if he had ever told them what had happened in Red Springs.

It was minutes away. The fire down below told him so.

It was said that in her heyday, Red Springs never experienced the pains of growing, nor did it share the simple joy of just being there. The town knew only the bittersweet sorrows of diminished yesterdays, blotted on the map of indifference.

Tiny Red Springs accepted nothing, and gave less. The sun rose, the sun set. One day would succeed another. There would be the gradual change of seasons, and another year would come and go.

HE HAD PLANNED ON LATE afternoon, but it was night when the youngster finally arrived, shouldering two of the bulky and clanking sacks, all while trying to roll-kick the modest-size keg down the middle of the road. The rain, having stopped earlier, began to fall again. It didn't matter to him. The rain could not wet or dampen the excitement that infused the young body. *There*—up ahead, there it was. The store. The engine, the core, the hub, the center of all activity—the heart and soul of Red Springs, North Carolina. The store—subject of dreams. Night and day; day and night— dreams. His dreams. There it was—beautiful, real. *There.* In reality, though, *there* was nothing more than a time-worn mass of planks pretending to be an edifice. *There* was a warped and decayed and stooped fabrication slanted precariously on the side of a bumpy and muddy road that had never known anything beyond a dismal, tiny-town existence that was now, mercifully, grinding to a snail-paced end.

Alone and aloof, there was a darkness about the place. It was further burdened by an overhang that swooped down in a two-staged maneuver and falsely claimed the title of *roof*.

But no longer. Its color, strength, patchwork, and protective qualities had long since surrendered to the Carolina sun, and all it could do now was just lie up there in a sapped indifference while holding on to a nail or two before sliding over the pillars and on down to the ground. The pillars, too, were of little help, but one of them did, feebly, manage to support the store's sign.

When the youngster was close enough to see the sign, it confirmed something beyond all wonderment. He could not read the wording, but there it was; he saw it and his young heart was pumping so fast he sent a wet hand to his chest in an effort to slow it down. He knew that the heart was the engine to life, and if it malfunctioned, everything would be over. It was a wasted and silly thought for anyone whose heart was as youthful and vigorous as his, but the urge to run or soar—or simply to just quicken the pace—was suppressed, and he decided to proceed with caution. What he did do, though, was something he always said he would do. There, right there in the middle of the lone Red Springs road, with the rain pounding on his back and the sacks, he fell to his knees and locked his fingers in prayer, "Thank you, Lord, Thank you, Lord. Thank you, Lord Jesus."

Now he could get on with the business at hand.

Quickly, efficiently, he labored the sacks around to the store's side, took a moment to collect himself, making certain his heart would remain functionally in place, and started to tiptoe back around to the front. Movement caught his eye. Hitched to the post was a mule. He needed a mule to complete his mission. This was, indeed, a day to gladden the heart.

He stopped and took another look up at the old sign that fadingly promoted C. D. McMillan's General Feed & Grain Store, C. D. McMillan, prop. He liked the sign even more because he now noticed that it had a little squeak to it. It also kept a nice lazing tempo with the rain-laced wind. Smiling, the youngster mounted the lone step and stood there on the much-thought-about stoop and searched the face of a door that showed the pains of a hundred nails. His mind slipped back to when he and Tess had started on the long journey. The first thing he thought about then was this very moment—here, now, wondering exactly what his approach would be. He had thought about, too—excuse me, he had actually *practiced*—a whole series of entrances, and, charitably, each one included the mule. The best one, he thought, was the one where he would congratulate the dear old wonderful beast of burden for getting them there, give her a big hug, cram her mouth with sugar, wrap her ears with a big red ribbon, take a deep breath, a running start and burst through the door, saying: "Here we is, folks!"

But what, his mind had suddenly allowed again, what if no one were in there? What if the ten or twelve locals who used to hang out at the store had passed on? What if all the people of long ago had moved away? What if all the Red Springers were dead? What if they were dead, dead, dead, dead, dead? It was a cruel, heartless, merciless thought, and he quickly dismissed it.

There were voices inside. The voices were not distinct, but if he could have heard them with clarity, he would have heard Silas repeat a refrain he used every time it rained.

"Lordy-lord-lord," he would say without change. "What I wouldn't do fer some hard likker an'a soft tiddy in this cold rain."

That would remind Shep to say, "That Mable shore had a soft pair."

To which McMillan would add, "An' had a rear that shook like two pigs on th' way to market."

Silas would always come back: "A b'hind that shook like moonlight on the Missi'sippi." He would take another moment and add, "I'd a marr'd her just for th' ride."

There would be a long silence, and then Shep would nudge, "Did'n she mar' that preacher-fella from Raleigh?"

"No," McMillan would generally say, moving off to the back of the store to get a log. "She marr'd that lumber mill fella from Charlotte."

"Shouldn'a let her get away," somebody would say.

"Shouldn'a let none'a'em get away."

"But they gone. All th' poon-tang in Red Springs done gone."

The conversation would die with: "J. D., y'think h'it's gonna snow anytime soon? We ain't had none in a coon's age."

"Ain't due."

Silas would bring it back: "One'a these days God's gonna get smart an' wash them li'l buggers with soap n' water b'fore he sends 'em down here. Notice how dark they was when they hit th' groun' that time?"

"Wash what with soap'n water, Silas?"

"Snowflakes."

They were the muffled voices that came from within. A confirming ear to the door told the youngster they were beautiful voices. There was a swelling inside him. He capped his muddied hands over his mouth until the swelling passed. When it did, there was a serious decision to make. What should be the approach? How should he go about entering? The words. What should be the words? But if he was unsure about one thing, he was certain about another: Despite the odds, the unbelievable odds, despite the heartaches, despite a virtual lifetime of gnawing and sleepless nights, he was where he was supposed to be, hearing the voices he wanted to hear, and that at this very moment he *had* to make an entrance, and he had to sit among them. Before moving he cautioned himself one more time. The mind—the mind. Don't forget to use the mind.

He touched the latch and set the door's hinges into a whining motion.

Just like that, a dream had come true.

three

THERE WERE FOUR OF THEM. One of them felt the chill that slid in with the opened door, and the one that was doing the talking droned to a slow stop. All eyes slid back to the source of the chill and whine. With anxious caution the youngster closed the door and stood there in a naked silence that anchored his feet and seized all thoughts of movement. For a long while he tried his best to say something—anything—but the words would not come. The mind was not working. Finally, in the effort to suppress any outward show of distress, he sent his clammy fingers to the corners of his lips and pressed them up in a position that faintly resembled a fixed smile.

In a moment, it was hoped, because of the new look, something would give, and under such an act he would join them around the potbelly stove. The moment was not yet upon them—or him, for that matter—and thus he could do nothing but hold to the one position and send his nervous eyes darting about the room.

The store, like the four of them as had been with the bridge, the sign, and everything else was giving out. There was no doubt about it, C. D. McMillan's store had all but thrown in the signal-ending sponge. The store had never really enjoyed a great day. Still, it was the end. Tobacco-stained bags of rat-nibbled feed, flour, corn meal, sugar, barley, beans, and rice lined the gloomy, barnlike room. To the rear, and under another leak, were two large, spigot-bearing kerosene drums. They were rusted and cob-webbed. The floor, heavy with sawdust, was so badly stained, the ordinary mind would have thought it was the depository of a loose-boweled horse. It would not have been the correct conclusion, because the stains were nothing more than misdirected spit—misdirected because, through the years, the aim had been for the top of the stove—for those little round, hard-to-hit lids that would take a good jaw of tobacco juice, give it the right sound and smell, bounce it merrily on top, and then sizzle it on down the sides.

It was not the sound, smell, or sizzle that had captured the youngster that evening, rather, it was the four of them: J.D., thin-featured and humorless; Silas, the only one not bearded, and a forever meddlesome and virtual nonstop talking machine; Shep, shaggy-haired and deceptively moonfaced; and then there was C. D. McMillan, the big-bellied, ruddy-faced storeowner. They were the dreamers of yesteryear—the good old days of servitude. But the times and the institution no longer existed and these Red Springers, last of the believers, last of the true back-wooders, raw, fidgety old codgers, warded off the end by sitting and standing around the stove, toeing in the sawdust, stroking beards, and soaking up heat in their narrow, cramped behinds.

With an inner fright that threatened to weaken his knees, the youngster sneezed, kicked in with a beaming smile of confidence, drip-dropped across the floor, and split-fingered a chair that was soaking from another leak. With the chair he had made it almost to the stove, when he froze and chanced a second look at them. They had not changed. Their eyes, still wide in astonishment, remained transfixed on the door. They could not have seen what they thought they saw. A color'd in Red Springs? Not only in Red Springs, but in *here*—? In the year of our Lord, 18—, 18 whatever year it is. *It* walked through the door of *McMillan's* store? At *night*? And *looking* like that? They had reason to question. They had more reason to question *its* looks. *It* was "colored," to be sure. But *it* did not have all the broad negretic features they had learned to despise those many ages ago. So, then, maybe *it* was a he. A *he* would be given the benefit of the doubt. And *he* was almost Creole-looking, not that they had ever seen a Creole, and not that they would have thought any higher of them even if they had seen one, but *he* could've been one of them. He was passable—to a degree. This one was a tad brash and nervy, and his voice and posture didn't droop with too much slackness—a non-colored trait if there ever was one. Maybe he was a lost Indian scout or something. Anything but a natural colored. Maybe something else. Maybe they were on to something. McMillan had heard there was a certain species of coloreds in South Carolina that looked, talked, and acted a little bit different from the North Carolina coloreds. He thought they were called "Gullahs" or something like that. Was he a Gullah?

The youngster had a pokerface, and eyes that created a sensation in depth. On his head, covering sandy-brown hair, danced the crushed derby. From a gooselike neck that snuck up from a frayed collar swung a loose maroon string tie. On a short, frail frame hung a used, oversized tuxedo with rolled-up cuffs that exposed heelless shoes and stockingless feet. There he stood, soaking, he and his outfit caked in the thick red North Carolina mud.

The silence in the store—the dumbfoundedness—was layered. So thick was it that the rain that fell in the back of the store and cut a path through the barley just to the right

of the sacks of flour sounded like little tom-toms giving
way to a waterfall.

The youngster navigated the chair over the last waterpath
and slid closer to the stove, joining the circle. He blew on
the soggy and saggy-bottomed cane and sat, and lifted the
palms of his hands close to the stove, thinking he would
grab a little warmth and then recapture their attention by
clearing his throat and giving them a simple "Hi'ya, fellas."
But then he decided against it, feeling that it would be best
to let *them* break the ice. Now that he was in there, and
could see them—and they could see him—why push it? he
thought. He had all the time in the world now, and he knew
the old-timers hadn't seen a strange face in years, and even
if they had, never could they have imagined this. They had
scratched, rehashed, and expertly commented on such diverse things as the weather, aches, cures, and the general
decline of male peckers and female posteriors. But never
this. The only thing that could have been of interest that
they had not over-covered through the years had been the
subject of slavery. The coloreds, Silas had stated, flatly,
"no longer was or is" and promoted the thought that a giant
dark cloud had come and swallowed up all the ungrateful
"freedom-seekin' bastids," and they would never be privy
to the good earth again and "any talk about them wouldn't
do nothin' but keep a bad memory afloat. They was dead,
gone, done with, so f'get the memory and thank God for
small favors." Silas had concluded that last bit with a touch
of irony. Irony reversed, because long before that "giant
dark cloud" had come, the same Silas had praised the same
God for the slaves, thanked him for their groundlike color,
and had gone on to state that if the Divine One had intended for him or any other blessed white man to work the
soil, he would have done the same to their color. Silas had
said that not realizing that North Carolina's soil ranged
from deep black to sandy white.

The old-timers were so silent for so long, the boy actually started to pinch one of them. Holding off for a quick test, he reared back in false but chummy comfort: "Aaah, th' charm of the old South. Ain't nothin' like it," he said, sugar-coating the charm to an empty response. He took his time, whistled a little bit, and came up with a musical "Is y'all got any music 'round here?—Maybe with a voice or two?—Sump'um kinda nostalgic? Dum-dum dee-dee. . . ."

He found himself swallowed in that same stiff silence that had crested at the door. But he had nothing to worry about because the mind was where he wanted it to be. He went back to whistling and shaking his booted wet foot. That lasted for a while, and then he sneezed and wedged himself in closer. He absently eyed the stove and said breezily, if not a mite manufactured: "I sure wish one'a these nice Mister somebodies still starin' at the door would find it in their nice li'l ol' hearts to turn 'round an' talk to a nice li'l ol' almos'-eleven-year-old soak'n wet color'd boy like the this nice color'd boy sittin' righ'cheer in front of this almos' nice li'l ol' potbelly stove in this almos' nice li'l ol' store with this almos' nice li'l ol' fire that's burnin' them use'd-t'be-almos'-nice li'l ol' logs."

It seemed like an eternity, but then, moist in a deep frost, all eyes had slipped and had fallen down, at, over, and around the young visitor. They had, in tandem, withdrawn from the door, and had been on him a minute longer than he had realized. Still, the stony silence that followed the eyes seemed to have lasted for another eternity. It would have lasted longer, but Silas just couldn't hold it any longer. His first inclination, after the youngster had sloshed across the floor, was to say: "There but for th' grace of Gawd went a duck." But he had forgotten what a duck looked like, and so he held up. But not this time:

"Whas a Nigra—?"

"Ah, ah, ah," the youngster scolded. "Not 'gra.' *Gro*."

"*Gro what?*"

"*Nee*-grow," he said, and went on to raise a damp finger:

"*Negro*. Of or related to a colored person," he said, in teacherlike fashion. "A *Colored Person*: a person of Negroid descent; of, pertaining to, or designation of a major ethnic division of the human species such as Negrito, Andamanse, and Melanesian—distinguished from members of other races by physical features without regard to language, or negritudiness. *Negritude:* an aesthetic and ideological concept affirming the independent nature, quality, and validity of black culture. *Culture:* the integrated pattern of human behavior that includes thought, speech, action, and artifacts, and depends upon man's capacity for learning and transmitting knowledge to succeeding generations." He took a breather and concluded, "Would y'all like to hear more?" Indeed the mind was working.

But theirs wasn't. They were numb. For a moment all one could hear was the rain seeking refuge inside. Again Silas felt duty bound to puncture the air. "Now, boys," he said. "Y'all know me. I know'd coloreds better'n a hog know'd Jesus. I used to be 'round coloreds nearly every day. Even helped lynch a few—an' that very thought takes me back to hearken the words of m'dear ol' granddaddy, 'cause he said this day was a-comin', if'n we didn' lynch a few more when we had the chance. But we didn't do it. I admit we was wrong. But now for me, Silas Crookashank, Americun, to sit here an' listen to some li'l black—"

"Ah, ah, ah. Yo' cuddly li'l visitor don't like that," the youngster quickly admonished. "The way you usin' it, black is a condition. I'm a person."

"That ought'a teach you t'keep that trap shut," McMillan said to Silas.

"It's mine. I kin do with it what I want."

"Gentlemen—puleeeze," the youngster interceded.

"Yewwwwwwshuttttuuuppp," they said in unison.

"I'm aghast," said the youngster.

"Keep y'behind closed!"

"Seal'd!"

Silas thought of something else. "Ain't nothin' worse than a nigger pass'n gas!"

"But, sir—"

"Don't!"

"Now, listen, boy—!" Silas said, preparing to say more, but J. D. broke in.

"Silas, he ain't gon' do nothin', now hush up so's we kin see what this fool is all about."

"You mean, see what this 'young man' is all about," the youngster corrected, easily. He said it and shifted an eye on the man, and then felt that he wouldn't do it again. Clearly J. D. was the taciturn leader of the group. He was a high-boned, emaciated-looking sort, but as far as the youngster was concerned, he was something to be feared. For sure, he would try not to look him directly in the eye again, but no matter what, this was not the time to abandon verve. "Now, then," he picked up. "I understand you are all—or rather *could* be historians."

Even Silas was delayed. "We *what*?"

"Historians—in—in a—a—manner of of—of—speakin'."

"An' that is got to do with?"

"History." And before they could ask another question, he threw in: "I know how well you've tried to hide it. But remember, build a better mousetrap and the world will beat a path to your door."

"Who you callin' a rat?"

"Ain't nobody callin' nobody a rat, Silas," Shep said.

"An' just what," Silas asked, "do you think go inta rat traps?"

Shep was stuck for an answer but sat there giving it serious thought. Moments later he was still stuck for an answer.

"Wha'cha call that there outfit thing that'cha wearin'?" Silas asked.

"A tuxedo. You wear 'em on special occasions."

"An' we special?"

"*Very* special."

The room fell into another temporary quiet. Silas knitted his brow.

"What was that thing you said we was?"

"Historians."Silas measured, "An' run it by me agin, hist'y is got to do with?"

"History."

"S'what I figgred," Silas lied, and took it a step further. "I just wanted to see if you really know'd what it was. See, when I was your age, I took a excess in that."

McMillan's face cracked. "You did what, Silas?" And then he never-minded him with a fluff of the hand, knowing as well as the others that Silas was Silas and anything he said beyond "good morning" had to be viewed with suspicion.

"Say, J.D.—y'know what?"

"McMillan, will you hush!" Silas barked. "We thinkin', ain't we', J.?"

"Silas, will you, for once in your life shut up!" J. D. said angrily.

"Please. For God's sake," added Shep.

"All y'all can just go straight to hell," Silas fired back.

"Gentlemen! Gentlemen! Gentlemen!" the youngster said, raising a quieting hand. "As historians and former leaders of the community, I find this bickering and episodic . . ."

"Epa'sawdik my rear end!" Silas flared. "An' if you don't keep your li'l trap shut, you gonna find yer li'l black rump tossed back out yonder in that rain. Y'li'l black, imp."

"*Silas!*" J. D. bellowed again.

"*What!*" Silas bellowed back.

The youngster rose indignantly. "I simply can't go on like this. I simply can't."

"Sit down and shut up!" said Silas, yanking on the tails of the tuxedo.

"If he shuts up, Silas, how'n th' blazes are we gonna find out what he's up to?" J. D. said harshly. "Now, quiet."

"I ain't doin' that. An' I ain't doin' the other. An' I don't care what he's up to," said Silas, still holding on to the youngster's tails.

"All right, then, boy. Get outta here."

"Listen, you li'l pickaninny, if you know what's good for you, you better not move a muscle," Silas said, and yanked him down, almost knocking the rest of the chair's wet cane away from the bottom. "Now, just sit right down there, and start talkin'. An' be glad I ain't got no rope handy."

"There's some in the back," advised McMillan.

"McMillan, will y'hush!"

"I'm mighty glad you got rope, sir," the youngster slipped in.

"Why?"

"Goes with the mule," the youngster said innocently.

"How you know I got a mule back there?"

"McMillan, hush!" Silas scolded. "Don't nobody care 'bout that broken-down nag. Just hush. Now, gwoan, boy; sit'cha tail right down there an' start talkin' 'bout what y'started to. An' don't stop til' I'm satisfied."

The youngster looked around nervously, almost as if seeking indirect advice from J. D.

"Gwoan," said Silas, pushing the youngster's legs around to face the stove, and thereby dropping his bottom almost through the chair.

"Well," the youngster started nervously, "what I—I—what I need from you is—is—is a li'l bit of y'alls 'community' history.—Say around 1867?"

He waited for the expected interruption, especially from Silas, but no one said anything. He shifted uneasily in the chair and continued. "Y'see, I'm a—a—writer. An' the tools of my trade is—gottem in here somewhere." He quickly sent his fingers pawing for the inside of his coat pocket.

While he was searching, Shep leaned over to McMillan. "Is we to undastan' it's now legal for color'ds to read 'n write?"

The youngster overheard it and beat McMillan to the answer. "Oh, yes. In fact, most *Negroes* are—"

"Nee-grows?"

"Yessuh. R'member: 'Of or related to a colored person?—A *colored person:* a person of Negroid descent?' Pertaining to the ethnic divisions of the human species, such as the Negrito, the Andamanse, and Melanesian? Y'all recall me just sayin' that? An' then I went on to s'plain negritude?"

Not a mouth moved.

"Good. Now, as I was about to say, sir, in response to your query—most *Negroes* are now occupied doing research on the Pleistocene period and its relationship to the existential existence of Homo Erectus to present-day man, emphasizing freedom of choice and responsibility for the consequences of previous acts."

There was a quiet. Silas's eyes danced to the ceiling. "Wonder what th' weather's like in Raleigh?"

The youngster then extracted a crumpled, much-too-small, soaking-wet notebook, a nub that represented a pencil, and an equally unfit-for-the-job, early-day version of *Roget's Thesaurus* and held them up for all to see. "*Rogret's Thesaurus!*" He announced grandly. "*Rogret's Thesaurus*—a must for the learned and the learning; a vital tool of the writing trade." He dug in again. This time he came up with a tiny, soggy, and thumb-worn dictionary. "The writer's bible," he said formally.

"Look mighty small for a Bible," Silas weighed.

"Silas!" J. D. cautioned, and nodded for the youngster to continue.

"I have these 'cause I er—er—I'm writin'."

"Writin'?"

" 'Bout slavery."

The word *slavery* pushed them into a deep, plunging, probing, double-checking tightness that caused the youngster to speedily come up with an explanation.

"See, I happen to believe slavery was a—a—a good thing. An'—I—an' I am er—er—I'm tryin'—no; *going* to convince people of that through my writin'."

The old-timers shifted somewhat warmly at the addition but still maintained a silence too uncomfortable for the youngster. Sensing a more favorable change was needed, he stood abruptly. "Ah! How utterly rude of me! What an oversight! How could I possibly expect you distinguished gents to relay the essence of your history without your being inspired. I beg your indulgence," he said, and grandly back-pedaled to the door.

"Where you goin'?" Silas demanded.

"On the other side of yon door, in the sack, lies the sweet mysteries of life. *Joie de vivre!*"

"Who?"

"*Joie de vivre!*"

"No."

"But, sir—?"

"I said no!" Silas said with much more firmness.

"But—but . . . ,"

"We don't care how minny times they 'wash d'feet'—we don' want no mo' coloreds in here!"

"It ain't colored, sir, it's somethin' to drink."

Loved it. Silas also loved what he heard earlier and could hardly wait for the door to close. He jumped up. "D'jew hear that, J. D.? D'jew hear them words? Th '*essen* of your n'story'! Wheeeeooooooweeee!"

"Never thought I'd live to see th' day one of 'em, would say slavery was good for 'em," McMillan added.

"Well, t'was good for 'em," Shep accented.

"We all know that," agreed Silas. "But I never thought

I'd ever hear one of 'em own up to it. I'm tellin' you, J.D., that boy's got a lotta smarts."

"An'a right fancy talkin' fella. *In. Dull. Gents.*"

"I don't take to be call'd *dull*, but that *gents* fits me to a T. An', J. D., did'ja see them writin' things?" Silas said, and then enthusiastically pantomimed writing in the palm of his hand. "Did just like that. Just like that, he did."

J. D. tossed a sour look his way. "I shore hope it won't like that."

"It was writin', J. D. I can vouch for it."

"*How?*" Inquired Silas.

Outside, the rain was angry again. The youngster's nose was getting a bit runny, but he was far too preoccupied to take notice. He was so preoccupied, in fact, he was actually on the side, sitting on the keg in the middle of a puddle, counting and separating bottles. The insiders were still at it.

"Imagine," Shep said, unable to get over it. "He likes slavery. Maybe h'its comin' back."

"Which I always predicted. An' for which they should be grateful," Silas said, and then shifted gears. "I wish th' boy could write. S'matter of fact, any colored who can string two x's t'gether ought'a start off writin' their apologies, just like he did."

"He didn't say he wrote no apology."

"He did!" Silas shot back. "Don't you ever listen'?"

"Th' boy ain't wrote nothin'."

"In that li'l book he helt up: *R'grets an' We's the Sorriest.*"

"Sounds like an apology t'me," said Shep.

It sounded like an apology to Silas. "Praise be!"

Praise be. It was the same phrase and same reaction he had used when he came back from Fayetteville, spinning the yarn about how all the blacks had been swallowed up by a dark cloud.

J. D. didn't say anything. He sat there motionless, refusing to say anything. J. D. was always last to comment, always wordless when something troubled his narrow-cheeked frame.

"What's ailin' ya, J.?" pestered Silas.

J. D. shook the question off and turned to McMillan. "Mac, see what that young'un is up to out there. Somethin' ain't right."

"How you figger that?"

"Hit's just too gawddamn weird. Him comin' in here soak'n wet, lookin' all crazy, and dressed up like a—a . . ."

"Rooster with a sheet on," Shep said, thinking of—and unable to pronounce the word: penguin.

"You know how minny years since anybody's come to this here town? You know how long's it been since we seen a color'd?"

"Well, I for one hope I don't see another'n," Silas said in contentment.

"Silas, won't you th' one who just said 'praise be'?" McMillan said flatly, quieting him.

"Mac, see what he's up to."

"I ain't goin' out yonder. H'its dark out there."

"You don't have to go *out* there," J. D. ordered. "Take a look out th' window."

McMillan tiptoed to the window and peered out into the darkness. "Can't see a daggummed thing."

Silas tilted his head around. "With them dirty windows and your eyesight, McMillan, you'd do a heap'a lot better goin' out an' feelin' y'way around."

McMillan fired back: "Why don't *you* go out there!"

"He won't go out there 'cause he scar't," Shep said. "He's always been scar't of coloreds in th' dark. All of y'all is always been scar't of coloreds."

"As any r'spectable white man should be," Silas said, and would have added more had he not been interrupted by the chill that accompanied the door opening. There was a moment of hesitation, and then the youngster smilingly entered, dragging one of the sacks behind him. With short, snappy strides, he moved directly for his position around the stove, dropped to his knees, untied the sack, and pulled out a gallon-size bottle topped by a wet red ribbon. "Cognac," he said, standing and waving the bottle before them.

"What in the world . . .?" McMillan started to say as he unseated himself to close the door—and take a suspicious glint outside.

The youngster held up the bottle ceremoniously high and pressed an admiring eye on the label. "Your cuddly lil' visitor has in his hands just what the doctor ordered. Cognac for my distinguished friends, and the friends of all mankind!" He took a look at McMillan and said, "An' I brung some licorice, figger'n that you might be out of it, but it got lost in the storm back yonder."

It was not that he had expected an ovation, but he had expected a tad more than what was delivered, which was nothing. The old-timers were far too riveted in a bewildered silence. But the youngster was unmoved and continued poetically. "Ah, cognac; sweet, sweet, cognac, the divine inspiration of lords and princes. Cognac, the blood of royalty; cognac, the diet of the deity—the dew of heaven and earth!" Again he waited for a reaction. It was to come from Silas.

"Boys, I'm gonna tell you somethin'," he said, breaking the spell and skirting the heart of the matter. "Yessireee— I'm gonna tell y'all somethin'. Now, I been sittin' here, quiet as a mouse. Those o' lips of mine have pretty much been seal'd since daybreak, an' they jus' don't up an' go into motion 'less they *really* got somethin' to go into motion over. Now, they jus' sent me a signal—sayin' they want to do somethin' unusual. They wants to go into motion."

"Wha'cha tryin' to say, Silas?"

"Hear me out, b'cause I'm about to break m'silence. Now, y'all know when these lips a'mine get itchy, there's more'n just fleas in th' soup. It means there's somethin' in th' soup ain't worthwhile eatin'—which means it's time for ol' Sile to take some unusual steps. It's time for ol' Sily-boy to start talkin'. Now, I a-sumes—I said I A-*sumes* y'all is ready f'me to crack th' ice, so to speak. I . . ."

"Silas?"

"What?"

"Please crack th' ice."

"I said I a-sumes—said I a-*sumes* y'all know when I start talkin'—an' do speak, in the few little words that I do speak, when I happens to speak, I speaks b'cause I speaks th' truth. When you hear ol' Sile say somethin', you know you can d'pend on it. Th' few times I decide to say some-thin', you know it is a well-thought-out process that I go through. I don't talk just to be talkin'. I'm a thinker; a lis-tener, which is the onlyest complaint my grandma ever had agin me. She said, 'Sile, you is too much of a list'ner. Too much of a thinker. Open up. Spread it around.' An' I said to her, 'Granny, I'm gonna do that—in due time.' I said th' day is comin' when I'm gonna stretch out, an' ain't gonna do nothin' but spread it around."

"Get to it, Silas!"

"Shush, 'cause all y'all is in deep luck. Today I'm finally gonna do what I promised m'dear ol' granny. I'm gonna do somethin' she thought I'd never do. On this here day—not t'morra, not th' day after, not next week, or the week after, not next month, or th' month after, not next year, or th' year after, or what follows after th' year after that follows the years after—but today, I'm gonna start spreadin' it around. On this here day, Silent Silas Crookashank, righ'cheer in McMillan's . . ."

"*Gahdammit*, Silas!" J. D. shouted.

"What?!"

"Will you get to the gawdang point!"

"*If* you would stop interruptin'!" Silas shot back heat-edly. "Now, like I *started* to say before jealousy overtook me. I ain't much for words. I ain't never been much for idle chitchat, an' when I say somethin', you know I mean every word of it. That's why I say it. When I tell you somethin', you can take it rightsmack to the bank, 'cause m'word is a good as gold. When I—"

"Silassss!"

"Allll right! All right." He was lost for a moment. "Now, where was I?"

"You was in th' bank," Shep reminded him. "But I don't know how, since we never had one."

"Or use for one," added Shep.

"Finish, Silas! An' I mean finish!" J. D. said.

"I'm gonna finish because I want to and NOT b'cause *Somebody* tells me to, but," he said to J. D., and recasting an eye on the youngster. "There ain't but one way of puttin' it. Pure an' simple: This nigger's crazy."

The youngster sputtered and almost dropped the bottle. "Sir!" He sputtered again. "I beg your pardon!"

"You can beg all you want," Silas said flatly, and leaned back precariously in the chair. "But, nigger, you crazy."

The youngster's face froze indignantly. "Why, I never!"

"An' I ain't either," Silas said, finishing the sentence for him. "But you can be sure of one thing. Nigger, you is out of your cotton-pickin' mind."

"But surely one of such condition would not attempt to gladden the hearts of his fellow man by offering him cognac."

"To begin with," Silas said, still leaning back, "I don't know what'cha talkin' about. In this part of the country, we speak Engl'sh."

"I was merely using the best of the language to offer you the best of drinks."

"An' that was your second mistake," Silas countered, and prepared for an arm-folding silence. "Your first was comin' in here."

McMillan checked with the quietly observing J. D. and then at the youngster. "Where'd you get that bottle?"

"I brought it with me."

"I can see that. But where'd you get it from?"

"Fayetteville."

"An' what'd you say was in it?"

"Cognac," replied the youngster as he displayed the label and seal for all to see. "I brought it for all y'all. An' see, it still's got the seal on it. It's real good stuff, I promise you it's real good stuff. Th' best drinkin' in the world. Try some."

Silas couldn't resist coming back to life. "We don't take to drinkin' with nigs. Nigs or any other kind'a foreigners."

"Sir," the youngster bristled. "You are insultin' the drinks of kings."

"I ain't never seen no king drinkin' it."

"That's 'cause you ain't never seen no king." J. D. said, breaking his silence and thereby doing much to further matters.

The thirst-growing old-timers knew that if J. D. was a reluctant talker, and even more reluctant over the youngster, he certainly was not a reluctant drinker. In his heydey—and before the canehobbler came to town—the stringbean of a man could outdrink the best Red Springs had to offer. And seldom was the day when he didn't wake up and down a quart before breakfast, and by sundown one was apt to find him plastered under the cornstalks. Anybody's cornstalks. But it had been years ago, long, bleak years, since the sweet flow of liquor had traveled his veins and sent his head to uncontrollable heights. And, too, it had been years since Red Springs had run dry, but, even so, like them, he had not forgotten the surge. So then it was good he had spoken up with a tinge of want in his voice.

"Let J. D. take a look at that bottle," Shep said eagerly.

The youngster, still a bit fearful of the thin one, held the bottle up for the taking. Silas had thought about reaching for it, but held back in favor of not appearing too eager. Shep did the honors.

"Exactly what is this here cognac?" J. D. said, removing the bottle from Shep's hands, and not exactly appreciating the notion that he was not the first to hold it.

"It's the best, sir."

"Th' best *what*?"

"It's likker, ain't it?"

"Oh, yessir. Cognac's a brandy, distilled from the wines of Charente and Charente-Maritime. But I forgot. The preferr'd pronunciation is cone-ee-yak-ee."

"Cone-ee-yak-ee. That's it." McMillan, the store owner, said, faking knowledge. "That's the real stuff, all right."

Silas couldn't hold back. "McMillan, how would you know?"

"It's a storekeep's solemn duty to know these things."

"It was also you solemn duty to learn how to read," said Silas, knowing it was not necessary to go further.

"Silas, you better keep a hog's distance away from me. I'm tellin' you for th' last time."

Silas leaned over restfully. "And then what?"

The youngster, thinking combat was imminent, pleaded, "Gentlemen, please."

"Yeeewww, shut up!" Silas blared, and tilted his chair forward. "Come to think of it, just who is you? Where you from? An' how come you know so much anyhow?"

The youngster shifted uneasily in his chair and started to say, "Well, sir—" but just as he was about to speak, J. D., after having studied the contents of the bottle, cleared his throat, held the bottle in the air, and shook it vigorously.

"Better go a mite easy on that, J.," Silas said with a cautiously anxious smile.

J. D. shook the bottle again.

"Howz she set, J.?" asked Shep in an overly friendly voice, and clearly indicated his willingness to be the first to taste the contents.

J. D. gave him a noncommittal look, returned the bottle

to the original position, and pretended to look away somewhat disinterestedly.

"Well?" said McMillan, hopeful of comment. But none came.

Silas exploded: "Gaddammit, J. D., is it good fer drinkin' or not?"

J. D. took his time, finally grinned, and broke the seal.

"Long time, no taste," said Silas. There was an enthusiastic grunt from Shep. McMillan decided he would wait until a more positive step was taken. It came.

J. D. grinned a little more, looked at the youngster and said, "What is it you wanted to know, boy?" He said it, and then to everybody's delight, he downed another healthy swig.

"I want to know a little of your community history— 'round 1867."

"That was a very good year, son," Silas said, keeping the contents of the bottle well in mind and sight, and at the same time leaning over and patting the youngster on the head and fatherly stressing the word *son*.

McMillan took note: "Silas, you ain't nothin' but a hypocrite. A back-slidin' hypocrite."

"I bet'cha one thing, I won't be a thirsty hypocrite," Silas said, now warmly smiling at the youngster and then taking further note of J. D.'s thirst. "I a-sumes—I said I *a-sumes* whatever is in that there bottle is all right fer me to be a-drinkin', eh, J.?"

J. D. took another drink. "It is."

"Y'mind," Silas said with fractured patience, "y'mind passin' it this a'way."

"I do."

"Well, you know," he said musically, "my lil' friend didn' bring th' bottle here just for you."

Shep agreed. "H'its for all'a us, ain't it, son?"

The youngster nodded. "Yessir. All y'all s'pose to drink hearty."

"Now, son," Silas warmly advised, "that ain't hardly enough likker for me t'be drinkin' hearty."

"But I got some more."

"You *what?*"

"I got some more outside. Lots of it."

"Why, you lil' angel, you," Shep joined in.

"Bless you, m'boy, bless you.—You look a lil' chilly, an' I notice y'nose is gettin' a lil' more runny. Look like y'might be gettin' new'–moany. Move on in. Get a lil' closer to some'a this heat."

"Silas, don't go blessin' an' heatin' 'em 'til we get it," McMillan said, "'cause the way J. D.'s goin', he'll drink a well dry."

"He ain't th' onlyest one who'll drink somebody dry," Shep accused.

"Don't be pointin' the finger at me," McMillan countered. "I never did drink as much as you. Fact, I didn'—and *don't* drink as much as anybody in here."

"That's because—in fact—you can't get it now," Silas said.

"I can make it if I want to."

"With what," Silas wanted to know. "Th' still's been busted for more'n eight years."

J. D. sleeved his lips. "Wouldn'a been if you hadn'a overloaded it."

"It won't overloaded," Silas retorted. "Th' mixture was too strong."

"An' you wanna know why? Whoever told you mixing cow dung with kerosene would make mash?"

"McMillan, th' trouble with you is, you never think modern. You take that there stuff in that there bottle there— what'd you say was in it, son?"

"Cognac. Pronounced 'cone-ee-yak-ee.' "

"Umhuh. An' that is—?"

"Brandy."

"An' you said brandy is made outta—?"

"Wine."

"An' wine comes from—?"

"Grapes."

"An' grapes is fertilized out of what, McMillan?"

McMillan refused to answer. "Plain ol' horse manure," Silas said, answering his own question. "An' if plain ol' horse manure is n'directly good for wine, then plain ol' cow dung is directly better for whiskey."

"Silas," Shep said dryly. "One thing's for certain. Ain't nobody else in this world like you. You the onlyest somebody I know who could look up a cow's rear an' tell the price of buttermilk."

"And when she's due," Silas said contentedly, and then sent his eyes wandering over to the bottle.

J. D. winked. That was a good sign. J. D. never winked when he wasn't pleased or when he wasn't ready to tease or make fun with Silas. "Mighty fancy-tastin' stuff, Sile. Must be m'ported," J. D. said as he took another belt. This one was a lot healthier than the last, and he almost caught the youngster off balance. "Speakin' of 'ported, where'd you say you was from?"

As the youngster had done once before, he sat there molded in an almost-stoic silence, staring at the flames that slithered through the vent openings on the stove door. McMillan had noticed this earlier and shot a participating look at the not totally unaware Shep. If they were puzzled, in a sense they had reason to be. The youngster had undergone several changes in the relatively short period. He had gone from the hesitantly buoyant charm of his entrance, to clumsy, ill-at-ease statements, to a remarkable quickness and sureness, to a seeming knowledge of them, and from the usage of rural black patois to varied stabs at eloquence. Under the circumstances it was only natural for him to have been fearful, and, of course, it was only natural to combat the outward show of fear through the age-old art of smiling—which he did at the outset, and while his cherubic poker face did not undergo a radical change, it seemed to have become frozen in a masklike exhibition of pleasantness. But his eyes were a different story, and even though they remained youthfully alert and magnificently hazel with that odd tinge of green, they nonetheless were devoid of a true inner happiness, and they seemed to have found contentment only in the direction of the rising flames.

McMillan repeated J. D.'s question. "Where'd you say you was from?"

The youngster shook his head from the fire in an almost sleep-awakening gesture. He heard the voice, but not the question. He had to be careful. He had already slipped once or twice—such as letting them know he had an interest in the mule, when, as a visitor, he should have had his own. And now with the cold, wet, and tiredness taking its toll, he was allowing his stamina to sag and his concentration to wander, and he was not being the catalyst. He had to be careful, too, because he had allowed them to occasionally drift too far afield, and that was not good. There was a long, long way to go and they were old and energies were easily sapped. Keep alert, he admonished himself, keep alert. "Er, what was the question, sir?"

"I said," McMillan said pointedly, "Where'd you come from?"

"Oh, er—er—I just came here to, er—check on a year . . ."

"It was 1867, you said."

"Yessir. To find out what happened. To find out a few things."

"About th' slaves." It was not a question.

"Yessir. About th' slaves."

"But slavery was over in 1867."

"That's just the point, sir," the youngster said, confusing them just a bit.

" . . . An' you say that slavery was a good thing?"

McMillan asked with growing curiosity, and then with another look to Shep, "An' you writin' to spread the word."

"Oh, yes, sir," he said with pleasant emphasis.

"Well, you a nigger after my own heart," complimented Silas as he unconcernedly interrupted the flow of questioning.

J. D. brought the bottle down again. "What brings you to Red Springs?"

"Well, sir," the youngster began without looking at any of them directly. "I was, er—um, er—see, I er—left home an' went t-t-to—Fayetteville—researchin'—an'—an' somebody told me th' name of this—Mr? Mr. Archy—"

"Archibald McBride?"

"Yessir. Mr. Archibald McBride."

A quick and hard silence fell over the room that lasted much too long to suit a young man already wired in seeming uncertainty. Now he could not look in their direction even if he wanted to. But they were not afraid to look at him. And they did. And they looked at one another, suppressing comment. Finally J. D. took another drink. Silas sent another mouthful of tobacco-induced saliva bouncing on the stove lid. McMillan watched the dancing spit for a while and then picked up a log and prepared to fuel the fire.

The youngster's uneasiness grew even more, but he had to press on.

Without urging from them, he mistily added, "I wanted to write about him because it was people like him that ruined the good institution of slavery."

"Oh?"

"Yessir. 'Cause he was a disaster. Y'might say, Archibald McBride killed a way of life."

"An' a fine howdy-doo-to-yew-too, suh," bumped Silas.

"Yessir," said the youngster more freely. "An' if th' good institution ever comes back, people'll know who to watch out for."

The added statement added more sparkle than a new-placed log on a fire. The old codgers were relatively comfortable now, and tacitly agreed that the young visitor was definitely on the right track. *He was a bit peculiar—but who knows what the world is comin' to? And despite his weird dress and hazel-eyed look and even stranger ways, he just might know something. He certainly could do no harm; and, as stated, he harbored no ill thoughts. He had no right to, because if slavery was at all bad—and it wasn't— but if it was bad at all, it still could not have affected him all that much—he was too young; so young, in fact, that maybe—just maybe he could be representing a change in policy. I mean he's free—but he ain't talkin' freedom. He's colored, but he ain't black. He ain't black-black either. So, then, he could be a mediator, or somethin'—like a go-between between the blacks and the black-blacks. History will prove that the black-blacks were treated shabbier than anybody else involved, but they loved slavery. Nobody ever listened to them. They were uprooted, dispatched, and freed without anyone giving a good gawddam. And that was wrong, hurtful, killing. The simple black moaned about freedom. They were part human, and somebody, quite rightly, became concerned. But they mistakenly allowed concern to transfer itself into appeasement and that was wrong—hurtful, killing. The nation had been torn asunder because of this folly, and it would take years to rectify itself. Because of the appeasement of a few—the blacks—a tradition died; the life of the South placed in jeopardy. The experiment failed. Admit it. Let's all admit it and move on. Let's get the country back on track. Let's show some concern for the black-blacks. They want to come back. Let's let 'em! Ignore the blacks, let the black-blacks come back an' everybody's happy. No more wars, natural disasters, or assassinations. The South will reclaim its rightful place of leadership, and the country will be on the move again. Rally 'round the flag, boys, we just found the solution. We're going to reinstitute the institution!*

"Praise be!" delayed Silas.

"Praise be to Jesus!"

"A special occa'sun!"

J. D. took another drink.

"Thank you, sirs."

"Is that th' way th' dress for special occa'suns in th' big sidy?"

"Oh, yessir. Got to," responded the young visitor. He knew that the old-timers had never seen a tuxedo before, perhaps a derby, but not a tux. It was wet, muddy, stringy, and despite having shrunk a tad, it was still about three sizes too large, but it did not faze him. He stood up, briefly readjusted his tie, and made a point of properly parting the long, dragging tails, and sat back down in the chair with the wet, giving cane. "Always wanna look y'best for special occasions. . . . Now, er—er, you gentlemen *did* know Mr. er—Archy—er, this er, this—this scalawag?"

"Y'gawdang right, we did," Silas said with rising indignation. "We know'd him, an we should'a cut his pecker off. We should'a cut it right off. That's what we should'a done. 'Cause he was ign'ant, just plain ign'ant. Th' damn fool. We should'a tied him to a tree and cut that lil' mike'cracopic worm he called a peed'r right off!"

The youngster swallowed uneasily. "That's—that's a—that's a rather harsh thought."

"Been even harsher if I'da thought about it at the time."

"What," probed the youngster gently, "what did this Mr. Archy do?"

"What he do? What'd he do?" Silas flared without answering the question.

"He turn't th' gawdamn slaves loose, that's what he did!" Shep said.

Silas came back: "An' it all start'd when he laid eyes on that there color'd heifer an' ended up lettin' her blow in his ear. That's the ver' minnit he start'd goin' crazy."

"But wasn't slavery over when he freed them?" inquired the youngster.

"It had done *been* over when he dunnit. That didn' make no difference. Th' slaves didn't know it! How'n hell's anybody gonna get any news down here. He didn' have to turn 'em loose! They ain't know'd nothin' about that there feller signin' them there papers."

"But they would have found out," said the youngster with more innocence his voice.

"When?" McMillan questioned. "Hell, *we* didn't know it 'til two years later. My granny never did know there was a r'loutionary war!"

"Mac?"

"Huh?"

"I'm s'prised that her grandson knows about it."

It took a while, but McMillan finally got it and then sent a hard look at Silas. He then moved to the rear of the stove for another log. Shep continued to eye the bottle, Silas unloaded another mouthful of tobacco juice on the stove and smeared dripping lips with the back of his hand, and said quite casually to J.D., "Say, J., you ever stick it to that first cook Archy had?"

J. D. gave it a dismissing thought and unthinkingly held the bottle out to Shep's outstretched hand. "Can't seem to r'collect."

"What about that fat fieldhand? Th' one that used to stand out there in th' fields like somethin' crazy, tryin' to get the others stirr'd up."

"An' quite properly died of a stroke. What was 'er name, Mac?"

"Elsie, sumthin' or 'nother. . . . Sweet Elsie Pratt! That's it. But r'member she didn' die of no stroke."

"Not 'less she died twice."

"Whatever. She was a big blob of blubber if there ever was one."

"Aw, groan an' tell th' truth, J. D.," McMillan said from the rear of the store, taking time out to rearrange a tub of rainwater. "You know you had that cook."

"I don't r'member none'a them people."

"Ain't nothin' for you to r'member. If Archy had it, you tried to get it."

"Oh, there was a couple of 'em that slipped by."

"I don't see how."

"Don't be pointin' th' finger at me, Shep, you won't no angel, y'self," J. D. said, reaching for the bottle.

"He'd a been a angel if Arch had'a caught him try'n to rub on that other gal's rear," Silas said. "Ol' Arch would'a wrapped a halo 'round his b'hind."

"Y'must be talkin' 'bout that Charlotte," McMillan said, returning to the stove.

"Umhum. That's the one," Silas said without so much as even attempting to clear for the wood. "I ain't never seen a many so crazy 'bout a black woman in all m'life. I 'member th' day he bought her at the auction: 'Stand back, everybody! Lemme through lemme through. Don't touch the merch'ndise. Don't put'cha a hand on m'goods!' Th' damn fool. You'da thought he was bringin' somethin' home that could give fresh buttermilk. Even when she was standin' on the auction block I didn' like her. Never seen a slave so uppity. She was even stannin' up there on th' block makin' up her own price! A slave sayin' what she won't an' what she will sell for! Stannin' up there actin' like a Amuricun! I never could stand her m'self."

"Silas?" McMillan said.

"Huh?"

"It t'was th' other way 'round. She could'n stand you."

McMillan knew that it was an accurate reminder. And despite the look, so did Silas. But J. D. was still commanding the bottle.

"Gawdangit, J. D., Gimme that bottle!"

"When I'm ready, Silas!"

"I want that bottle, an' I want it now!"

"You ain't gonna get it now!"

Silas leapt up, almost knocking the youngster's chair

over. He remained calm. "Gentlemen, I told you there was more where that came from."

Silas looked at him wordlessly, and then narrowed an eye, set for serious business. The youngster's move was simple. He leaned over, dug in the sack, and easily withdrew two more bottles.

Silas sat back down; his face broke new wrinkles. "Hee, hee, hee, boy, you is about to kill me with kindness. Cone-ee-yake-ee. Right under this ol' nose a'mine. I like that, hee, hee, hee. I like that. Hee, hee. I'd like it even better with some pickles."

"Thank you, sir," said the youngster, still holding the bottles and clumsily clanking them in his lap. "But, now, is it possible to talk about Mr. Archy's last days?"

Silas reached for a bottle. "Why, shore."

"An', Ben's, too?" said the youngster tactfully and before releasing the bottle.

The old-timers didn't like the youngster's last request.

J. D. asked, "Why Ben?"

"What's he got to do with this here thing?" Shep asked.

"Oh, er—er, well—there was certain kinds of slaves that weren't good for slavery either," the youngster replied.

"Oh? Well, it's Archy's *first* days, *without* Ben, that we'll talk about. *If* we talk a'tall."

"Yes, sir. But from a writin' point of view—"

"Now, you hold on. We know what we want to talk about, an' what we don't," Silas interrupted, fully aware that more bottles had clanked in the sack.

"Yessir, but concentrating on Mr. Archy's last days. Think of what you'll be doing for slavery. You just can't have th' white side of th' story. You gotta have th' Negro's, too. . . . Colored's. Sorry."

"Listen, boy, if you want th' hound to hunt, you better . . ."

"Oh, please, sir. Please. I gotta have the *whole* story. Everybody's story. Please talk about, unc—I mean Ben.

Please, y'all—you gotta include him in the story! Please. It won't be real without him. We gotta have him. We jus' gotta."

"You testin' my patience, boy. It's *our* way or hit th' door."

"Please don't do that, sir." He was almost crying when he said it. But the fire down below told him he was placing every single thing he had worked for in jeopardy. Wisely, he relented. "Okay, we don't have to talk about him. Ben was just an' old hump-backed servant. Ignorant. Useless. A weed. Certainly not good for the image."

"A low-down, good-fer-nuthin', broken-back African scalawag if there ever was one," Silas said. "An' I repeat— *if* we do any talkin' a'tall, it'll be about Archy. This is a white man's country. It'll be a white man's history."

Suddenly the youngster bolted as if stricken with a thought. His eyes widened. "What if—what if—" The solution was close, but not completely there. He had to fully work it out in his mind first. He got up, circled the stove, and bypassed a couple of water-catching buckets. He returned to his wet seat, rubbing his hands urgently. He blew on them a few times, sat, stood up, marched to the back of the store, came back, and sat again. Something was really brewing. The moment grew. He stood, and then exploded: *"Yyyyesss!"* The voice hit with such a force, the old-timers almost ducked for cover. In fact, Silas got so concerned that he got up and went to the back of the store to relieve himself in the hole next to the basket of onions.

"Yes! Yes, yes, yes!"

The youngster repeated the yes-yes-yes's no less than thirteen times. Each time they were accompanied by a jerking, accentuating body motion that except for Silas making preparation back in the corner had the old-timers thinking true safety was being on the other side of the door. "Why didn't I think of this before! What a solution! Great! Sparklin'! Am I on a roll, or not?! Gentlemen: Here's what

we got—an you're just gonna love it to death. Toooo death!
What if—what if . . . Oh, boy, this is jusssst great! It's
tooooo good! Sensational! . . . What if your cuddly lil' visitor told you the story? Huh? How 'bout that?! You sit back,
relax, keep th' home fires burnin', an' let yo' cuddly' lil'
almos'-eleven-year-old visitor be yo' guide to th' past.
How 'bout that? I tell *you* the story! Let *me* tell *you* the
story! Let's see if the information *I've* pieced together is
correct. I'll tell *you* the story with the clear-cut under-
standin' that you have the privilege of stoppin' me at any
point if I am wrong. Mind you, what I'll be sayin' comes
from talkin' with the good *white* folks in Fayetteville, and
from my own lil' ol' imagination. Now, naturally I won't
write everythin' I say, and I wouldn't write anythin' that
would tend to 'unfairly' bring disfavor upon you. An'
sometimes what I'll be sayin' will be to confirm certain
facts—confidential facts. Agreed?"

They were caught in his enthusiasm, but they wouldn't
agree—just yet.

A little more selling was needed. "I see teamwork in our
future. You keep on sippin', and I'll keep on talkin'—
tellin' a tale that was dear long ago. An' in the end? History
will have to recall how fittin' it is."

"Don't quite get'cha, boy," McMillan said.

The youngster, feeling that he had said a little too much,
started searching for a response. Fortunately J. D. interceded.

Feeling little or no pain, J. D. requested another bottle.
The youngster eagerly complied, knowing that another one
would put him over the top. That was all that was needed.
J. D. was the leader, and if J. D. went along, the others
would go along. Still, before he cracked the seal, the thin
one slipped him a question he thought he had already
answered.

"Where'd you say you was from?" he asked in that cold
voice.

"Er . . . um . . . er—Charlotte, sir. . . . I'm from *Charlotte*," the youngster replied.

"That's a long way for a colored to be trav'lin'," McMillan said with suspicion.

"A *mighty* long way, sir."

"How long'd it take you to come from Charlotte?"

"Nine months."

"To come from Charlotte to Red Springs took that long?" Shep said, wide-eyed.

"Yessir. To come from Charlotte took *nine* months."

"An' this here likker, this cone-eey-yak-ee, what's somebody like you doin' with it?"

"Th' gov'nor gave it to me," the youngster said, hoping for a sale.

"The who?" Shep prodded.

"Th' gov'nor."

"What's he do for a livin'?"

"Er, he's th' chief officer of the state."

"State?"

"Like *ham* n'eggs?"

"Er, no, sir. *State*. A territory. North Carolina is a state."

"Oh."

"An' I was on th' gov'nor's—th' chief officer of the state's staff back in Fayetteville," the youngster said.

J. D. said, "Doin' what?"

"Overseein' th' tobacca plants. Oooops, s'cuse me—overseein' the tabacca *processin'* plants."

McMillan said, "Hot damn! Hotttt damnnn! Y'all know what that means?! If they processin', that means that th' machines is here an' they runnin'. Th' machines is in North Carolina! They'll be in Red Springs b'fore you know it! I better start gittin' the store ready. An you actually *seen* th' machines?"

"Yessir. Makin' cigars an' cigarettes."

"Praise be to Jesus!" Silas grunted from the back of the

store. He was now peeling an onion while squatting low and grunting hard over the hole.

It was Silas who tightened his posterior muscles, scorched his tonsils, but it could have been anyone of them—including J. D. For years they had heard about the newfangled machines that was going to revolutionize the South. And if it was in Fayetteville, or any of those big cities—surely Red Springs couldn't be far behind. What a great, great, great day a'comin'. Give 'em all another bottle, son. No. Now is the time for the keg. Go get the keg and roll it right down the middle of the store, through the puddles and on down to the stove. And then go on with your story, son. Go on with your story. But first:

Silas asked. "Wha's in that keg?"

"Beer."

"That dog won't hunt."

"Wha's in them other things?"

"Alcohol."

"Likker?"

"Yessir."

"How would you like tu a'proch this story, son?"

"Th' beginnin' of th' end."

"Th' floor is yourn."

"Thank you, sir. Now, y'all notice I have a slight cold, an' my voice might get a little weak. An' sometimes, when I'm sayin' things, it might sound like I got a lump in my throat and tears in my eyes—but it's all due to th' cold."

"Er, I might find m'self th' same way, son," Silas said. "Whenever I think of Archy and darkies I allus gets a lil' tear in m'throat an'a lump in my eyes. Th' cold only makes it worse. Er—is that 'nuff drinkin' there to carry me through?"

"Should be, sir. If not, durin' intermission I'll get more."

"Boy, that's why I likes you," Silas said, rearing back comfortably in his chair with a foot on the keg and a spare bottle under his arm. "Like I said, you thinks like a white man. Gwoan. Finish killin' me with kindness."

"I intend to," the youngster slipped in quickly. "Now, I must say at the outset that I do believe and strongly suspect that you gentlemen are, in your own ways, all heroes, but you're just too modest to admit it. I think you claim—an' rightly *deserve*—the title of heroes, because you have altered the course of history. There has been a change in Red Springs, and you are responsible for it."

But he could not go on with the story without interruption. Silas said, "Seee, seee, seee. I told'ja. This boy thinks like a white man."

"Thank you, sir. Now, as to the story itself, I am led to believe that many years ago the sun was shining brightly on the outskirts of town. The slaves had long since departed—"

Silas said, "Hold up there. How do a 'leven-year-old runt know what th' sun was doin' here minny years ago? An' about them slaves—er, Shep, pass me that other bottle of cony'akki."

"Silas, gaddmmit!" J. D. said. "You already got a bottle in your hand, one under your arm, another one under th' gawdamn chair, an' y'damn foot on the keg! Now, will you shut up an' let this idiot get to the story, f'gahdsakes!"

"If you gonna tell a story, y'might as well get it right," Silas said.

McMillan said, "What difference do it make to you what th' slaves was doin'. You ain't never had a plum' nickel to buy one nohow!"

"An' you ain't, either," Silas said. "Ain't non'a y'all sittin' 'round this here stove had 'nuff brains or money to git no slaves!"

"I had 'nuff brains to get this store!" McMillan said.

"This heap?" Silas said. "This thing'd make a pig puke and give rats th' runs."

"It sav'd your b'hind more'n once!" McMillan said.

"Aw, hush!" Silas said. "You ain't doin' nothin' but showin' off in front of this lil' frog-faced young'un!"

"Gentlemenz," the youngster said.

"You. Shut. Up. Hush. I'm tired of listenin', anyhow."

"If he hushes, Silas, how'n th' blazes is he ever gonna tell the damn'd story?! Now, go on, boy," J. D. said.

"An' hurrup," Silas said.

"Thank you, sir," the youngster said. "Now, then, the slaves had long since departed. But before that, Miss Mildred, the lady of the house, had died of her own hands. Her main slave, Charlotte, ill-reputed servicer of Mr. Archy, and mother of Moses, had died during childbirth—giving birth to Moses."

Silas said, "Keep it simple, son. Keep it simple."

"Yessir. Main slave Charlotte was succeeded in death by the beloved slave, Sweet Elsie Pratt—fearless midwife to all the slave womenfolk, and teacher and helper to all the slave children."

"Elsie Pratt. That sassy, fat tub o' lard. Glad we put her outt'a misery," Silas said.

"Silas, will you quit it," J. D. said.

"It's *my* history."

"It ain't your history," J. D. said.

"It's Red Springs's history," McMillan said.

"An' I'm a citizen of?" Silas asked.

"Dammit, Silas!," J. D. said.

"Dammit, y'self!"

"Shut up, Silas!"

"I shall continue when you gentlemen are ready."

"You will continue *now*, or you will hit the road!"

"But, sir—?"

"C'tinue, young'un!" J. D. said. *"Without* no more interruptions!"

"Thank you, sir. Now, the effects of all this had severely crippled Mr. Archy's plantation. Still, the fool Ben, th' old hump-back black—son of Africa, the second largest continent in the Eastern Hemisphere—"

"Where'd y'say that was?" Silas asked.

"Gahdammit! Silassss!" J. D. yelled.

"South of Europe and between the Atlantic and Indian oceans . . ."

"S'too close to th' store for me," Silas said.

"Silas, for once in y'life, please—please shut up!"

"Now, Ben would . . . every day of his life . . . be in the harsh fields laboring. Main Fool Mr. Archy, his only task in life on those rich, beautiful mornings of long ago, was simply to rise, and, as was his custom . . ."

f o u r

THUS IN THAT STRANGE SETTING did the strange copper-colored youngster with the strange eyes and odd dress tell his story.

He was not the simpleton the men had thought. This was a master storyteller at work, and he spoke of many things, his voice aging with the telling. Trancelike, he sent their minds back, way back. He touched on the history of Red Springs, the early days of slavery, the arrival of Mr. Archy, and of a place just outside of town, the plantation.

The main body of his story began with the quiet of an early morning when the sun, just making its appearance, deepened the greenery and made the entire world a place of beauty. Even Red Springs. It was nothing short of remarkable. His description moved their minds slowly; from over the expanse, all the way to the tips of row upon row of sky-nodding cornstalks. And then, slowly, hypnotically, he focused in on an old and decrepit shack, or farmhouse if you will, that fittingly backdropped the panorama. It was Ben's house, Mr. Archy's loyal laborer, still there after the days of slavery, still beholden to a lonely old white man who had long ago sopped him of will, spirit, and freedom. But the oldsters were not permitted to tarry, and he ingeniously led them well away to the big house.

It was the plantation, magnificent in its day, but again, as he said, its day was no longer here. Like everything else, it suggested the days of slavery, the days when the linen-suited plantation master would ease out onto the porch and send his eyes sweeping in the black dots toiling in the un-limited fields. Like a work of art, the stubby plants of the genus nicotiana stretched on and on, running even beyond the puffed downy fibers called cotton with its oil-rich seeds and caressable whiteness. Standing over all, said the boy, was the corn. He was most detailed and passionate in talk-ing about the corn and the stalks that used to stand tall and sentrylike and would sometimes send their leafy arms out to touch innocence as it raced to a creek that was not too far away. And one time, he said with a strange sadness in his voice as he gazed at the stove's fire, the cornstalks retarded progress. They slashed at innocence. The old-timers did not understand this, but he talked on, as he was now not to be questioned.

Again and again he reminded them that the days of beauty were no longer here, and that everything around the big place had suffered. The house had been reduced to ruin, seemingly sticking together only because of memory. Fit-tingly, it was set deep in a circular yard, and two huge oaks shadowed it in ghostlike fashion. Most of the windows were boarded, and those that were not were too stained to permit the free flow of sunlight that angled through the bare tree limbs. The weeds licked uncontrollably at the base of the old place, laid claim to the yard, and had now gone so far as to reduce the once-manicured walkway to a path. At the end of the path and just off to the left, before getting to the opening that led to the cornfields, there was a modest grave site with two headstones curiously facing each other. And there was a further oddity: One of the headstones was somewhat well attended with a patch of flowers that sprouted from its base and boasted the inscription, *CHAR-LOTTE—MY LOVE*; the other had been totally neglected. The small inscription read: *MILDRED R. I. P.* And it seemed as if someone had had second thoughts about the "R. I. P." because the lettering had been prankishly defaced.

But if the outside of the big place was bad, the inside was a complete disaster, with no place being worse than the kitchen. It was dark, dirty, dingy, and, according to the young storyteller, it was where Mr. Archy spent most of his time.

ARCHIBALD MCBRIDE WAS CROTCHETY AND pushing hard on the last of the good years. Thin-featured and bowed, he could often be counted on to mumble suspected bits of profanity while he moseyed around the kitchen packing a lunch. Judging from the concerned and caring manner in which he sliced the bread, measured the lettuce, and counted the crumbs, he gave the impression that he was preparing for a day of fishing. But the impression was quickly dispelled when he picked up his rifle, ritualistically blew on it, snugged it under his arm, grabbed the bag, and ambled out into the hall. As always, he would stop in the big, dreary living room and focus an eye on one of the two faded portraits that adorned the mantel above the fireplace.

Sometimes he would stand for minutes staring at his beloved Charlotte, a bright, ever-smiling, bouncy black girl who could not have been a day older than eighteen. Impishly attractive, it was suggested that she had been a slave, but she definitely was not cut from the slave mold, mostly because her big, bright, mischievous eyes hinted strongly at the happy-go-lucky devildom of "uppityness."

In direct contrast to her, and slightly to the sun-starved rear, was the hard face of Miss Mildred, a sternly seasoned, and, at all costs, a not-too-easy-to-digest, ruddy-faced white woman.

Miss Mildred, as she had preferred to be addressed, sort

of typified the wives of the period. And though, in life, she had unquestionably been *Mrs.* Archibald McBride, their eyes would never meet, and thus Mr. Archy would always leave the room in reasonable peace, and always he would come back, give the photo a second thought, curse the memory, and drift back out to the porch. There he would take a long, sun-squinting look off into the fields of tobacco and corn. The distance would reduce Ben, the sweating, field-laboring, hump-backed old black, to a dot. Always Mr. Archy would withdraw the look with a frown and amble off the porch in the opposite direction; always he would follow the path that led to the gravestones. Always he would stop and give Charlotte's headstone a lovingly warm pat. Always Mildred's would receive a nose-bending frown, and, then, always he would amble on to the distant and weedy creek that snaked around the vast acreage that separated the cornfields and stretched all the way to his laborer's shack. Yards upstream, and without any wasted motions, he would survey the area and drop to his knees and eye the water. Then he would dip a finger in it, taste it, frown, and stand, cussing to the high heavens. Still cussing, still frowning, still eyeing the creek, still retasting the finger, and, in his mind, still feeling the same sensation in his mouth, he would back away to another prearranged spot along the same patch of weeds at the edge of the creek and assume the duck-hunting position. And there, the bent old man would wait. Soon the boy would come.

THE BOY IN QUESTION WAS Moses, and Ben was his uncle, and in the winter, years ago, when times were slow and when he was no longer summoned to the big house, the uncle would counter the briskness of the hard winds by stuffing the cracks of the old place with burlap and by dutifully positioning himself in front of the kitchen stove and quite suitably spin out countless tales as to how he, with minor help from Gen. Robert E. Lee, had won a distant

war. Ben was great in those days, leading the hard-riding,
saber-swinging cavalry romping across dusty borders, seiz-
ing commands and thundering on through a host of nooks
and crannies before charging up hill after hill to victory.

Ben was indeed great. Anyone able to sit around a stove
and re-win a war that had never occurred, stage battles that
had never been fought, *had* to be great, and was worthy of
commendation. The commendation would come in the
memory of Moses.

Pathetically, Ben had never even been close to a camp, a
saber, a cavalry, or even something as lowly as a canteen.
Because of who he was, and what he was, and like all the
rest of the slave-reared farmers tucked away from the rest
of the world, the poor old man had not been anywhere,
ever seen anything, or done anything except greet the sun
by plowing, or hoeing, or seeding, or weeding Mr. Archy's
vast and stubborn soil. He had learned of Lee and the war
only through overhearing some of Mr. Archy's visitors.

But the boy, Moses, didn't know this, and surely he
wouldn't have cared. There was no reason for his young
mind to have been saddled with such an issue as sifting fact
from fiction. All that concerned him was that they, without
doubt, were the best stories imaginable. Though no even
slightly accurate, they were the kind of stories that quick-
ened the boy's pulse and fired his imagination to such an
extent that when summer came, he would sit on the porch
and stare out into the broad fields of swaying corn and convince himself that the stalks were a mass body of enemy
troops on the move. Quickly, he'd find his hoe, shove it between his spindly legs, slap his hip, and holler, "Giddy-up!"
In an instant the long ride would begin. Methodically, he'd
go around and around the front yard, kicking up whiffs of
dust, and then he'd widen the circle to include the huge oak
that cornered the porch. Then, picking up speed, he'd round
the house, encircle the pump and the outhouse. Now, like a
true cavalryman, he'd zip through the shed, cut across the

road and nip the edges of the tobacco plants, and then he'd
slap with full fury through the rows and rows of cornstalks.

It would be a long while, but the boy would eventually
reach the last row of corn. He felt the sensation of victory.
After resting and palming away the little beads of sweat
that lined his forehead, he would clutch his "horse" and tip
across the thickets to hunt for a few berries. Then he'd
mosey over to the creek. It was right then and there, according to Mr. Archy, where he would commit his third and
most grievous wrong. The first two centered around his
having nothing to do but race up and down the cornfield
all day, which, at times, the elder man could barely tolerate—not out of kindness, but out of a simple state of confusion. But the third wrong was not acceptable in any fashion.
And what galled him most was the fashion in which it was
done. The boy, according to Mr. Archy, would stand at the
creek and permit the mud to ooze through his toes and all
over his feet, and then, quoting the man, "He'd whip it out
an' pee in it."

This was not a totally inaccurate observation.

There were times when the boy would slip out his little
slightly less-than-dark instrument, finger it sweetly, and
arch a thin and salty mixture with the larger and more
pleasantly colored body of water. But it did not occur quite
as often as Mr. Archy had alleged. First of all, it was a
physical impossibility. The boy just didn't have it in him,
and even if he did, Mr. Archy was not always around to see
what was going on (or, as the case might have been, coming out), even though he was not beyond trying. Thus Mr.
Archy's routine of getting up before sunrise, packing his
lunch, stumbling to the creek, and tasting the water explained why he spent so much time at sunrise hunched over
and glinting for the boy through parted weeds.

Unfortunately the position wouldn't last much longer
than sunrise. The intensity of the sun, the lulling constancy
of the creek's flowing waters, and the stillness of the woods

ll conspired against him and robbed him of his vigil. The ld man would inevitably roll over and sleep for hours. Worse, though, he was quite capable of snoring with all the ndiluted robustness of a bull, which worked against him as ell. Sometimes the boy would be "giddy-uppin" through he last rows of corn, hear something that sounded very uch like a wounded bull, and waste no time getting back the old farmhouse. There were times, too, when Mr. rchy's snoring wasn't operating at full volume and the oy would come, rest his horse, tip across the thickets, luck the berries, stand in the mud, slip it out, quite nicely lieve himself, and head for home.

Not that he had ever been, but it was nice not getting aught, thereby preventing the distinct thoughts of a long, ollar-tight drag back through the fields, depending, of ourse, on the strength and mood of the old man at the time f apprehension. But aside from that, there was no real eed to rush, because shortly after sundown, and after Ben nd the mule had shuffled in tiredly and settled down, Mr. rchy would pull his buckboard into the yard and say that e caught the boy, anyway. This did not happen frequently, ecause some nights the boy would be there when the uncle ulled in back, eagerly waiting to feed the mule. Some- mes the boy was so eager he'd take the hay on the inside f the shack, hoping that the mule would have good enough nse to come inside and get it. Disappointed, he'd swing ut of the back where a door once stood:

"Think she can eat all'a this, Unca Benny?"

"Think so, son," the uncle would say without the benefit f checking. The boy would plop the pile down on the round. Then the uncle would look. "Should'a put it in th' ough, son."

"But if she can't eat it off'a the table, Bessie likes to eat ff'a th' ground. She wanna be like a horse when she grows ."

"If she told you that, she's th' damdest mule I ever di
see."

This exchange would cause the boy to look at the mul
as if to say "Bess, tell 'im what'cha like."

But more often than not, Mr. Archy would be there
waiting out front. Ben knew it. Without even seeing him
Ben knew that just before dark, the man would be there—
waiting. The old black man would stop whatever he wa
doing and shuffle to the front, go up on the porch, slump
down in his rocker, and wait on the man who did nothing
all day. Mr. Archy wouldn't rush it though. Taking plenty
of time, squinting his eyes in the direction of the porch, set
ting the mood, Mr. Archy said, "Caught the boy pee'n i
the water again, Ben."

Ben, not believing, not disbelieving, not pushing, no
questioning, chiming delicately: "Sho can't unnerstan' that
Mr. Archy."

"Ain't nothin' for you to understand. Th' water'
salty'er' n hell," Mr. Archy would assert flatly, and creal
down from the buckboard, simultaneously waving of
Ben's mild effort to come down for an assist. There woul
be a long silence, and then he would plod around to the rea
to check and see if the mule had been fed. He would the
continue. "Bet he even pees in that well over there."

"No'e don', Mr. Archy," Ben would say, having traile
the man. And speaking as if the hard, brutal days of slaver
had never left.

"In the bed?"

"Nosuh, Mr. Archy."

"Where's he do number two?"

"Nowheres, suh."

" 'Nowheres, huh?' Damdes' thing I ever seen in m'life
runnin' up an' down the fields like somethin' crazy, pee'
on everything." He would then shove one hand deep int
his hip pocket, and run the other one along his long, sag

ging chin, and lead back around to the front of the house. "What we gonna do about him, Ben?"

"Aw, he alrigh', Mr. Archy."

"I still say he ain't gettin' th' proper tendin'."

"He is, Mr. Archy."

Ben would climb back up to his rocker, allowing the man more thought.

"I can do a lot for th' boy, Ben."

"I knows it, Mr. Archy."

He'd take more time. And then he'd say slowly, "Would be somethin' if I took him, huh, Ben?"

"Sho would, Mr. Archy," Ben lied.

"S'pect I better leave well enough alone. S'pect I better stop this fool talk, huh, Ben?"

"S'pect so, Mr. Archy."

Mr. Archy would move closer to the buckboard, search the air, and dig deeper: "What's he do all day, Ben?"

"Ooooh, 'bout th' same as any boy'd do," Ben would sing. "Lotta runnin' an' jumpin'. 'Bout th' same as any boy'd do, I s'pose."

And then he would turn: "How come he ain't learnin' how to work the fields, Ben? How come he ain't learnin' how to work 'em like you, an' like the others used to do? You can't work them fields by yourself. That's why this whole goddamn place is a wreck. It used to be th' biggest and best kept place in all'a North Carolina. People used to come from miles and miles just to see Archibald McBride's plantation. An' now look at it! It ain't nothin'!"

"It needs workins, Mr. Archy."

"It needs workin', an' one man can't do it all by hisself. How come you don't take that young'un out there. Why ain't he out there, Ben? Why? How come he ain't out there, Ben? He ain't big enough to lift more'n a tobacca leaf, but how come he ain't out there?"

"You tolt me not to never take 'im out there, Mr. Archy."

"Yes, I did," he would say absently. "Yes, I did, didn't

I? You're right, Ben. You're right." His mind would wander, taking plenty of time before saying anything else. Then, when he finally spoke again, his body would seem weighted and his voice dropped almost inaudibly low. Then it would rise. "S'pect she wouldn't like it, him being out there. S'pect she wouldn't like it at all. An' ain't no reason for him to be out there. Ain't no reason a'tall. An' I don't wanna catch him out there, y'hear, Ben. Y'hear me? I don't want him ever out there. Even when he grows up, I don't want 'im out there in them fields, y'got that, Ben? Y'got that?"

"Yessuh, Mr. Archy; he won't never be out there. I promises you that."

He would lower the voice again. "I owe the woman too much. I owed the boy's mother a lot, didn't I, Ben?"

"You owed her a lot, Mr. Archy."

"Sure owed that woman a lot. But y'cant say just 'cause I didn't get th' chance to pay her, I forgot her. Y'cant say that. Nobody can ever say that. An' nobody can say there's been another woman in that house 'cept Mildred since it happened either. An' there won't be another one in that house as long's I'm livin'. Ain't that right, Ben?"

"S'right, Mr. Archy," Ben would say, as if he had a choice.

"She was a good woman, won't she, Ben? A damn good woman. Won't nobody could walk in that house an' take care a'things the way she used to do. Never had to tell her what to do. She'd jus' walked in an' did whatever needed to be done. Just like it was her own. Guess in a way of speakin', it was hers, huh, Ben?"

"Guess so, Mr. Archy."

"She was a good woman an' that there feller was lucky to have somebody as good as she was. But y'know, speakin' of him, somethin' deep down inside of me tells me that I owed him a little somethin' too. I mean, sometimes I get to thinkin' about the whole thing an' I wonder if he ever understood. Ben, you was a slave. Would you've understood?"

"I would'a understood, Mr. Archy."

"He didn't mind, did he, Ben? You think he did? Maybe he did mind, but he never said nothin'. Never said a word. Said nothin', and just went on an' did his work. An' did it real good too. Like yourself, Ben, he just went on an' did what he was s'pose to do. An' then he left."

"Left without sayin' a word, Mr. Archy. The onlyest slave of yourn to do it."

"T'was a long time ago, huh, Ben?"

"'Long time ago, Mr. Archy."

"Seems like only yesterday. Guess that's 'cause it's been botherin' me more'n more lately. I ain't 'shamed to say it hurts me. It hurt me then, and it hurts me now. But I'm gonna tell you somethin', Ben. I ain't gonna worry 'bout it no more 'cause Lord knows if anybody's paid for doin' wrong, it's been me. Ain't nobody in these parts done paid the price I have. I gave up everythin'. Everythin', didn't I, Ben?"

"Everythin', Mr. Archy."

"Everythin' just so's I could get a little piece a'mind. An' th' thing is, everybody, every man in th' South's, done th' same as me. But ain't none of 'em paid the price I have. Now, I ain't tryin' to say that all the white men's done had babies by colored wimmins I ain't sayin' that a'tall. But I do say all of 'em had a colored woman. An' I know for a fact that when most of 'em found out that the woman was due, they got rid of 'em, babies n'all! Did you know that, Ben? Did you know that? Well, they did! An' if you don't believe me, I can take you on th' other side'a Red Springs an' show you where some of the bodies was thrown away or burr'd."

"I done heard 'bout 'em, Mr. Archy."

"Dang right, you have, an' so's everybody else. But they look at me as though I'm some fool for not doin' the same.

But I didn't. I didn't, an' I'm proud to say I wouldn'a done it for nothin' in the world. An' I hope the boy grows up with enough sense to understand it too." He would pause, and sadly add: "Hemorrhage to death. What a ghaddamn way to die."

But on that, Ben would say nothing.

Mr. Archy would let it soak for a while and then he'd recharge. "But dammit to hell, it's killing me. I tell'ya, it's beatin' me to death. Oh, I know what you're thinkin', Ben, I know what you're thinkin'. You want me to think about the boy. Well, I done thought about him. Ain't a day goes by that I don't think about him, an' you know what? I don't give a damn about him. If it wasn't for him, it wouldn'a happened. She'd still be here. Look at 'im. Look at 'im, Ben! Do he look like me? Do he? Do he look like he was worth a life? Do you die givin' birth to somethin' like that?! Do you? Y'gawddamn right, you don't! Look at 'im! What'n th' gawddamn hell would I do with somethin' like that? What would I do with a little black-ass young'un? I'll tell you what'd I do! I'd go plum' crazy. Crazy! So keep 'im outta my sight, Ben. I don't care what you do with 'im, just keep 'im outta my sight. He's yours. Make 'im do what you want 'im to do. He belongs to you, Ben. He ain't mine. The boy belongs to you, Ben." He'd let it go and say ever so wistfully, "Lord, my God, how I wish she could've been saved."

"Wish so too, Mr. Archy."

The conversation would die again. From the rear would come the head-hanging youngster. He would slip an eye on the man commanding the scene and climb up on the darkened porch to snuggle up to his uncle. Purposely, Mr. Archy would not notice him.

"What a night that must have been."

"It was a rough one, Mr. Archy."

"A goddamn plantation full'a slaves, an' you couldn'a

find one of 'em. An' when you got back from lookin' for help, it was too late."

"Too late, Mr. Archy."

"An' not a midwife in sight?"

"Not a one."

"An' it rain'd that night?"

"Storm'd."

"That's why I hate storms to this day."

"Me too, Mr. Archy."

"If"—he tried to collect his thoughts—"If only you could'a found—what was that loud, fat one's name?"

"Elsie Pratt. But she won't here at th' time."

"If you could'a found somebody like her—somebody—*anybody*—somebody that could'a taken charge—somebody who knew 'bout birthin', Charlotte wouldn'a—she'd still be here—She'd still be alive."

"She'd still be alive, Mr. Archy."

"An' you had to d'liver th' boy by yourself."

"By m'self."

"All alone."

"All alone, Mr. Archy."

"All alone. An' from a dead woman."

"Yassuh."

"Poor Charlotte," Mr. Archy would always conclude. He would collect himself and climb back aboard the buckboard. And say quietly: "I loved her, Ben."

And Ben would be just as quiet: "I knows you did, Mr. Archy."

He would pause again, and then he'd say, "I never loved Mildred."

To which Ben would reply, "I knows you didn', Mr. Archy."

Now he would clutch the reins. The heavy air of nostalgia would take its toll. "Ben," he would say. "Ben—Ben, do you remember what y'all used to do for me?"

"I 'members, Mr. Archy."

"Do you think . . . ?" He would not lose the thought; rather, he would sit there, searching the air. Prolonged moments, and he'd ease back. "Do you think . . . Ben, do you think you could do just a little bit of it for me now? Just a little bit, Ben—just a little bit for the bossman."

"Yessuh, Mr. Archy."

And from out of the darkness of the porch, the tired old broken-backed black man would sing to the beat and conscience-stricken white man:

> *"Go down, Mo'ses*
> *Way down in*
> *Egyp'lan'. . . .*
> *Tell ol' pharaoh*
> *To let*
> *My peeple go. . . ."*

And as this was sung softly, together the two minds would roll back to what someone had referred to as the good old days. The good old days of slavery, when his plantation stood as a symbol of the South: big, white, and proud and sprinkled nicely with obedient, sunup-to-sundown blacks toiling at the land. Those were the days when he confusingly ruled, when he could, in secret, love an insouciant black girl but would not permit the others to leave the boundaries of the plantation. They were the latter days too, when he would not allow them to go as far as tiny Red Springs in fear they would find out that slavery had, in fact, been over for four long years. He was not there at the start of slavery, but he was there on time. He was there, and, in his first few years after marriage, he ruled when the good and decent—the linen-suited as well as the putrid and smelly—would drift in for a visit, and he would dispatch Ben on the mission of rounding up all the female slaves so that the visitors from "the big sidy" could be properly entertained. And if they didn't feel so disposed, he would trot out into the fields to round up a few of the more physically endowed male slaves for the females so that the "big sidy" visitors could watch a show of unrestricted lewdness.

And those were the days, too, when, prompted from God knows what, he would order the slaves to momentarily stop their back-breaking work and surround his porch with song.

It did not have to be on a moonlit night:

> *"Go down, Mo'ses,*
> *Way down in*
> *Egyp'lan'. . . .*
> *Tell ol'pharaoh*
> *To let*
> *My peeple go. . . ."*

"An' I let 'em go, didn't I, Ben?"

"Yes, suh, Mr. Archy."

"If Mildred had been livin', it never would'a happen'd, would it, Ben?"

"No, suh, Mr. Archy."

"She didn't like a damn thing I did, did she, Ben?"

"No, suh. Mr Archy."

"Did you ever know anythin' that woman want'd, Ben?"

"Never know'd, Mr. Archy."

"Neither did I, Ben. Neither did I." He would wait, and then he would say, "I long for the old days. . . . But I did somethin' good, didn't I Ben?"

"Yes, you did, Mr. Archy."

"I did somethin' right."

"Real right, Mr. Archy."

"Ben—Ben—Ben, do you think—Ben, can you—? Ben, do you—could you just—just a lil'bit?"

He did not have to finish the question.

Again—low, and haunting:

"Go down, Mo'ses,
Way down in
Egyp'lan'. . . .
Tell ol'pharaoh
To let
My peeple go. . . ."

"An I let 'em go didn't I, Ben?"

"Yes, y'did, Mr. Archy," Ben said quietly. "You let 'em go."

"Night, Ben."

"Night, Mr. Archy."

The boy snuggled in closer to his uncle, and was equally quiet in his delivery. "Night, Mr. Boss man," said the boy.

But the man on the buckboard did not want to listen.

He was gone. If they didn't eat, Ben and the boy would retire for the night. The full measure of darkness would swing down and clamp a special kind of silence on everything except the frogs, the crickets, and the mosquitoes.

The rest of Red Springs, North Carolina, would sleep.

f i v e

TIME PUSHED FORTH A MODEST but welcomed change on the plantation. Before the days of servitude were over, Mr. Archy had acquired a few additional slaves from a farmer in nearby Shannon who had drunk himself into bankruptcy. With the added help, Ben no longer had to go and nurse the fields on Sundays; he did, however, have to spend a few hours at the main house, tidying up a few odds and ends, and covering areas overlooked by the house staff. But those chores were generally over well before noon, and Sundays, in the main, would find him on the porch relaxing in his rocker and somnolently sifting through a batch of youthful questions. The boy, Moses, had not quite reached the age where he could tie things together, but it was at that time of life when the world was expanding and Ben was no longer able to avoid questions about Mr. Archy, and more important—to him, at least—he was no longer able to romp across the dusty battlefields and charge armies without question. Not that the boy doubted him, or that the stories were any less spirited or interesting, but it was a matter of youthful syllogistics that prompted him to ask more questions.

"Un'ca Benny," he asked one typically beautiful and lazy Sunday afternoon as he sat on the edge of the porch undoing a knot he had tied on the hind legs of a petrified frog. "Was Mr. Archy ever a gennel in th' army?"

"Heavens, no, boy. Whatever made you think of somethin' like that?"

"'Cause he's always tellin' you what to do."

"That's 'cause my position's changed."

"If it hadn'a changed, could you tell him what to do?"

"I could."

"Sho' wish you was a gennel."

And with that, the frog croaked once and lightly hopped away.

The frog, though, pointed to one of the little oddities of Sundays. Ben did not mind the boy playing with frogs or worms or anything else he normally entertained himself with. But on the day of the sabbath he didn't want the rough stuff. No running or jumping or stories. It was, he contended, against the will of God. This was odd, because the boy had once asked him about New Hope Church and Ben had replied, rather tautly, "T'aint worth talkin' 'bout." The issue was closed.

Ben's attitude toward the church no doubt stemmed from the attitude the church members had toward him, which dated a long way back.

Hints of freedom were in the air back then. Understandably, it was a time of utter jubilation, and in those incredible, those wild and hectic days, laced with whooping and shouting and singing and merriment that seemed like they would never end, the blacks did not hesitate to praise God to the highest. Every single night, New Hope Baptist Church bristled with activity. But Sunday was the day of all days. No self-respecting black would let high noon shine upon him outside the door of New Hope Baptist. The aged, the weak, the crippled, would hobble into New Hope, and in most cases, be more than adequately prepared to spend the day listening to—and for—the word of God. They did not have nor could they read hymnals or Bibles, but Reverend Terrell, fired as no Baptist preacher in the whole South, would unleash a sermon that would have the congregation shouting beyond all measure. Monday morning would roll around and all the working "how-do-u-do's" would be reverently flavored with such comments as:

"Sho' was a good Sunda' service we had, won't it?"

"We re-new'd."

"Freedom day is a-comin'."

"Glory!"

"I feels it. I feels it! *Good God a'mighty, I feels it!*"

There was one person, however, who was not renewed, and did not "feel it" at all: Ben. The blacks had tossed him out of favor long before thoughts of obtaining freedom, at that time charging him with such diverse and unseemly activities as snooping, snitching, withholding information, and for being overly subservient to Mr. Archy. The conflict gained impetus one Sunday about a year before freedom was granted. Out of the spirit of good fellowship, a missionary group extended a "conditional" invitation to Mr. Archy's main man to attend a brief evening service. Mainman Ben waited almost a year before honoring the invitation, but he did it on a Sunday morning.

New Hope was not a beautiful church. Owing to a lack of proper building materials and workmanship, it leaned toward the distressed side. To the Red Springers, although it could not be seen from the main road, it was an "eyesore." Worse, in their words, it was an "escape hatch that sits plumb in the middle of Archy's place betwixt the road and Red Springs right where we can't see what's going on."

The observation was not entirely correct. The church, sitting not on Mr. Archy's property or even Red Springs's land, for that matter, was built on the "no-man's" section just forward of a swamp, which discouraged escape, and the church's main function, which it did with commendable

struggle, was to serve as a place of worship. It was not de-
signed for anything else.

Again, like any slave-constructed church, New Hope was
a church of hope and spirit, and it rightly merited the best
Sunday finery—which, essentially did not differ from the
weekday finery of overalls and torn print dresses. But at
least the attempt was made to wash them in a kettle of soap
made from lye and grease or something of similar potency
before Sunday morning rolled around.

Ben's grunt of the year before finally led to a visit. When
he slow-walked up to the door that sweaty and humid Sunday morning, he was dressed—and smelling—no better
than he would had he scheduled a visit to the nearest pigsty.
Sweet Elsie Pratt was heard to say that there was enough
dirt under his fingernails to grow groceries. Whether the
observation was true or not had never been established. It
was known, however, that the moment he walked through
the door, the politely nosy and surreptitious head-turnings
normally associated with congregations were completely
abandoned. Necks strained and eyes rolled as though Satan
himself had breezed in. And just about like Satan would
have done, Ben nonchalantly strolled on past the eyes,
necks, and intended-to-be-heard "ooooohs," and plopped
down on the deacon's bench, tossed a thick wad of tobacco
in his mouth, and sat uninvolved throughout the ceremony.
When it was over, still like Satan, they politely but firmly
escorted him down the aisle and out the door. Ben, needless
to say, never returned to New Hope. So against the church
did Ben become that one day, while visiting the store,
McMillan had asked him when and where the slaves held
their meetings. Ben told him everything he wanted to
know.

It would prove costly.

Ben would have remained aloof and in relative isolation,
spending his time on the fields or in his shack or some-

where around the planation had it not been for Sweet Elsie Pratt.

Sweet Elsie, as she chose to be called, was a two-fisted, nonprized ex-slave from "the big sidy" of Lumberton, North Carolina, population: 985. She was proud, heavy-hipped, and an avid snuff-dipper. After escaping (with secret blessings from her former slavemasters), Sweet Elsie arrived in Red Springs after having fallen woefully short of her original destination of New York City, some five hundred and eight miles away. But not being one to let such an insignificant thing as misdirection upset her, and thankful because the swamp hadn't consumed her, Elsie more or less decided to make the best of outer Red Springs and set about the most improbable task of blending in with the rest of the slaves at Mr. Archy's plantation while importantly and quite incorrectly assuming there was a price on her head. It would have been somewhat disturbing for Elsie to have learned that all three of her masters had, in fact, planned her escape for months and were quite displeased she was slow in taking the bait.

In what had been an extraordinarily short period of time though, and while strategically remaining out of Mr. Archy's view, Sweet Elsie managed to install herself leader of the tiny-town slaves, and some say that had it not been for her leadership, Mr. Archy never would have released them, which, of course, lends itself to serious doubt. While Elsie might have been responsible for prodding the slaves to think about freedom, it was not through her initiative, or the slaves, for that matter, who had caused Mr. Archy to free them. But to the dear lady's credit, she came to the plantation with a knowledge of something the McBride slaves had no knowledge of: freedom.

Bold for the times, she was primarily responsible for the many uneasy "freedom" meetings that were held in New Hope, and on the fields she brought to the plantation spirit and color.

In a lot of ways, Sweet Elsie Pratt was a born leader. She had a strong voice and a face that glistened, and when not troubled, could have been described as jolly and infectious. But the face could not benefit from the attributes because most of the time it was kneaded in agitation and aggravation. As a speaker she was a stem-winder. No one could pull her off stage. At the meetings in church, and always speaking from the pulpit and in a voice soaking in condemnation, she would always start with the question: do you know what freedom is? No matter how many times she asked the question there would always be a lone, thin voice, more than likely coming from the church's last pew. The voice would take forever to speak out the word "no'am," and you could almost see it ducking back outside as it answered. But the no'am, meaning No Ma'am, would start it. Elsie would rear back from the pulpit, and voooom. Eight minutes of salty impieties would get her warmed up, and then she would be just about ready to launch into a subject that, at about the time she was through, would have her breathing as though coronary arrest was imminent.

The subject would be the white man. Sweet Elsie Pratt *did not* like the white man. Church etiquette aside, she would cuss him and all that was his. She would cuss him, his mother, his father, go easy on the children, come back and cuss his relatives, his possessions, and anything he might own in the future. She would fall back and cuss any and all of his ancestors, foreign and domestic. There was not a thing about the white man or the white man's family tree that she found acceptable. There were times when she got so carried away with her dislike of the white man that Reverend Terrell, New Hope's pastor, knowing better than to make the approach on his own, would signal the deacons to sit her down. Getting Sweet Elsie Pratt to sit down was not an easy assignment. Very often the deacons, having made the approach with fear and head-hanging dismay, would find themselves in the same category as the white man, and she would take a swing and send the pastor and the deacons scrambling. One day she took a swing, she missed, picked up the pulpit and sent everybody running. When she finished, there wasn't anything left in church but the sound of the tambourine. And that was coming from outside. It was in the path of the running congregation.

It was said that it was because of Sweet Elsie that the church had come under several attacks by the Red Springers. More than likely it was true, but Elsie couldn't be stopped. She brazenly decided to hold the meeting in what she thought was the less obvious place, in the direct center of Mr. Archy's fields. Naturally the meetings were supposed to be top-secret and therefore did not include Ben. He and Mr. Archy would have had to have been deaf not to have heard her, because even out there Elsie had a voice that rang like a cannon. When she laughed, as she sometimes did, or stressed a point, or reached back for an apt description of the white man, she sounded like a cannon exploding. The biggest boom, however, was reserved for when she talked about Ben and Mr. Archy, so the trick as learned in church, was to pump her with as many niceties as possible during the course of the meetings, and at all costs, avoid mentioning Ben and Mr. Archy and the white man.

For some reason during that last year, it seemed that Sweet Elsie had mellowed, because she actually spoke to Ben in a civil tongue once. In fact, she was the one who had extended the original invitation to Ben to attend church (ironically it was she who extended the original arm in escorting him out of church that muggy Sunday afternoon). Elsie probably would have ignored Ben altogether had it not been for a rumor that popped up sometime later concerning Mr. Archy having fathered a child by a cute, far-too-young, and much-too-frisky housekeeper who had rejected her slave lover in favor of the plantation owner.

Worse, Ben was keeping the child because the young
mother had died during childbirth.

Sweet Elsie thought such a thing too preposterous to be
believed and probably would have passed on it had it been
anyone else other than Mr. Archy. Since it was him, and
knowing that the man couldn't be trusted, she decided to
investigate—as any good busybody would have done.

Taking the mile trip and catching Ben in the fields one
particularly hot and dry afternoon, Elsie got one of the
more sudden shocks of life when she learned that not only
was there truth to the rumor, but that the girl had died during childbirth, and Ben was there when she died. To soothe
matters (surely with Miss Mildred in mind), Ben tried to
give a halfhearted explanation. Elsie wouldn't have any of
it. She screamed, cursed, and called him every name in the
book. She rolled up her sleeves, threw up her fists, and
dared him to defend himself. He couldn't.

"*Where's th' child?!*"

"He wit' me, Elsie!"

"Wit' who! I don't see no baby 'round here!"

"He at th' house."

"What house?!"

"My house."

"Your house?!"

"S'where he is. He can take care'a hisself."

The response was so outrageous she could no longer
speak. Instead, she grabbed Ben and almost threw him on
the wagon. All she could think about was seeing a tiny,
crib-size infant wrapped in swaddling clothing and crying
out for maternal care.

When the wagon pulled into the yard, the boy had already completed a jaunt through the fields, and had made
his customary deposit in the creek and was now back, nap-
ping comfortably on the porch.

Elsie, upon seeing the stretched out figure, screamed:
"Lan' sakes alive, boy, where you come from?!"

Almost like one would greet thunder, the boy rolled over and opened his eyes, focused, and scrambled to his feet. "Hi'ya, Un'ca Benny," he said, flashing a what-you-doin'-in-so-early grin, and then extending a courteous who's-you nod to the fat visitor.

Elsie was flabbergasted. "S'that him, Ben? Is that him?"

"Yep, that's him," Ben said proudly.

"H'it just can't be," said Elsie. "You shore that's him?"

"Umhum," said Ben.

"Where you from, boy?" Elsie asked.

"The cav'ry."

"Th' who?" Elsie asked, not having the slightest idea who or what the cavalry was.

"Th' cav'ry in th' army."

"Oh, you don't say? An' how long is you gonna be with us?" Elsie asked.

"'Til th' nex' war."

It was love at first sight. She absolutely adored him, and her questions were endless. *What'cha name? How'd you get'cha name? How old is you? Where y'been hidin'? Is Ben been good t'you? How's your eatin'? Been t'church? Wha'cha do all day? Is Mr. Archy been by t'see you? You wanna go home with me?* and on and on. She concluded that he was a "smart, lil' fella," hugged and kissed him royally, and vowed that she would always be there for him.

And he was smitten with her. Sweet Elsie had hugged him, kissed him, and asked him questions. No one had ever done that before.

From Sweet Elsie's point of view, it was fortunate that he was a "smart lil' fella." Had he not been, and was more like the helpless infant she had imagined, Ben and Mr. Archy would have been in trouble. On the way in from the fields, Sweet Elsie had made up her mind to take the child. Unknown to her, such an act could have been accomplished only over Ben's dead body, and because he stood in the fields in seeming helplessness did not mean that under serious threat of losing the boy he wouldn't have challenged death itself. The point being that his attitude in the field was just another oddity in the long line of inextricable things about Ben.

Happily no other problems arose that day and, ironically, what had started out on a note of utter hostility flowered into something special for all of them; for as the day drew to a close, the fine, uncharted seeds of need had subtly taken hold, and when Elsie left well after midnight, something wonderful nibbled at her—as it did Ben—and it was an altogether new and different feeling. It was not as bubbly or springy or bucolic or idyllic as privileged for the young; rather, it was something warm and cozy, something strong enough to ward off the loneliness of the long evenings and the pitiful process of aging. That's what it was; something for the old and the growing old.

Like the moon that followed her and slid behind dirt-poor old New Hope and silhouetted her as she stopped the wagon to go inside, she knew the beauty of what she felt that day, and sealed by a tingling evening, would last. After being on her knees and giving thanks to a good and giving God, she would hurry to the slave quarters and get her things. She did not have much, but now Sweet Elsie Pratt had a home to go to. Soon, very soon, for the first time in her life, she would know a man, and she would have a man; they would have each other. In the morning when she awakened, they would have a son. If all went well in the coming years, perhaps the old church could stand one more great event. It would be good for the three of them. It would be good for family.

All did not go well in the coming years.

All did not go well those hours after midnight. Like the church, Sweet Elsie Pratt died at the hands of a wagonload of Red Springers. It was their third attack on the little church where the big lady had stood and spoke for freedom.

The flames were short and blustery.

six

WHILE RED SPRINGS SLEPT IN obscurity and remained oblivious of everything but the change of seasons, the days passed without much happening at the plantation. Ben did not linger on the memory of Sweet Elsie, and only once or twice did he recall that night. When he did, it was with the shallowness and fleetingness of unformed vapor. He had accepted it all for what it was, as something that had happened and, like the vicissitudinous winds of life, things come; things go. To question life further would be fruitless. If Elsie had remained, it would have been different. Perhaps there could have been something, something even deeper than he had imagined—something for him; something for her. But it did not happen. It was over.

And so, with the boy at his side, Ben would spend his evenings sitting on the porch, inwardly alone, absently sifting through a batch of questions and quietly rocking with an uncluttered mind. Like the slowing of a clock, the former planation master had been coming into the yard later and later. That was just fine with Ben.

More and more Mr. Archy's days were weighted with

loneliness. His nights, unfittingly set up by the slow crawl of uneventful evenings, grew in length and had begun to wrestle with a troubled mind. He would never admit it, but it would have helped if the boy would have been at the creek when day was dying—when, seemingly, activity was needed most. But lately, certainly since Sweet Elsie Pratt, the boy was seldom there, preferring to spend his time waiting for his uncle to come in from the fields so that together they could bring down the shades of night.

There was no question about it, the boy missed Sweet Elsie Pratt. He often asked when she was coming back, and he wondered, too, if she had ever been inside the big house. He hadn't.

Unlike before, though, maybe the boy would've been welcomed in the house because Mr. Archy needed something to break the monotony of everyday living. There was simply nothing to do. Nothing to say to anyone. The nothingness was getting worse. There was a time, too, when Mr. Archy actually asked himself, did he really want the place; and then he looked as if he were dissatisfied with the answer his mind was leading him to. Coinciding with that, he had now fallen into the pattern of waiting late into the day, of mounting the buckboard, circling the entire plantation, coming back to the house, and slowly taking the route leading to Ben's place. In the yard, he wouldn't climb down and go around to the back like he used to; rather, he would stay aboard and consume minutes before saying anything. Dutifully, Ben would wait. Cautiously, the boy would try to remain inconspicuous behind Ben's rocker.

"Y'say t'morrow is town day, Ben?"

Ben hadn't said anything. But he'd lie: "Y'suh. We runnin' pretty low."

"Ben . . . Ben . . ." He'd drop it and sit there with a wandering mind.

Ben knew what he was going to ask. "Yassuh, Mr. Archy?"

"Ben . . . Ben . . . do y'think—Ben, you s'pose it'd be all right if I went in?"

It was not all right, and Ben knew it. Red Springs and Archibald McBride were pure trouble, and why he persisted in going there was beyond the black one's comprehension. On this subject, Ben would always try to avoid the answer.

"Huh, Ben? Y'think it'll be all right?"

Still Ben would give no answer, mainly because Mr. Archy didn't want one.

"I s'pose it'd be all right," Mr. Archy would say. "You stay an' tend to th' fields. I'll go." He lowered his eyes tiredly and fingered loosely on the reins as Ben rocked slowly.

"Ain't allus been like this, huh, Ben?"

Ben could answer that one. "Nosuh, Mr. Archy."

From the buckboard, Mr. Archy looked away again. He then looked up on the darkened porch, and then, as the boy found courage enough to come from behind the rocker to straddle one of the two beams that held the porch in relative distance from the house, the plantation owner started again: "Do you die givin' birth to somethin' like that?" It was, as usual, not so much of a question as it was a statement. "Y'better keep 'im out of my sight, Ben. I don't care what you do with 'im—just keep 'im outta my sight, y'got that, Ben? You got that?"

Ben got it, but Ben wouldn't respond. Nor would the boy. They had heard it before, and they would hear it again. But despite the harshness of content and tone, never once did it overly disturb the child. He didn't welcome it, but it didn't truly upset him. It could not be said that he had not understood, that protected by the coat of youth he was impervious to the barrage, it could not be said that he did not know at least something of this man's ire. No, it couldn't be said. What could be said, though, was that Sweet Elsie Pratt—sensible Elsie Pratt had—confirmed something in him that he didn't understand. The night she went away, she had talked about the hope of man, and the inevitable goodness of man. This was a time to remember. But even if he did not remember, even if he did not understand the question of man, even if he didn't get the significance of what was being said, it was not that important. After all, the child knew something the man didn't know. Deep down inside, he liked him.

"Night, Ben."

"Night, Mr. Archy."

seven

THE NEXT DAY'S MORNING PEEKED out with a kind of sleepy-eyed lateness, hung for a while, then hoisted a slow but generous sun that found Ben at Mr. Archy's place, readying the buckboard for the trip into town. A moment later, a disgruntled Mr. Archy came out adjusting a hat that corresponded with his crumpled white seersucker suit. He took only a fleeting glance at the headstones and, totally ignoring Ben, climbed aboard and stung the mare's rear away. Ben looked after him for a long, unreadable moment and then mounted his wagon and headed back to the fields.

The Red Springs store was precisely four and three quarter miles from the big house, and save for the midway point where, deep off the road, only the charred ruins of New Hope remained, it could have been considered a calming trip, made all the more peaceful by endless stretches of wild but scented greenery.

Normally it was Ben's job to make the monthly, and sometimes bi-monthly, supply trip because Mr. Archy had once vowed that the only way he would ever set foot in dried-up Red Springs again was as a stretched-out dead

body. He made no mention of what was to be done in the
event the body was not stretched out. The thought never
troubled anyone. It was even less of a concern of Silas's, as
he and a few others sat on the stoop of McMillan's store
that day.

WITH HIS FEET LAZILY SOAKING in the pickle barrel, Silas
happened to peer off in the direction of the approaching
buckboard. For some reason, he didn't comment to the others and waited for man and horse to come within squinting
distance.

When they were closer, Silas two-toed a pickle from the
bottom, grabbed it, popped it into his mouth, and leaned
farther forward for a better view.

Another oldster spotted the buckboard. It was Archibald
McBride's, all right, and now even the others could hardly
wait for the man on-board to close in on the stoop before
uttering the appropriate greetings.

"Well, well, well," Silas started off, "look what th' sun's
done brung out. A dead body."

The other men complemented the remark by chuckling
lightly and registering a derisive "Mornin' to ye, y'ole
polecat. How y'be?"

Mr. Archy refused to look in their direction, climbed
down from the buckboard, and quietly tied the mare to the
hitching post.

"Didn' s'pect to ever see you back in th' Springs, Mr.
McBride. Somethin' wrong at'cha place?" Silas said,
munching on the pickle while shifting a sly eye at the other
men who urged him on. Silas nodded agreeably and waited.
Then, just as Mr. Archy's foot touched the first of the two
steps leading to the stoop, Silas winked for the benefit of
the others. "I heard you done took to ownin' up to your lil'
blackberry."

He knew that remark would get him. And it did. Mr.
Archy reddened with the intensity of a beet. He stopped

short in his tracks, his jaws muscled in tightness. But he didn't turn. He simply held there, rigid. He took the second step and held again. *Don't*, he said to himself.

The shabby interior of the store never gave evidence of having enjoyed better days, and the musty atmosphere remained the same—the same as when the youngster had started telling the story.

It was the height of summer, but J. D., Shep, and the newly added Tonic and Okra were perched around the unlit stove, engaged in idle chatter with three other old-growing codgers along with a strapping, slow-moving, and dim-witted character by the name of Cruddup, who, at thirty-eight, represented the youth of the group. Both Okra, who had a head like a bullet, and Tonic, untrusted because his high cheekbones made him look like an Indian, were about twenty years older than Cruddup.

McMillan was behind the counter, and the only other person in the store, and not exactly doing much for the female gender, was a wee-bosomed, fragile little lady with an angelic face and heavenly thoughts. She represented Red Springs's churchgoing uppercrust. Sometime ago McMillan had once nailed her on a sack of flour in the back of the store and promoted the good act the next day by showing the stains to Silas, who in turn claimed the tiny spot as his own.

"S'all for t'day," she said sweetly, arming the sack of groceries.

"Okay." McMillan said, and respectfully waited for her to withdraw from the counter so that he could run over and confirm lust by poking Cruddup in the ribs.

The eyes remained on the long-skirted and backside-starved rear as it completed the move from the counter to the door.

Cruddup shot his imagination up to fanciful heights and wheezed to McMillan, "What'd you say they looked like?"

"Bigger'n watermelons," McMillan lied.

"Hot damn!" said Okra.

In further exaggeration, McMillan pushed his arms out barrellike. Cruddup vibrated at the demonstration: "Hotttt dammmmmm!"

The salacious air came to an abrupt end. Just as she fully disappeared outside, tilting her birdlike nose in the air at Mr. Archy, in he came. There was a nudging silence. He said nothing, and went to the counter. There he waited. And waited. Finally he slammed a fist down. "McMillan, am I gonna get service, or are you gonna stand over there like the idiot you're known to be!"

"You ain't in no position to come in here an' orderin' people around, McBride!" McMillan said.

"It's *Mister* McBride!" Mr. Archy said.

Shep grunted. "'Mister'—now, ain't that th' last word."

"Shep, when I'm talkin' to you, I'll go back to hog callin'."

"You'd do better goin' back an' findin' some'a them pigs you used t'sleep with," Shep said.

Mr. Archy shot for the stove poker. "I'll kill you, y'bas- tard."

Cruddup, Okra, and Tonic sprung to their feet and grabbed him.

"If you got any sense, Archy, you'll get'cha can outta here. An' *stay* out. I done told you that a long time ago!"

"You don't tell me where I can go an' where I can't. I built this town."

J. D. leapt up: "You ain't built a dawddang thing!"

"Not a damn thing!" echoed Silas from the door, still munching on the pickle, his feet still damp from the pickle brine. "Mac, don'cha let'em have a dang-blasted thing. Nuttin'."

"Nuttin'," echoed the suspected half-breed.

"An' y'aint built this town! You allus sayin' it! An' you allus wrong! Wha'cha did is kil't it! Y'kil't Red Springs. Y'kilt th' finest spot th' Lord ever done number two on!"

Silas snorted, and then strutted around like a peacock, emulating Archy's moves, as if he'd been there that day. "Folks," Silas said, "t'day is th' day I'm gonna free you. T'day is th' day you gonna be'a thankin' Archibald McBride for a long, long time. Well, you see how they thanked you. Y'see how they thanked Red Springs? Ya dum' bastid!" He reloaded and refired. "They ain't a nigger in sight! Not one! Exceptin' that hunch'a yours. An' he's too dum' an' cripple to even know how to move on!"

The men agreed and, sure that the points were driven home, backed off a little—not much, just enough to permit a thorough soaking of the words. Silas continued to encircle the group. "Y'better leave while th' leavin' is good."

J. D. ordered, "Give 'em what he wants so's he can get outta here."

"Why give 'im anythin'?" Cruddup said without releasing his hold. "Let th' black buck a'his come an' get it."

"He ain't a 'buck'! He's got a name, you jackass!"

"He ain't got nothin'! An' we don't want him in here," Cruddup said.

"An' we don't want you in here, Archy!" J. D. said.

"If'n you got any business here, you gonna have to send th' hunch."

"He's not a 'hunch!'" Mr. Archy said.

"He's a hunch, Archy! A black, buck hunch!" Silas accidentally dropped the pickle as he raced around the stove for a nose-to-nose confrontation: "What would you call somebody bent over with a bump on his back bigger'n Miss Cora's behind?! A hunch!"

"Get'cha filthy breath outta my face!" Mr. Archy demanded.

"Th' color'ds was filthy, Archy!" Silas said. He got closer. "'Member them, Archy? R'member color'ds? Slaves? Them things that'cha freed?"

"'Member that black heifer that drove y'out'cha mind?" Cruddup got closer.

"An' drove Mildred to committin' suicide?" J. D. said.

"Y'poor ol' wife, Mildred," Silas picked up. "A white woman. Gone. D'ceased. Pois'oned by her own self."

"That's somethin' else agin you, Archy," Okra said, trying to emulate Silas.

"A bony-fied daughter of Red Springs, a maid'n of th' South! Kilt herself!" Silas said, adding emphasis by picking up the sawdust-caked pickle and cramming it back into his mouth. "An' beside stealin' all her money an' makin' her commit suicide, you ruined th' best set o'pink cheeks this side of the Miss'sippi!"

Mr. Archy's face tightened, and he said, "You bastards! You rotten, low-down, good-for-nothin' bastards!"

J. D. crinkled his nose and sent a blotch of dark saliva splattering in the center of the man's face. Mr. Archy stood motionless. J. D. took it one step further. He rolled his tongue around his tobacco-darkened mouth and heaved another load at him, and without waiting for a reaction, he turned his back. "Drag his ass out'a here," J. D. said.

Wisely, Mr. Archy left under his own power. On the way back to the plantation, he was far too angry to think about what happened that day. But it was a day that the men in the store would never forget. It was the day, as they had alleged, when Mr. Archy made that godawful decision, that terrible decision that retarded a town and crippled a way of life. A decision that stabbed the fields and robbed them of a right. A decision that hurt like a giant, wayward boomerang that zoomed from his plantation to the heart of Red Springs and splattered and collapsed the posture of a hundred worlds and then U-turned back to the starting point. And Silas, as nutty as he was, had every right to strut and bring the point home: Archibald McBride freed the slaves. Though McBride delayed their emancipation by many years—he freed them just the same.

The chorus of naysayers had changed over the years, but the contents had not.

Dammit to hell, Archibald McBride! You didn't *have* to
do it! What'n th' hell was ailin' you! Didn' you *know* how
well off we was? Didn' you know how well off *you* was?
ee-zus H. Ker-rice! You din' have to be sittin' up there on
that big ol' pillar'd porch of yours that day, sippin' rum an'
lemonade an' starin' out at th' darkies pluckin' away out in
them distant fields and have to worry. They was happy,
Arch! An' *you* was happy! An' Ben, sittin' there at your
feet, *he* was happy! An us, with our combined twenny-nine
slaves, *we* was happy! *Everybody* was happy! Life was a
bed of roses! Don'cha like roses, Arch? . . . Arch? Archy,
did th' rum a'fect you that much? Or was it that lil' black
heifer, Charlotte? Did she drive you *totally* out'cha mind by
workin' on you at night when Mildred won't there? An'
speakin' of Mildred, Arch, where was she that night an'
day that'cha freed 'em? Somebody said she'd made a *second* trip into Fayetteville. Why? An' with some kinda papers, Archy? An' who was that with her, Arch? Who drove
her? Why was they there? How come Mildred won't there
to put a stop to that nonsense? She was nuts, but she was a
woman of th' South. She said she didn' like slaves, but we
now better. She wouldn'a let you turn 'em loose. She'd a
come got us, an' you *know* what we'd a done. We'd a tied
you and that black heifer to a tree an' tarr'd an' feather'd
th' life out'a both'a y'all. Speakin' of Mildred, for one
more lil' thing, Archy. Didn' somethin' happen in Fayetteville that none'a us know about, includin' you? But let's
get back to that god-awful day you call'd "freedom day,"
that day that you shock'd 'em, an' like Silas was sayin',
when you stood on th' porch actin' like you was th'
preacherman.

IT MUST BE SAID THAT the preceding account did not occur.
The false hearsay as to how Mr. Archy went about freeing
the slaves had been around for so long that now it had cemented itself as fact. What was true, and not a figment of

somebody's imagination, was that on the day in question
Ben, as ordered, had been all around the plantation round
ing up the slaves. His last stop was at the edge of both
fields. Without ceremony he hollered out to the workers
"Mr. Archy say come there!"

It was just that simple, but the slaves knew something
was up. The tipoff came from house boy number two (aged
forty-seven). Houseboy number one had stolen enough
goods to keep him in happy independence for about a year
He had pilfered everything that wasn't nailed down from
the storage house, and kept the booty buried underneath
some self-made gravemarkers. What gave him away was
the newly dug dirt and some names he had x'd on the
wood. They were a little too familiar.

One day, led by Reverend Terrell, New Hope's pastor
and brother Cromardy, the church's head deacon, a group
went to the cemetery and dug for name confirmation.

The church services that Sunday were characterized by
an unmistakable threat of eternal damnation—which would
be expedited by the clear-cut rule: Stealing from the master
was an act punishable by hanging. If the culprit wasn't fin
gered, the selection would be done by the logic of opportu
nity and/or lottery. Not trusting the latter, houseboy number
two tearfully explained the errors of houseboy number
one's ways and went on to relay his personal suspicion
about Mr. Archy's impending decision.

Houseboy number one was forgiven, but he was never
heard from again.

eight

OCILITY AND OBEDIENCE WERE THE hallmarks of being a
ood slave. Archibald McBride had very good slaves, and
was a monumental day in the lives of the very good
aves. They had quite properly gathered around the porch
s very good slaves, different this time, because they had
ope and anticipation. Some thought a speech was in order.
thers thought a ceremony of some sort. Perhaps a docu-
ent or a piece of paper would be given, one that they were
ot able to read, but something to hold on to, something
at they could show the world that they were members of
umankind, that they had names, birth dates, family; that
ey belonged, and had belongings. That they were free,
nd that as a people no longer had to worry about the
hips, the chains, the ropes, the guns, the swamps, the
ean-jawed traps, and the tracking bloodhounds. They did
ot have to worry about being tarred and feathered.

No longer would there be the fear of running through the
oods and thickets and encountering all the things that
nspired against ungranted freedom; that there would be a
demptive moral compass, a compass of a renewed spirit,

pointing the way, advising that although you are a free people, your rejoicing should be held at a minimum because the unshackled troubles are not over. But saying first that I, as a slaver, was wrong. *We*, as slavers of over four million of God's children, were wrong, and saying, too that a nation that condoned the institution, a nation that was founded on the principles of equality and justness, abandoned decency and ignored its covenant, was wrong. On behalf of that nation, my people, and myself, I offer my apology, and along with it, something to sustain you as you go your separate ways in a land whose customs and way you do not know, and among a people that will remain forever hostile to you and all that will be yours.

But Mr. Archy never said any of that. In fact, Mr. Archy never even came out on the porch that day. He sent Ben back out. The simple message his man-servant delivered was ever so quiet.

"Mr. Archy said y'all free."

WHEN BEN ARRIVED AT THE store, the setting had not changed from when Mr. Archy had arrived. He didn't expect change. But he did expect trouble, because when Mr. Archy came back, he was wordless. He quietly drove into the fields, gave him the money without saying anything and he left. That was not a good sign.

The same three or four lazing old-timers were up on the stoop decorating the front of the store, and Silas, just off to the left, was back resoaking his feet in the pickle barrel and at the same time played footsies with three newly deceased flies that floated on top of the brine all while taking in the sights. Looking off to his right, as he had done with Mr. Archy, he peered off, saw Ben's wagon approaching and unnecessarily cleared his throat to Okra, Cruddup, and Tonic: "Ol' Arch did send th' hunch, after all, didn' he?" Silas said.

When Ben got there, he didn't look at any of them di

rectly, he simply pulled the wagon up front, climbed down, and quietly started hitching the wagon to the post. Silas waited until he had finished and said, "Lemme ask ya somethin', Hunchy ol' boy. How come when Archy freed th' othern's, you didn' scat out outta here with 'em? Wouldn'a been 'cause you was scare't of what they would'a done to you, since you almost broke y'back bowin' an' scrapin' to Arch?"

Ben wisely said nothing, knowing that any word from him would only inflame matters.

"How come?"

Ben still wouldn't say anything.

Okra shouted, "Mr. Silas done ask'd you a question, boy!"

Ben took his time. "Mr. Silas," Ben said. "I think this ol' back got this a'way when I was still in my mama's belly, when she was runnin' an' hurtin' from slavers an' trouble-makin' peoples like you. Now it's my back, an' I'm free. I think I got th' right to bend it an' scrape it to anybody I want."

Silas almost fell out of the pickle barrel. "Lordy-Lord, Lord, Lord, Lord! Whas done happen to us? Whas done happen to th' good ol' U.S. of A.? Help us, somebody! They runnin' wild! They kil't th' town, an' now they aimin' for the country, all eight States! Lordy-Lord, Lord, Lord, Lord. Why, oh Lord, why? Why would'ja let me weaken to my knees without wearin' my Sunday best an' prayin' for d'liverence from raccoons and colored folks if you won't tryin' to hurt me in some way. I love you Lord Jesus, but my load is gettin' too heavy to bear. An' I a-sumes, I said I a-*sumes* you knows it. Amen and good day. Yours truly, Silas Crookashank. Hey, Doc, J. D., Shep, y'all come ou'cheer!"

"Whas'up?" J. D. could be heard yelling from inside.

"We unda attack!" Silas yelled back, and continued over-doing it to the others. "What'd I tell y'all? Didn' I tell y'all they'd start gettin' uppity. Didn' I tell you? Huh? Huh? Huh?"

The newly arrived man with the cane hobbled out. "Whas' trouble?" he said.

"Him! Y'shudda heard 'im, Doc! My Lord, y'shudda heard 'im!" said Silas, pointing and jumping up and down.

J. D. came out, followed by four others. "What'd he do?" J. D. asked.

"Takin' to sassin' folks," Silas said.

"You's a liar, an' you knows it, Mr. Silas," Ben said.

"J'hear that? J'hear that? See! See! See! Ain't even been free long enough to use soap 'n water, an cussin' a white man already. Lord, why you punishin' us like this? Why, O Lordy-Lord? Father of Pickles an' All Things That Ain't Greasy, help us! Help us, Lord Jesus!" Silas said.

J. D. waited until Silas's sense of high drama had receded, studied the black man for a moment, and said quietly, "You just talked yourself from comin' in, Ben."

Ben responded just as quietly and with a look to the store owner, he said, "I didn' hear Mr. McMillan say nothin' about it."

"He ain't got to. You *ain't* welcom'd!" Leveled Doc the cane hobbler.

McMillan quietly said, "Better git, Ben."

Ben was surprised. Mr. McMillan, he always thought, was a bit more reasonable than the rest of the Red Springers. There were times when he had been there and the man had actually engaged him in conversation; such as the time when he inquired about the meetings at the church. One time he even went so far as to say he had heard that there was a new little boy on the plantation. Ben had explained that the child was his, and that he was in good care. Mr. McMillan wished him luck, gave him a little piece of licorice, and told him to make sure that the boy got it. Indeed, McMillan was the best of the bunch; the licorice and the church inquiry were nice gestures, Ben thought. He also remembered the boy so loved the candy that he wanted to buy some at a later time and McMillan said he was out of it and wouldn't be carrying it anymore.

The old black man climbed aboard the wagon, and thought about it again. Still, at the time, giving candy for the boy, and asking about the church were mighty nice gestures, indeed at the time. Perhaps the store owner would have a change of heart one day.

Apparently the store owner was not thinking the same thing.

"Git," McMillan repeated.

"An' don't even think of bringin' y'black ass back here a'gin," the cane holder said with finality.

nine

"TH' BASTARDS. THE ROTTEN, LOW-DOWN, dirty, good-for-nothin', bastards," fumed Mr. Archy, already waiting in his front yard, and without Ben having to say anything, he stood there fuming.

"I ought'a go into town an' shotgun every single one of 'em. Th' no-count bastards!"

Ben sat, his hands still wrapped in the reins. "Maybe," he said slowly, "maybe we ought'a go to Fayetteville, Mr. Archy."

"Th' hell we will!" Mr. Archy fired. "We ain't goin' a gawdamn place but back to Red Springs."

"That's gonna spell a lot'a trouble, suh."

"You ever known me to be afraid of trouble?"

"Nosuh, but—"

"'*But*' hell!" Mr. Archy said, and spun back into the house. Inside, he went directly for the shotgun and went into the pantry drawer for the shells. On his way back out he crammed the chamber and jammed the rest of the shells into his jacket pocket.

"Let's go, Ben," he said, hurrying off the porch.

"Y'kno, Mr. Archy," Ben said with true reasoning in his voice. "I was just thinkin' if we goin' back to town, why not wait 'til it gets dark."

Mr. Archy hopped on the wagon. "For what reason?"

"Maybe Mr. McMillan'll be alone an' I can talk to 'im."

"Are you really that dumb? Gimme a *real* what-for?"

"Well—" Ben said.

"Wait for what, Ben! For *what*?"

"I'm thinkin'."

"*You* don't think. *I* think! Now, let's go."

"Mr. Archy. Please let's not do it. Please let's don't go. An' I ain't sayin' it b'cause I'm scared. But there's trouble there. An' there's a heap of them, an' only two of us."

"Move th' wagon!"

"Mr. Archy—"

"Move this gawddamn wagon, Ben!"

"Suh?"

"I said, *move* the wagon!"

"Think about what I said b'fore, Mr. Archy. We don't *have* to go to that store. It's better to go to Lumberton anyhow. There's more stuff there. It'll only take us an hour more. Then there's Fayetteville."

"You gonna move this wagon?"

"You th' boss man, suh, but I ain't gonna move it. An' I ain't gonna let you move it. I jus' can't."

"You ain't gonna *let* me? Why, you—!" And with that, the plantation owner punctuated his feelings by lifting his foot and cramming it into the laborer's side, knocking him clear out of the wagon. Mr. Archy then slid over, leaned out, and in a fit of boiling anger blasted: "You don't '*let*' Archibald McBride *do* a gawddamn thing! I freed you, but you are still a gawddam slave, and a slave don't *let* me or no white man *do* nothin'! Y'understand that you black bastard?"

Ben remained crookedly motionless on the ground and

made no attempt to counter the man. Mr. Archy blistered him again.

"*Get up!*"

Still Ben wouldn't move.

"*Gawdammit, I said 'up'!*"

The old black man slowly answered the command by stiffly unlumbering from the hard dirt. Once up, and taking his own good time, he carefully put his foot on the step as though to make the swing to sit down. Instead, he sent a frightening and stinging back-handed slap across the white man's face. He slapped him again, and hopped back down.

Mr. Archy reacted in horror and, in doing so, accidentally kicked the breaking lever forward. In panic, the mare bolted and galloped forward. Mr. Archy fought for the reins. Controlling but not stopping the fast-moving vehicle, he shouted back, "I'm gonna kill youuuu, Ben! Y'hear me? When I get back, you're dead! When I get back, you're dead! Dead! Dead! Your hear meeee, Bennnn! You're dead!"

Ben heard him, but one would have never known it. Not giving vent to his feelings one way or the other, he simply stayed on the ground and turned his head to the most unexpected direction. He settled on the headstones.

t e n

THE RIDE BACK INTO RED Springs had been a blur.

"That Archibald McBride has got to be th' dummes' thing I've ever seen in my life," Silas announced from his regular spot on the stoop.

The wagon was blistering the final approach.

"Hey, J. D. y'all come on out! Th' man is crazy. Plum' loco," Silas said.

The old man with the cane was there and led the others out to the stoop. J. D., trailing, waited for the wagon to get closer. "That's far enough, Archibald McBride," J. D. said.

Mr. Archy ignored him and brought the wagon to a stop. It was ill advised. The old man with the cane led the charge. That, too, was ill advised. He broke from the porch, cane held high, and promptly fell down the two steps, and was out.

"Now, y'see what you done done, Archy; You done kil't th' only doctor in Red Springs! Y'done kil't a man o' th' cloth!" Silas said, coming down to check the man's condition.

Silas was wrong on both counts. The man with the cane

was not dead, and was not a doctor. He laid claim to the title, but a doctor he was not. He was a former Klansman and snake-oil salesman from Mississippi who had arrived in town some forty years before. He was lost and thought Red Springs was the port of the Cape Fear River. Someone peered into the back of his wagon, saw the little bottles of oils that bounced on top of two sheets and a pointed hat, and promptly announced that there was a doctor in town.

Silas withdrew an ear from the man's right shoulder. "His heart ain't no more. It is my solum duty t'say th' doc is dead," Silas said.

Mr. Archy stepped over the body and tried to push past the idiocy. He was blocked. "Out of my way, you worthless piece'a trash!" Mr. Archy said.

"You is a killer, Archibald McBride! An' th' biggest piece'a trash born a foot pass th' Mason-Dixon is you. An' don't you f'get it!" Silas continued.

"He won't f'get it," said Tonic. "He's got somethin' home to keep 'im reminded."

"I'm gonna tell you somethin'," Mr. Archy said. "An' it goes for all'a you—to include this ignoramus on th' ground. An' don't y'all f'git it. Some of th' slave children that left Red Springs had light skin. They didn' get light skin by bathin' in milk or usin' bakin' soda or flour. Ev'ry last one of you at least *tried* to have a colored woman—an' more than a few of 'em is dead and buried because you animals couldn' take no for an answer."

"But none'a us would'a had they lil' black bastards," J. D. said with his usual cruelty.

"Or would'a kept 'em, if we did," Shep said.

Pointless to argue the matter further, Mr. Archy tried again to push his way up the two steps. Cruddup blocked him with his body. On the move, J. D., Shep, and Tonic grabbed him around the waist and collar. A clumsy, staggering old-timer's struggle ensued, culminating with the main two, J. D. and Mr. Archy, spinning off the stoop and then down to the side of the wagon, where Cruddup rejoined them by tossing J. D. aside and pressing his full body weight against the older man. He sent the body arching toward the seat. Fully encouraged by the group, Cruddup pressed harder. Mr. Archy tried desperately to fight the stronger man off. He couldn't. Mr. Archy appeared to be going down.

"Now, y'gottem! Y'gottem now, Cruddy-crud!" Silas said, jumping up and down, leading the cheering. "That'szit! That'szit! That'szit!"

"Hog-tie 'im, Crud! Break his back!" Shep hollered.

"Nail'im to th' wheel!" encouraged McMillan.

"Tie his pecker to th' spokes!" Silas said.

The encouragement continued. Cruddup, lifted the man and landed a blow to the side of his head. Mr. Archy's head reeled back in pain and drops of blood cornered his mouth. Cruddup released him for a fraction of a second. The body slid partway down. Cruddup then charged in with a bear hold. Mr. Archy was gasping for air. The men whooped louder. Cruddup pressed harder. Struggling and pushing himself up Mr. Archy was finally able to free an arm, dip it in the wagon, and send his fingers pawing and stretching for the rifle under the seat. He barely got a hand on it, and when he was fully able to grasp it, he clutched it by the barrel, braced himself, and pushed his body forward, simultaneously unloading a mouthful of bloodied spit directly into his oppressor's eye. Cruddup dipped back defensively and, in an instant, Mr. Archy sent a hard blow to the man's head with the butt of the weapon. The big oaf reeled back dizzily and clutched his head in pain. The men fell silent as Cruddup staggered around and then slumped to the ground.

After the initial stunning moments had worn off, J. D. spat at Mr. Archy and called him an "unfair, lowdown, dirty dog," and urged the group to "git 'im."

Silas backed him by shouting, "Wha'cha'll waitin' on? He done kilt't *two* peoples!"

"Git'im!" J. D. ordered again.

"Tie his pecker to the spokes!" Silas shouted.

The group made a tentative move. Mr. Archy leveled the rifle. "One step in my direction an' I'll blow a hole right through you."

"Archibald McBride, you ain't got th' nerve!" J. D. said.

"Try me."

No one would.

They stood there crouchlike, each of them waiting for the other to make the move forward. Nobody moved—nobody except the "dead" man, who had been overlooked and was now coming to.

Back at the standoff, Mr. Archy shouldered some of the blood away from his mouth and made a feigning move, as if to get back on the wagon. The group started to close in.

Mr. Archy leveled the weapon: "Don'cha be no fool."

"Takes courage t'pull a trigger, Archy," J. D. said, "an' that's somethin' you ain't never had."

"One more step an' I'm gonna have your life."

"You scare't, Archibald McBride; y'scare't," Silas hollered over, having slipped back to the barrel and was now alternately fanning, kicking, and sending his pickle-inspired little toe digging up Cruddup's drippingly crowded nasal passage. "Y'jus' plain scare't—an' y'aint doin' nothin' but runnin' off at th' mouth!"

"Try me."

Archibald McBride meant business, and the rest of them knew it. They held off. As they stood there, their attention shifted from the muzzle of the rifle to Silas's antics with the prostrate Cruddup.

"Get up, y'lazy good-fer-nothin'! Get up! Y'sleepin' on th' job!"

"Silas, th' man's hurt!" McMillan shouted.

"That ain't no excuse!" Silas blurted back, and then proceeded to kick the man. "Get up, y'lousy, good-fer-nothin', hog-smellin' lunkhead! I said *up!*"

"Silas, can't you *see* th' man's hurt!" McMillan said again.

"What I *see* is him sleepin'!" Silas retorted while giving another kick to Cruddup's rear end. "Up, I said. We got work t'do!"

Finally, Cruddup reeled back into consciousness, and under Silas's barrage he staggered to his feet, clutching his head and moaning, "Where I'm at? Where I'm at?"

"Where th' hell y'think? Where y'big dum' b'hind is allus been!" Silas said, aiming and delivering another kick. "Now, git back over there an' finish wha'cha start'd."

The big man looked around and tried vainly to bring the surroundings into focus.

Had he been able to see, he would have seen Mr. Archy had already climbed aboard the wagon and was preparing to rid himself of the nonsense.

Shep was the first one to spot him. "See, y'runnin', Archy, jus' like th' coward y'allus been!"

Mr. Archy stopped. "Nobody calls me a coward."

"Then why you runnin'?" Shep said.

Quietly, businesslike, Mr. Archy picked up his rifle, and climbed back down. "Your move," he said.

Once again everyone was circled; and once again everyone was afraid to make the move.

The other man who had been knocked senseless by his fall from the two stairs, and the man whom Silas had pronounced dead, was on his hands and knees, patting the dirt for his cane. Silas was standing on it. "Move," the man said softly. Apparently Silas didn't hear him. "*Dammit, I said move!*"

The big dumb one charged, responding to the command. And in that same instant, Mr. Archy's big, booming shot sent the body back wickedly. It contorted in the air and fell lifelessly to the ground. No one, including Mr. Archy himself, had ever thought such a thing would happen. He, as they, were all talk. To kill someone (anyone other than the totally accepted practice of dropping an errant slave) had never been a way of life in Red Springs. Hatreds, dislikes, disagreements, mistrusts: All of those things had been allowed to smolder, fester, simmer, and to occupy idle minds, and occasionally take the form of air-bloated threats, that would eventually follow them to the grave, and there to rest. But now that was gone too.

Silas, J. D., Shep, McMillan, and the other four or five men now realized that another change had come to Red Springs, the isolated little place that had been reared in peace, nurtured in slavery, and sabotaged to death by the unholiness of one Archibald McBride. Now he'd done it again.

MR. ARCHY CAME TO THE slow realization that a man was dead. He looked at the body again, and then at the men. In panic he withdrew and scrambled aboard the wagon under their still-stunned eyes. Pulling tightly at the reins and bearing down hard on the mare's rear with the strap, the buckboard spun around and drove off recklessly.

Of the men, J. D. was first to collect himself. "Well, that did it," he said.

"I never thought this kinda thing would ever happen in th' Red Springs," intoned McMillan.

"McMillan go in back an' get'cha wagon," ordered J. D.

"An' while you back there, Mac, git some kerosene," said Silas.

"An' rags," J. D. said.

"Them you wearin' will do nicely," Silas added on his way to pick the dead man's pockets.

In short order the wagon was loaded. The cane hobbler, back to life and seeking support on the kerosene drum, said: "Mac, don't feel like there's 'nuff kerosene in here."

"S'nuff."

J. D. climbed from over the backseat and gave the drum a look. "Ain't 'nuff kerosene in here to singe a bug's nuts. Y'all go get some bottles an' fill it all th' way up," J. D. said with menace. "We goin' to start a fire, not a roast."

eleven

NEVER HAD MR. ARCHY FRACTURED the road as he did that day. It was all the more difficult because he was driving Ben's wagon and not the buckboard. He hadn't driven a wagon in over thirty years, but still he was able to manage. The entire countryside whizzed by in a blur, and he gave no thought to slowing the pace. He knew the towners would be coming soon. When he finally reached the plantation area, he did not veer to the left as he had done earlier; rather, he stung the mare over to the smaller road that led to Ben's place; and before even getting to the yard, he was yelling for Ben. "Ben! Benn! Bennn!"

When the wagon rumbled into the yard, he was still calling for his black servant. "Ben! Ben!" He continued shouting as the wagon came to a rolling stop. Quickly, he hopped down and went to the door, which was never closed in summer. "Bennnnnnnn!" He heard nothing in return, so he whirled back to the wagon. Aboard, he stood and squinted off into the fields. He did not see Ben. He sped off anyway, hoping a closer look would find him.

But Ben was not to be found in the fields that day. He

and the boy were spending the afternoon at the bank of the creek, something he had never done in his entire life.

Moses was so excited by his uncle being at the creek that he didn't know whether to stand, or sit, or kneel, or squat—and for a while tried to do all four at the same time. He elected to sit only after Ben had assured him that sitting was a luxury the other three couldn't afford. The boy sat, but he still wasn't quite content. He wanted his uncle to participate—to run, jump, ride, and to lead the cavalry. The uncle, of course, would have none of that. Still, there was unbridled joy in having the wrinkled and leathered and tired old love right there beside him right there in his favorite spot in all the world: the creek.

They were at the creek, and they weren't being bothered by anyone. A great occasion like that, though, had to be questioned. He started off by asking why was he there, and where was Bess and the wagon. Then the boy rattled off what must have seemed like a thousand questions, and each one was followed by a plunking of a pebble into the water. Unca Ben, why this? Why that? What is that? What is this? How come this? How come that? Who was this? Who was that? The questions went on and on. But each time he would come back with the unhurried refrain, "Unca Benny . . . it shore is good you here."

It *was* good. The loneliness of the long summer days had come to an end—for both of them. As Ben had explained, he would be spending more time with him. They would enjoy the creek together, and although it was not much, whatever they had, from this day forward, they would enjoy it together. In answer to a "how-come" question, the uncle had been honest enough to say or had delicately suggested, that there would be a slight change taking place, and that he had done something not to Mr. Archy's liking, and that the consequences could be far-reaching. He even hinted that they might have to go and live in the woods and make do off of the land. That was not the worst thing the boy could have heard. In fact, in thinking it over, it was downright pleasing and he couldn't wait until the subject was further explored. Although the tone of voice the uncle had used was not exactly uplifting, the subject matter certainly was, and that sent him through a series of more questions. The uncle gently steered him back to the possibility of dire consequences, and added that if anything ever happened to him, he was to grow up strong, and be just and honest in everything that he did. Strange, thought the boy. That was the same thing that Sweet Elsie Pratt had told him that long-ago night just before she left. *Wonder where she went? Wonder when she's comin' back?* God, how he missed her.

"UNCA BENNY." A DELAYED THOUGHT was made audible. "What is just, and what is right?"

They were not the easy questions. He was born shackled to tradition. Was that right? He would go through life without privilege. Was that just?

"I s'pect you'll learn in time, son."

That was not the answer the boy was looking for. Nor was it the answer Ben would have usually given. That in itself was not right, nor just. The boy sat there and permitted the cool mud to ease through his toes, he felt a wee bit slighted. He wouldn't pursue the matter though. Rather, his mind went back to something the uncle had touched on when he first got there—something he had said before the living-in-the-woods idea—and something he had said with far more conviction. "But if you did go to Fayetteville to stay—well, y'didn' say nothin' 'bout me goin' too?"

It should have been an automatic assumption that anywhere the uncle went, he would go too. But, again, there was something about the way the uncle had said it.

Ben, obviously confused too, remained there in the prone position, his eyes planted upward. "Well, like I said b'fore, no matter where I go, I'm gonna always come back an' spend time with you. We gonna spend more time togeth'r than we ever did before," Ben said.

"Unca Benny, you tryin' to say if you went away from here, I can't go?"

"Well, son, tek'nically speakin', I can't take you away."

Ben wanted to say more but couldn't, and even if he could, it was too late to stop the tears that flooded the young eyes and cherubic face. Youth spoke. He wanted to run. He did not think about riding his horse. He did not think about being a soldier and charging. All he could think about was motion: his legs in motion, carrying him away from a world teetering on the verge of collapse; and he could hear the sound, that awful tumbling and rolling and shattering sound of something being destroyed. It was not the thought of being alone. It was far more tragic; a love—a belonging was being destroyed.

"Unca Benny, you wouldn't really leave me, would you?"

The old man got up and went to be close to him. And then he hugged him.

"Never in a million years, son. Never in a million years."

twelve

WHILE MR. ARCHY SEARCHED THE fields for his laborer, searching maniacally, row by row, thinking maybe he would find Ben sleeping under a patch of corn, the Red Springers had already wagoned in to his place and had commenced rolling the big kerosene drum on the porch. Tonic and Okra had already taken the smaller containers upstairs and had begun soaking the furniture under the running commentary of the cane hobbler, who, though bandaged and still feeling the effects of the fall, had taken it upon himself to be scout.

Purposely spilling as much kerosene from the air hole as possible, McMillan and Shep, under the direction of Commander Silas, tilted the drum through the door and rolled it down the long hallway to the kitchen, where they encountered unneeded difficulty getting through. McMillan became discouraged after several tries and suggested going all the way back to Red Springs for smaller containers.

"Y'gawddang nut," Silas flared. "We fill'd it up! An' all y'gotta do now is find somethin' t'punch another hole in it and let it drip from right there!"

"Y'ever tried punchin' a hole in a kerosene drum?" McMillan shot back.

"It's a hell'va lot quicker'n goin'—"

"Silas!" J. D. yelled, rightly cutting him off. "Just *bend* over an' *re*move th' screw cap!"

"I didn' know it had one," said McMillan, the storekeep and owner of the drum.

The bandaged man with the cane hobbled by, and said, "Shep, you an' McMillan find a couppla pots an' pans an' take some'a that stuff an' help 'em upstairs. Hurrup."

McMillan, doing as ordered, found the pots and pans on the bottom shelf of the pantry—and thinking about a resale, started wiping and blowing off the dust.

"McMillan, dangblastit!" Silas said. "We ain't here for dinnah!"

During the pandemonium, J. D. went to the stairway and hollered up, "Okay—c'mon down. We gotta go. Arch'll be back any minnit!"

"J. D., where d'ya s'pose—"

He broke it off. J. D. didn't have any more of an idea as to where Archy was than he did. But what stopped Silas was something he spotted in the living room. It was always his intention to pocket a few loose items, but it was the two portraits that grabbed his attention. In the South, it just didn't happen. It just didn't happen that a plantation owner would have a portrait of a black girl so prominently displayed. And, to make matters worse, it occupied a better position than his wife's. Silas would have thought worse had he seen the gravestones; still, he was so disgusted, he couldn't even steal anything.

Outside, everyone was contentedly in place. McMillan was about to inch the wagon away. The man with the cane, and the bandage that had now slipped down and seriously impaired his vision, had felt his way to the driver's seat, and assuming they were on the road, he was ordering McMillan to put on some speed. McMillan was trying to get around to telling him that they were not yet moving, when J. D., rather soberly, came up with an inquiry: "Ain't y'all forgettin' somethin'?" He had asked it as though they had all day to spare.

McMillan stopped the now inching wagon. "What?" he asked.

Except for the man with the cane and impaired vision who was busy wondering where daylight went, they all looked at one another.

Nobody had forgotten anything.

J. D. raised his voice. "Y'all *ain't* forgot nothin'?"

"Yeah," said Silas. "We f'got to find Archy so's we could tie him to a tree and cut his pecker off."

"Is that wh'cha came here for?"

"We came here," sputtered the cane man now struggling with the bandage. "We came here t'set th' place on fire."

"Do you *see* anything burnin'?"

The cane man, struggling with the head bandage that had slopped down and covered his eyes, wanted to say, "I can't *see* anything." Silas beat him to the punch.

"It ain't burnin'!"

"Dammit!" J. D. fired. "Will somebody get off'a this wagon an' go an' set fire to the gawddamn house!"

No one had a match. They sat there in stony silence, eyeing each other, accusing each other. Of all the dumb, stupid, idiotic things to do—

It was up to Tonic, the half breed in denial, to rescue them. Every house had to have a match. They couldn't fire the stove or light the kerosene lamps without them. Quietly the man who had always hid the Indian side of his heritage hopped down from the wagon and walked the few yards back to the house. He took his time going inside. A moment later he was back out and waited with the others. Together they waited a moment more. Soon a slither of flame crawled up the left front window's curtain. Maybe it was the sight of the flame, but no one said anything at the time,

and they felt nothing but a strangeness as the slither grew
and reached over to the next window and then joined the
forces that blew from the foyer. Soon there was an explosion, and the entire house was seized by a great roar that
spearheaded a wicked burst of flames that spewed from
every opening. It was the end of the McBride plantation.
Strangely, though, for all it meant, there would be no parting shots from the Red Springers. When the flames became
too hot, the bandaged man with the cane said, "Let's go."

And they were gone.

IN THE FIELDS MR. ARCHY was still traversing the endless rows
in search of his laborer and had now gone so far as to conduct
the search on his hands and knees. Ben had to be somewhere.
But Ben, as he had been since the earlier incident, was at the
creek, dozing. So, in a sense, Mr. Archy's suspicion did con-
tain an element of validity. But, conversely, in all the years he
had been out in the fields, never once did he entertain the
thought of taking a nap, quick or otherwise. The old black
man was supposed to be out in the fields working—and that
was exactly what he did; even when the pains of sickness
racked his body and the curse of fever dimmed his vision and
sapped his strength, Ben was out there, working. Though he
was no longer a slave he was still a product of the institution.
The rules of the institution were simple: slaves had no right to
get sick; those that did—well, let 'em die.

At the creek Ben dozed contentedly. The boy, simply for
the sake of wanting something to do, and not wanting to
leave his uncle's side, got his hoe and playfully swung it
over his head. Tilting it up, and angling it in the direction of
the house, he spotted the smoke rising over the shrubbery
and billowing in the distance. He tried to get his uncle's attention. And then the smoke really got serious. "You better
take a look, Unca Benny," he said, nudging him.

Ben wouldn't move.

The smoke spiraled higher. "Look! Unca Benny, look!"

Slowly getting the message, after the boy had said it again, Ben rolled over and sleepily shielded his eyes. There was no doubt about it, fire was in the air. Quickly he scrambled to his feet, looked up, and saw that the source was far beyond the underbrush and it had to be the plantation house that was burning. For an instant he started to hurry in that direction, but he held back. Anticipating the move, the boy had already started to make the long run.

"Hold it, son!" Ben called.

The boy, legs still in motion, running in place, looked at him quizzically.

"We goin' home," Ben said surprisingly.

"But, Unca Benny—"

"We goin' home, son," Ben said again, this time with more stress.

The boy was stunned. "*Home?*"

"Yes," said Ben, and pointed. "An' home is this a'way."

"Why? Why? Why?" the boy demanded. He wanted to know why the uncle wouldn't fire off with him; why he wanted to turn his back and go the other way. Although it could not be seen from the creek, he knew it was the plantation house burning. He had been told over and over again, fire was the worse thing that could ever happen to anybody. There was a fire at Mr. Archy's. Mr. Archy needed help. He needed it desperately. The plantation was going to burn to the ground. He reminded the uncle that he had said if someone needed help—anyone—help them. Don't be afraid. Well, he wanted to help, and he was not afraid.

The hunched old man did not want to disappoint the boy further. He could not find the words to explain his feelings and those that lay deeper. He looked at the smoke, and then at the boy. Slowly he turned and walked away. The anxious and confused boy looked after him for a bit, and then at the smoke that had now darkened the sky. He would go there. He had to hurry.

*   *   *

WHEN MR. ARCHY FIRST SAW the billowing smoke he was at
the extreme far end of the tobacco field. He was still on his
hands and knees, looking for the old black man under the
draping tobacco leaves, and what was to delay his move
more was the fact that he had strayed too far from the
wagon. In truth, even if Mr. Archy had arrived at the house
earlier than he did, it would not have mattered. There was
nothing he could do. The house could not have been saved
under any circumstances.

It did not take long for the heat to give testament to the
awesome and consummate power of fire. First to be seen,
and burning in the foreground, was his horse. His legs had
become trapped in the overturned buckboard, and they both
went down in flames.

The heat shot out and singed everything around it, so
much so that when Mr. Archy's wagon did try to come into
the yard, it was stopped even before getting to the outer
edge. Crazed, the old man stood up wild-eyed and bore
down hard with the whip and yanked angrily at the reins.
The frightened mare would go no farther. The man cracked
her again. This time the animal responded by summoning
her reserves. She hawed menacingly, arched her back, and
bolted, throwing the wagon askew and sending the man
sprawling to the ground. Though down, he would not stop.
With his eyes riveted on the house, he started to crawl forward, his belly clinging to the ground. The closer he got,
the more madly the heat blistered out. He would continue
to fight forward until the heat became absolutely unbear-
able, when it seemed as if his entire body had been picked
up and devilishly thrown into some sort of man-devouring
oven, when the heat parched his skin and seized the pas-
sageway to his lungs—and it was only then that he stopped
the forward progress. He had stopped, but he would not
turn around. Instead, he lowered his mouth to a crooked
arm and set the free fist pounding in the dirt.

When the boy arrived, panting on the outer edge, the man was still pounding in the dirt, uttering over and over and over: "Th' bastards. Th' bastards. The dirty, rotten, lowdown, good-for-nothin' bastards—"

Moses knew he was sinking fast.

"Mr. Archy—Mr. Archy—" the boy screamed and screamed. He was not heard. Another gust of scathing heat spewed out. Now the situation was beyond desperate. The boy tried to move in again. He was stopped. "Heat rises," his uncle used to say when they sat close to the kitchen stove during those long story-telling winters. And so he fell to the ground and began crawling to rescue an old man who had nothing to do all day but try to catch him peeing in the creek and later sit up there on that buckboard with the pretty horse and call him a lil' black bastard—words and thoughts he did not fully understand, and from a man who now, except for his throat-rattling coughing, fell silent and motionless. He had to hurry. The heat told him not to. It was more oppressive now and, mixed with a white, almost clearless smoke, it undulated along the ground snakelike. Moses was suffocating. He had enough in him for his thin and muffled voice to say: "Hold on, Mr. Archy. Hold on, I'm coming." He didn't know how, but he was determined to find a way. *Off with your clothes,* something told him. It was a female voice. It continued. *Now take the clothes off and use the clothes to shield yourself.* He did just that.

When he finally reached the plantation owner, his little body could not move him. He tried pulling and yanking on the arms, the legs; he moved to the head and then back down to the torso. No matter how hard he tried, he could move the unconscious body only an inch or so. Now he could do nothing but cough and cry, and soon he was about to lose all reason. *This is not the time,* said the voice. He knew she was right. *Think,* she said again. Quickly, now, beyond childlike efficiency, he tied his trouser legs protectively around the man's head and raced back to safety.

When he first arrived, he had seen the mule entangled in
the wagon and reins. Bess was the answer. He quickly went
to her, freed her from the entanglement, and tried to lead
her back to the burning house. But the mule was too frightened and yanked for freedom. The only other choice was to
mount her, aim her in the opposite direction, close her
blinders as much as possible, and then quickly spin her
around and charge back for Mr. Archy—hopefully reaching
him before the mare would again panic and before the man
would die. He tried, but the effort failed; he was too small
to even mount the mule. Time was running out, and there
was no time to race all the way across the fields to summon
his uncle. He didn't have enough time to even make it to
the creek. Still, he did not panic. Again he was helped by
the voice. She simply said: *Think*. Steadying Bess, he went
back to the wagon and frantically dug into the carry box;
and sure enough there was a rope inside. He quickly got it
and tied one end to the reins and coaxed the mule back to
the area. Bess sensed that she did not have to go all the way
in. Placing herself in jeopardy, she was cooperative enough
to come in closer than she had before. She came in close
enough for the boy to tie the tope around the man's body
The plantation owner was pulled to safety.

"HI, MR. BOSS MAN," SAID the boy, his childish exuberance
back, his eyes unmoving.

They were at his favorite spot, the creek. They had been
there for a long while and the boy remained propped up on
his elbows, his caring eyes not leaving the man for a second. It was a long time, too, before the seeping dawn of reality had slowly returned to the old man. When he came to
he more or less hoisted himself up to a quasi-sitting position and was cognizant enough to wet-eye his surroundings
The loss of the house had not dawned on him yet and he
filled the initial moments rueing the sight that greeted him
The boy, not quite three feet away, squatting in his face

Not only that, he was still naked. So, now, not only did the man have to contend with the boy doing number one (peeing) in the creek, damned if he wasn't all set to do number two.

Small wonder the man was not touched by the boy's childish exuberance or by the friendliness of the greeting, or anything else he had to offer. When the loss of the house did begin to settle on his cobwebbed mind, Mr. Archy became even more disgruntled. The reason stemmed from the deep-seated belief that the boy was the source of all his troubles. The fact that he, Mr. Archy, selected a black woman to have an ongoing illicit relationship with didn't enter into his thinking at all; it was the result—the boy, that nagging residue of the affair, that constantly warped his mind.

They sat face-to-face.

"Anything I can do, Mr. Archy?"

Mr. Archy had no evidence that number two had taken place—yet—and so he figured he would cut him off at the pass: "Y'can begin by not peein' in my creek."

"'K," said the boy, unable to recall the last time he made a little deposit. Feeling good about it, he picked up a pebble and started to toss it in, but he held up. "Mind if I toss this in?"

There would be no further conversation with the man. He got up and stumbled away.

The move did not stop the boy's concern: "If you lookin' for y'horse, ain't nothin' I can do 'bout that. But if you lookin' for Bess, she's this a'way," he said, helpfully pointing. "An' if you lookin' for th' wagon, h'its back that way—but th' wheel on it is broken. But we can fix it, an' 'least we'll still have somethin' to ride on."

The man did not stop. He ambled on without looking back. Without looking back even at the ruins of the house.

The boy scooped up a handful of pebbles, laid back, and arched them individually into the water.

Soon the urge would come.

thirteen

USK SETTLED CALMLY IF NOT gloomily around Ben's place;
n came the lamp and the shadowed figure moved away
om the window.

Ben had moved from the one room to the kitchen.

Ben's kitchen was the center of activity. It said it all. It
as the utter depths of poverty. With its stained floor giving
ay to an old Thatcher stove whose chimney nervously
uched a roof that was independent of anything secure, it al-
ost defied description. The walls had never warmed to
allpaper, paint, or varnish, and the shelves that housed the
w cooking and eating utensils sagged to U-bolt propor-
ons. In the corner nearest the stove was a pile of chopped
ood, and in the far corner there was a tub that represented a
nk. In the center of the room was a homemade table with
vo weak chairs, and there was nothing else. Swinging into
e adjacent room, the bedroom, there was a huge, high-
osted wooden bed that suffered from age and was covered
y a multicolored—and multisoiled—quilt that, despite its
any colors, failed in the attempt to match anything. Diago-
ally across from the bed was a large trunk and next to it a

bottom-hanging, high-backed rocking chair that angled away from the loose-bricked fireplace. A lone kerosene lamp nested on a small round table just a few feet forward of the front wall and flanking window. All over the tiny room, including the ceiling, there were faded patches of burlap, paper and straw jammed protectively in a host of cracks and crevices.

Ben, who had just stepped outside to answer the call of nature, quietly returned with a pair of damp overalls, and lost his head in the big trunk. He was still scratching and pulling when Mr. Archy's voice rang from the yard. Oddly, the voice was not as harsh as it could have been; to be sure, it had an almost solicitous tinge to it—but still, it was Mr. Archy's. Unnecessarily, Ben decided to go to the window for a confirming look, and just as unnecessarily he shuffled back to the trunk. It was only after he had finished what he had started that he responded, and even then he was not sure about his plan of action. The voice called again—and again oddly, the voice did not become stronger; it didn't yell out, it didn't command, it continued in that same strange tone.

The texture of the voice was noticed even more when Ben went outside to see the man. Out there, there was an even bigger oddity. Mr. McBride was on the porch. Even though he owned it, he had never been that close to the house before. But, to go back, the first thing Ben had noticed was that the man who had threatened to kill him was not loud, and he did not have his shotgun. He didn't believe Mr. Archy would have actually used the gun, but he was wise enough to know the irrational mind couldn't be trusted.

He would wait to see what the man had to say.

"Ben," Mr. Archy said hesitantly, his hair unruly and his mind far from being settled.

"Now, Mr. Archy," Ben interrupted, and in violation of his promise to wait. "If you come here to—"

Mr. Archy stopped him with a wave of the hand. "F'get all that—we'll tend to that later. Right now I need your help."

"If you talkin' 'bout goin' after Mr. Silas an' them, I ain't gonna do it."

"You *ain't* gonna do it?"

"Nosuh."

Neither one of them spoke with harshness, yet everything was said with conviction, and Mr. Archy, although seemingly on the verge, didn't flare up at the refusal; rather, he stood quietly and searched the presence of the man who would not look at him directly in the eye. He then stared out into the dark. "Ben, what's got into you lately?"

"Nuttin'."

"But you're tellin' me what you ain't gonna do."

"I know that. An' I'm tellin' *you* I ain't goin' into town for to fightin'—an' I don't care what you say."

Still with patience: "You ain't ailin', is you?"

"Nosuh."

"Y'feelin' all right'?"

"Never felt better."

"No; you can't be feelin' well. So let's just forget 'bout what you said for now."

"I ain't gon' f'get nuttin'—an' I done told you I'm feelin' fine."

"Naw, Ben, y'aint. Y'aint been yourself lately. Y'must be sick or somethin'. Somethin' ain't right. I'll tell you what—gwoan back inside an' lay down for a spell. We'll get to that bunch later. Be better if we wait, anyhow."

"I ain't gon' lay down, an' I ain't goin' inta town after them peoples later on—or any time after later on."

"Now I *know* you ain't feelin' right, tellin' me what you ain't gon' do after what all they done done t'my place. Or do you know what they done?"

"Saw th' smoke from th' creek."

"From th' creek! From th' creek!" Mr. Archy said, hotly shedding the mask of patience and calling hard for the old ways.

"Umhum," Ben said, still maintaining composure. "S'matter a'fact, I was layin' down at th' time."

"You mean," Mr. Archy flustered, "you mean you was *layin' down* restin' your black behind while they was burnin' my place down to the gawddam ground?"

"I s'pose that's a pretty fair way of puttin' it," Ben said, calmly moving away from the door and comfortably sitting. "'Ceptin' I didn't know they was burnin' it at first. Then when I did figgure it out, it didn' bother me none."

"Ben, do you know what you're sayin'? Do you have any *idea* what you're sayin'?"

"Shore do," Ben said, rocking easily and ignoring hard glares. "But'cha know, I figgered if they didn't shoot you when you went into town, they'd do somethin' like that. An' I also figgered that if they did do somethin' like that, I won't gon try an' stop 'em."

"'You won't gon try an' stop 'em,'" echoed Mr. Archy.

"Nope. 'Cause if I r'member correctly, you departin' words this mornin'—y'said that you was gonna kill me— 'course I didn' pay that no mind—but I *did* pay a'tention to that thing you said about bein' free but still bein' a slave— an'a slave, you said, don't tell no white man what to do. Now, do I have to r'mind you what Mr. Silas and them is?"

"Ben, you're an ass, a *dum' black stupid ass!*"

Ben looked up coolly at the man who was bearing down hard, and slowly shook his head. "Mr. Archy," he started to say, comfortably crossing his legs and folding his arms above his head. "This is just one'a them days where we jus' don't seem t'be agreein' a'tall. Ben *was* a ass, but Ben ain' no ass no mo'."

"Where you get off talkin' like this! Y'crazy or somethin'? Y'outcha mind?"

Ben sprung forward in the chair: "I ain't th' one that's crazy, Archibald McBride, *you* is! An' you even crazier if y'think I'm gonna spend th' rest of m'life kowtowin' to you.

I ain't *gotta* do that no mo'. An' I ain't *gonna* do that no mo'. I don't need you, Archibald McBride. You need me!"

"I *need* who?"

"Me! *Ben*—your ol' darkie!" Ben said, jabbing himself in the chest. "An' as dum', black, an' stupid as this ol' darkie is, *you* can't git along without me!"

"Nigger, I'll have you lynched."

"By who? You can't do it yourself! An' I purposely—*purposely*—let'cha screw y'self up with Mr. Silas an' them. You can't go to Lumberton, an' there's too many of my kinda folks in Fayetteville. An' you *know* they don't like you!"

"Maybe they don't, Ben, maybe they don't. But if it comes to sidin' with somebody, I don't think I'd have th' problems you would."

"We may be dumb through the next ten centuries, Mr. Archy, but God help the day when my people start pickin' the ex-slave master over th' ex-slave."

"You don't know your people. An' as far as that ten—"

Mr. Archy let it drop because it was getting away from the real issue. It was not his thought, but ten centuries might have been stretching it. Ben did have a point though. A very good point.

What Mr. Archy wanted to say, and it would have been interesting had he pursued it, was: "An' as far as that ten centuries goes, your people ain't gonna last *one* century, from what I've seen let alone ten." He would have said it at any other time, but here he declined in favor of settling for a moment, thinking things over. And then, as if he had no other choice, he said quietly: "Ben, I want you off my property."

Ben responded as if he knew it was coming. "I'da been off a long time ago, Mr. Archy, 'cept—"

"'Cept what?" The loudness was about to come again. "Need? I ask'd myself that forty years ago! What do I need you for? You ain't got a pot to piss in!"

"An' you ain't either. An' if you don't believe me, open up your nose an' smell th' smoke! You know what that smoke means? The smoke means the end, Archibald McBride, th' end. Your end!"

"My end?" He even chuckled for a bit, and then he came back: "The 'end' my b'hind." Mr. Archy said it as though holding something in reserve. He made a move, stared out at the fields, and came back again: "In case you forgot, I got land—somethin' you an' nobody like you will ever understan'."

"I undastans one thing," Ben said, topping him. "You ain't got nothin'."

"Land, Ben *land*—look at it! G'woan, look!" Mr. Archy said, gesticulating widely. "Land—l-a-n—land! I got land!"

"Mr. Archy, suh," Ben said quietly.

"Every inch, every yard, every mile—everything you can lay your eyes on, I—*me*—Archibald McBride owns it! I own lan'!"

"I beg you pardon, Mr. McBride." Ben tried to continue with surprising ease, but in a way to strongly emphasize a point to a man going downhill. "You don't own nothin'."

"Can y'see it!" Ben was right. The mind was slipping.

"Mr. Archy—"

"*Lan'*."

"I sees, Mr. Archy, but—"

"Damn right, you do!"

"But what I sees ain't yourn."

"You lookin' at *lan'*."

"But th' lan' ain't yourn."

"Land Ben!" Mr. Archy shouted, his mind now positively slipping away.

"Mr. Archy?"

"*Lan'*."

"Mr. Archy!"

"*Land!*"

"Th' lan', Mr. McBride," Ben said, coming back, and still with ever so much calm. "Th lan'—*all* of it—b'longs to a lil' black boy by th' name of Moses."

But it would not register. Mr. Archy's mind had snapped.

"Lan', Ben; l-a-n. Go 'head! Set fire to it! Light it up! Haw, haw, haw. See! Ho, ho, ho. See what I mean? Ho, ho, ho. Hey, you in Red Springs. Hear me talkin' to you? Send 'em back! C'mon back, McMillan. You, too Shep, Silas, J. D.! Hey, an' what about you, Tonic? An' that ignorant ass with the cane! An' you, Okra, bring y'matches. Cruddup, raise y'self from the dead. Get up! Get up, you lazy, good-for-nothin' slob! C'mon—All y'all, let's have a fire! Let's burn Archibald McBride's lan'. Let's burn th' sunovabitch to th' groun'. Burn th' bastard outta Red Springs, run 'im out of North Carolina. Run this sunovabitch clean on out of th' country and all th' way back to Scotland. Back to his mamma's belly! Haw, haw, haw. . . . But wait-a-minnit. Hold it, Ben. Arch ain't going nowhere. Archibald McBride is still here. An so's his gawdamn lan'!—Hey, you slaves—c'mon back! They couldn' kill Archy an' the lan' can't burn! They couldn't burn th' lan'—so y'all come on back an' *steal* it! Hee, hee, hee. Hee, heee, heee . . . Land! Ben, land! Mine!"

And so it went for a long while. The man, circling the yard, screaming, gesturing, banging on the wagon, and pounding in the dirt. It was so bad that Ben had to leave the porch. He went inside to his bedroom and sat on the trunk, peering out every now and then, making sure that the man did not hurt himself. And when he quieted down, he would come back out. What he had to tell the planation owner could not wait, and if he was at all well enough to hear it, he would tell him.

When he got back out to the porch, Mr. Archy had stopped, and was sitting on the step, looking off—and as though nothing ever happened. Ben did not wait to ask if he wanted to hear what he had started to say earlier, but he did feel he should make a small inquiry:

"Mr. Archy," he said easily. "Is you all righ'?"

"Are you?" Mr. Archy said in return.

"Yessuh."

"Well, if you're fine, I'm better. I'll allus *be* better."

"I'm glad to hear that, suh," Ben said, sitting and feeling that the time was right. "B'cause, what I was tryin' to say to you, is that th' lan' is in Moses's name."

Mr. Archy continued to stare straight ahead.

"Th' lan' b'long's to th' boy Mr. Archy."

"Th' lan' belongs to *who*?"

"Moses."

"Come agin?"

"Moses *owns* th' lan'."

"Who?"

"Moses."

"Moses. Th' boy?"

"Yassuh."

"Now I know you sick," he wanted to say laughing, but he couldn't.

"No, I ain't. Th' boy *owns* th' lan'."

"S'little far-fetch'd, ain't it?"

"Nosuh. Not if th' boy's in your family."

Mr. Archy's face tightened. His mind went back, but he did not take off in a tirade. His mouth was in a kind of half-fixed position that seemed to wave off Ben's credibility.

"Nigger, you even crazier'n I thought." He looked a little strange when he said the word. He shook his head and walked to the edge of the yard.

That was another interesting thing about Mr. Archy. He wasn't thinking about it at the time but he seldom used the term *nigger*. Oh, he used it all right—he used it twice on Ben. But he never used it with the everyday frequency of the average white or plantation owner. *Nigger* was a term that was just downright base. He loathed it. There was nothing about it that he liked. Of course, he knew that it had an attachment to the word *Niger*—that far-off river in distant Africa, but most of the slaves didn't even come from that area. Some even came from Cuba, Haiti, the Bahamas—from all over the Caribbean, so he often wondered about the appropriateness of it. No one ever called them Caribs. He often wondered, too, why the slaves would have even answered to something so repugnant as *nigger*. Of course, they would have been shot, or lynched, or whatever life-ending measure was convenient at the time of infraction—infraction meaning not properly responding or being obediently respectful when addressed, but the slaves could have found another way to bury the term. For instance, he thought, why not just simply play dumb? They didn't understand the language anyway. And if one or two of the slaves had been shot or lynched for the cause, so be it. The whites couldn't have killed them all. It would have been economically unfeasible. Why buy something for a day and then go home and shoot it? But there was no getting around it, to his way of thinking *nigger* was just simply a bad, ungainly word. The blacks should have used some kind of—not intelligence, but *mother wit* perhaps? Give the term back to the people who gave it to them. Simple. It was such a thought that also had him wondering how long the connection to slavery would last. Not long, he once concluded, but then he heard a new batch of slaves from Ghana calling each other niggers. They were not offended. Oftentimes they laughed. Stupid, stupid, stupid. The connection, he reassessed, would last forever.

With his mind fully loaded, Mr. Archy returned to the step and sat.

Ben picked up from right where he left off: "I may be crazy, Mr. Archy, but th' boy own's th' land." And before Mr. Archy could question it, he added: "His maw helped him get it."

There was something in the way the black man had said it. Something that caused Mr. Archy to hold his temper and a mind that was on the verge of exploding again. Still thinking, he got up and strayed back to the yard's edge and rolled back the years. "His maw?" He turned back to Ben. "Y'mean Charlotte?"

"S'right," Ben said knowingly, and louder so that the man

could hear him clearly but yet in a manner that sent the other man's mind back to the edge:

"Nigger, you done lost your mind."

"Like I said b'fore, Mr. Archy, mabbe I is, but that don't change nothin'. Th' boy own's th' lan'."

"Fool, don't you know a slave didn' own nothin'." He then walked back to the porch and said in what he thought was edifying clarity, "An' don't you know a slave couldn'a given anythin' away, especially nothin' of mine?"

"But y'wife could."

Ben said it with such a quiet confidence that it remolded the contours of the man's face and reddened it to an unhealthy degree. He turned his head to question logic, but he couldn't say a word. He came back, slid down, and slumped over to the edge of the porch, and there he sat for a long while, gazing at nothing while churning old thoughts through his mind. Mildred, as he had known her, was a hateful, mindless old witch with nothing but spite in a warped heart. There were things she would have done to hurt him. But give away land? Violate the law and give it to a boy born in slavery? No, anything or anybody but that. More certain, she never never would have given anything away that could have even been remotely connected to Charlotte.

"Y'lying, Ben."

"Then go to Fayetteville, Mr. Archy."

"Ain't necessary. Ain't necessary, a'tall."

"Go to Fayetteville, Mr. Archy."

Once again there was something in the way the old black man said *Go to Fayetteville, Mr. Archy.* He had said it with so much poise, so much calm, with such a calculated confidence that it became a downright challenge. Fayetteville was the county seat. If there were any records at all, Fayetteville would have them. But, no, the whole thing is just too absurd. "Mildred couldn'a done nothin' like that."

"Yessuh, she could," Ben said quietly.

"She wouldn'a."

"But she did."

"Even if she wânted to, she couldn'a. She couldn'a. It ain't legal." And then he thought about it. The conclusion wasn't all that satisfactory. Hesitantly, he said again: "She couldn'a."

"Miss Mildred found a way t'give th' boy th' land, Mr. Archy."

"She couldn'a."

They were to go back and forth, and Ben wanted to end it. But not Mr. Archy.

"I know wh'cha tryin' to do, Ben, but it ain't gon' work. Mildred wouldn'a done nothin' like that to me." It had changed from *couldn'a* to *wouldn'a*. There was a chink in the armor.

"Mr. Archy," Ben said with hopeful finality. "Think of what you did to her."

That got him. Then again, everything Ben had said seemed to've merged with a certain kind of well-laid knowledge. His total posture was one of utter ease and contrasted bluntly with that of the man who couldn't find a way to respond to the last statement. One thing was certain, the air of absurdity had vanished and that look of wild impossibility gave way to moving clouds of doubt. What bothered Mr. Archy more now was that the boy who, dragging his hoe behind him, came drifting in from a prolonged stay at the creek. He stopped and delivered a light "here I am" wave at the two men. They did not respond to him, not even commenting on his lack of clothing. Sensing his presence was not acknowledged, let alone not being appreciated, he continued to his room to put on his last pair of pants and came out to the rear and stayed there, looking every bit as though he had been saddled with the chore of rearranging raindrops.

"She wouldn'a done nothin' like that. I know she wouldn't— she just couldn't," Mr. Archy said, and almost with the depths of a plea continued on to say: "Y'lyin', Ben. Y'gotta be lyin'."

"Then like I said, Mr. Archy, go to Fayetteville. You'll finds th' truth is in Fayetteville."

What a god-awful moment that was. He wanted Ben to say—and somewhere deep in his mind he thought he heard him say: "Yessuh, Mr. Archy, I'm lyin', I'm makin' this whole thing up. I'm crazy, an' I don't know what I'm talkin' about. An' Mr. Archy, suh, I'm sorry I caused you hurt by stirrin' up all'a these bad memories 'bout when th' boy was born. It didn' bother Miss Mildred. An' even if it did, there won't nothin' she could'a done about it, anyhow. She was smart, very smart, but even she couldn'a fix a way t'give nuthin' to no son of a slave."

"What's that you jus' said, Ben?"

"I didn't say nuttin', Mr. Archy."

"Yes, you did—that last part—repeat it, Ben. Wha-what was it? Ben—Ben, what was that? Huh, Ben. Huh? R'peat wha'cha just said."

"When I said what I said, Mr. Archy—I said th' truth is in Fayetteville."

"Yes," he said absently, his mind was away. "Yes—that's where th' truth would be. . . ."

"In Fayetteville," Ben added quietly.

"In Fayetteville."

"In Fayetteville."

"Ben—" he started to say again. It was dropped, and the conversation between the two men came to an end.

Tomorrow morning he would be in Fayetteville.

THEY HAD ONLY THE ONE wagon now, and Ben dutifully prepared it for the long forty-mile trip which, because of the hour, would have to be overnight.

Mr. Archy thanked him for the effort, checked to see that the lanterns were fore and aft, and except for the crunch of the wheels in the dirt and the cry of aged wood, the wagon rolled away slowly and soundlessly.

Ben stood looking after him for a long period, and then

ambled to the backyard to collect an armload of wood. Moses sprang out to help him, but rested his case by chin-sitting on the step.

"Where was you all'a that time, son?"

"Th' creek."

"D'jew put out th' fire?"

"Wanted to, but Mr. Archy didn' want no help," he said, somewhat puzzled and without making reference to the rescue.

"Well, I can undastan' that."

"Well, I can't."

Ben allowed the remark to pass without comment.

"How come you didn' wanna go over there?"

"Jus' tired, I guess."

"But you was gettin' plenty rest by th' creek, an' you ain't never done that b'fore?"

"Son, as you get older, things change."

"That th' reason you didn't go?"

"I s'pose you can say that," the uncle said, not wishing to pursue the matter.

"Well, since I done said it, how'cum you didn' go?"

"Now, now," Ben said, trying to end it. "A lil' feller like y'self shouldn' be worrin' 'bout things like that."

"I ain't worried," he responded casually. "I jus' wanna know why you didn' wanna go."

"Questions, questions, questions. Y'hungry, boy?"

"Been hungry all day."

"Well, now, let's jus' put a stop to that right now. Gonna fix you somethin' d'licious."

The boy popped up excitedly: "Like what?"

"Now, y'gotta be careful," Ben said, aiming him back into the kitchen. "'Cause this here day is a *very* special day."

"T'is? What is it?"

"Let's jus' say it's special. An' since it is special, we might as well eat special. What's y'favorite, Mist'r Moses?"

The boy who was about to scoot up to his chair stopped

and turned. "Mist'r? Unca Benny, you jus' call'd me a Mist'r."

"You is a Mist'r."

"Oh, no, Unca Benny. Mr. Archy is a Mist'r."

"An' so is you. An' he ain't no better'n you, is he?"

"Well, now, I don't know—"

"I know. An' I know you got every righ' t'be call'd that— an' don't you ever let anybody take that away from you, y'hear?"

At that point the boy was too occupied rolling the sweet sound of the word around in his mind. "Mis'ter"—he tried phrasing it in different ways—"Mist'errr—Mizzt'r—Mus'-tur? I'm one'a them?"

"All of 'em."

"'All of 'em?' Hottt zzziggidy!"

Ben smiled as he shirttailed one of the grubby pots from the shelf. "Now, Mizzt'r, what'll it be?"

"Ummmm—Er . . . Ummmmmm—er! Rice, bacon, an' peas!"

"But we have that 'most every day."

"But it's still my favorite."

The boy was smiling happily. Ben waltzed over and got a pail. "Would th' Mist'errr like to t'get us some water from th' pump?"

"Th' Mist'errr be gone!" the boy said eagerly and with his chest puffed out. The pump reminded him of something else he liked—the world beneath the pump. It always held a strange fascination. You could look down the big hole for hours and not see a thing, but when you tossed a rock in it, or a stone, or some tools, or some corn, or a can, or a snake, or a frog, or mule dung—almost anything—you'd hear a *kerrrrrplunk*.

Fascinating.

Worms, beetles, ants, bees, butterflies, grasshoppers, Junebugs, chicken feathers and/or droppings, wouldn't do that. No *kerplunk*.

Not fascinating.

When the boy returned, and after trying out a new ker-plunk with a bottled firefly, Ben had already tossed the kerosene liberally over the chunks of wood and the fire had begun to roar up the stove's narrow tin chimney. Smoke squatted heavily over the room, and it, along with the fire, sent his mind back to Mr. Archy's place. But that was over, and he wondered how the fire started in the first place.

"Unca Benny, how y'think that fire started over at Mr. Archy's place?"

Ben busied himself evasively. "Dunno, son," he said, and then wondered if Silas and J. D. and Shep and McMillan and all the others were satisfied. And if, pray tell, they had anything else in mind. He purposely lost the thought by concentrating on the heavily salted strips of meat that he took out of the lard can and slapped in the pot that bounced on the stove. Since, in cooking, Ben was impressed with directness, he never troubled himself to wash or closely inspect anything, and it was probably due to the long-held belief that anything foreign clinging to meat could do nothing but enhance the flavor.

"Unca Benny," the boy said, thoughtfully curled on top of the table. "Is t'morrow a special day too?"

"From here on out, every day is a special day."

"Then that mean we can have our other favorite food in th' mornin'?"

"Grits?"

"Nooooo."

"Okra?"

"Nooooo."

"How 'bout mustard greens an' peanuts?"

"Sounds good, but nooooo."

"Corn pons?"

"Like them too, but noooo. C'mon, Unca Benny. Our re-ally, really, really, really, really-really favorite."

"Dumplins an' collard greens!"

"Noooo."

"Bread 'n lard?!"

"Nooooo."

"Bread 'n buttermilk?!"

"C'mon, Unca Benny!"

"Then what?"

"Fatback 'n blackstrap molasses!" he said, forgetting he would walk eight acres for cracklin' bread and okra. And another two for pork rinds or pigs' feet. And if he had been thinking right at all, he would have said licorice—lightly fried. How that came about was when McMillan gave Ben that little bit of licorice that time, Ben brought it home and fried it with the rest of the food. The boy ate it, fell in love, and looked as though he'd walk on water for another piece. He still would.

"Fatback 'n blackstrap molasses!"

"Oh, sure," Ben said, glad that the boy had forgotten about the licorice. Feeling good, and again not exactly going by the book, he dumped a kettle of partially shelled peas into the water, and as an afterthought added a ladle full of dark, spotted lard. "Yessuh, we can have as much of anythin' as we want. An' you know somethin' else? We can eat as long as we want to. I don't have to go in the fields no mo'."

"Y'aint?"

"Nope."

"Y'mean y'kin stay 'round here all day?"

"Ummhum."

"Hotttziggidy!"

"Yep, I ain't goin' back in them fields no mo'. Them fields done see th' last of y'ol'unca Benny."

"Is Mr. Archy gon' tend to 'em?"

"Wouldn' think so."

"Who gon' tend to 'em?"

"Beats me."

"Hmmmm . . . well, h'its shore nice you ain't gotta go out there," he said happily. "An' h'its shore is nice of Mr. Archy not to let you go out there. Is that what y'all was talkin' bout? He seemed a lil' mad."

"Not exactly."

"Then what? Did he get mad at your singin'?"

"No. T'wont that."

"Y'kno, I like that song," he started singing, "*Go down Moses*" and said, "It's got my name in it."

"Glad you do."

"Y'reckon that's why Mr. Archy likes it?"

"Don't think so."

He took his time coming up with, "Unca Benny, do I have a last name?"

"No."

"You have one?"

"Color'd folks don't have last names."

"Sweet Elsie Pratt had one."

"T'wont hers."

He rolled over on the table. "That's one thing I'd really like to have. A last name." He took a moment more. He gave it more thought and asked, "Did Sweet Elsie Pratt like my name?"

"S'pect so."

"Wished I know'd where she went." He moved, and put a thoughtful hand under his head. "I miss her."

Ben would not comment. The boy plowed on.

"What was my mamma like?"

"Tol't you b'fore, son—you never had one."

It was coldly delivered; it was coldly received. The boy fell quiet. And then he started humming: " 'Go down, *Mo-ses* . . .' " He broke it off and fell quiet again. More quiet moments passed and, unable to sit without fidgeting and animatedly thinking, he got up and circled aimlessly around the table, and then bounced outside for a quick whiff of the quiet night air. He was out there for a full ten minutes, at the pump, searching, thinking; he then scooted back in and moseyed over to the stove to savor the sweet smell of the pot's contents. There was only one bad thing about a good meal, he thought. It just takes too long to cook.

He elbowed his way back up on the table: "Unca Benny, you think Mr. Archy eats as good as us?"

"Not quite, m'boy."

"How come?"

"Welllll, a man like that pr'bly ain't got the taste."

"Wha'cha think he eats?"

"Lotta funny things."

"S'what I figgered . . . no fatback an' blackstrap molasses. An' no corn pons." He evaluated it for a moment, and added: "Jus' can't undastan' people like that."

"Well, don't be in no hurry, son," Ben said as he sampled another mouthful from the pot and applied the final touches before removing the pot to the table. "I ain't too sure he can undastan' you."

The boy was too busy thinking to have gotten the last part of the statement. Thoughtfully, he drummed his fingers on the table and mused, rather disconsolately, as Ben slid a battered tin plate in front of him "No corn pons—an' noooo fatback 'n molasses. An' I bet he ain't never ever heard of fried licorice."

Poor Mr. Archy.

AND A POOR MR. ARCHY it was. At that point in time he was stroking the wagon to Fayetteville and, among other things, he was not all that happy with the mode of transportation. The mule was deplorable and slow, and far worse than the highsprung buckboard, Ben's old wagon shook and creaked miserably and surely didn't look as if it would make it even part of the way to Fayetteville. He had no such thoughts when he used the wagon going to and certainly when he left Red Springs that morning. But now the ride ate at him, and it would be a long journey, cutting six miles on the other side of Red Springs before even getting to Lumberton. Even so, the tiny burg would be closed by the time he passed through, and there was only one other town in his path. No question, the ride would be nothing but one dark and miserable pain with nothing to soothe him but the monotony of yesterday's South. Accompanying him, too, were intermittent thoughts of Mildred and that unholy day she decided they would marry. They had taken this same road. That was a bad day then; this was a bad day now—and, coupled with that, were all the strains and pressures of a woefully newfound concern. What a miserable day this had been. There was the bitter confrontation with Silas and J. D. and that numbskulled bunch, culminating with a shooting—no, a killing; the outrageous and shocking insolence of Ben; the burning down of his place; the loss of his horse and the buckboard; and on top of all that, there was that pesky little pee-dripping son of— son of who's? Certainly not mine. I don't have to own up to anything like that. Gads, what a day. But the most stabbing of all—the thing that really did it, the killer, the thing that got right down to the gritty core and wrenched every single nerve and seized every single solitary fiber in his gaunt old body and sat his conscience talking, were those words. What words they were—Ooooh, what satanic-sounding, brutal, and savagely cruel words: "Th' lan' ain't yourn. Th' lan' ain't yourn, Mr. McBride. Th' lan' ain't yourn."

"But, now, wait a minute. Wait just a gawdammm minnit! How'n hell would he know if it ain't mine or not? How could he know? How would a broken-down, shiftless ol' nigger know what I own? How *could* he know? He can't read; he can't write; he ain't been a gawdamn place outside'a Red Springs 'cept for th' time when Priminger found him hidin' outside'a Rennert—or whatever th' hell he was. An'—an' he was too gawdamn dumb to leave th' plantation when the others left, an' ain't nobody been back to see 'im, includin' that big black tub o'lard Elsie whatsername; and it's for sure that Silas an' them don't know a damn thing—an' even if they did, they wouldn' tell that black bastard! I must be out of my cotton-pickin' mind to listen to that fool!"

It was as if a Greek tragedy was at work:

"Fool, are you out'ta your mind?"

"No."

"Admit you're tellin' a gawdamn lie!"

"I ain't tellin' no lie."

"You're a damn liar!"

"I ain't."

"You tellin' me that's *not* my lan'?"

"That's right."

"How come it ain't?!"

"Mrs. McBride turn't it over to th' boy."

"Th' hell she did!"

"Then go to Fayetteville, Mr. Archy."

"Why?"

"Th' lan' ain't yourn."

"You're a gawdamn liar!"

"I ain't."

"The hell you ain't. Th' lan' is mine!"

"Th' lan' ain't yourn."

"It is! I, me, Archibald McBride, son of a Scot, owns it! Every gawdamn speck—mine. Two thousand and ten acres—mine—all mine! As far as the eye can see—mine, I, me, Archibald McBride! Y'got that, Ben! You got that, you broken-backed, lyin', ignorant, gawdamn slave! Ha-ha-ha; you got that—*slave!* Ha-ha-ha. You got that?"

"I got it, Mr. Archy. But th' question is, do you?"

"Stop it, stop it, stop it!"

"Why, you don't own nothin'."

"I Doooo. I Dooooo. I Dooooooo."

"How come a white man like you don't own nothin'?"

"I own lan'!"

"No, y'don't."

"You're a liar! A liar! You're a black, broken-back, sun-whipped liar!"

"Th' lan' ain't yourn, Mr. Archy."

"Gawwddammmm, yoouuuu! If I had my bullwhip, I'd beat'cha like I never beat a slave b'fore!"

"Beat on, Mr. Archy, but th' lan' ain't yourn."

"It is, it is, it is, it is, it is, it is, it is, it iiiissssss!"

"Go to Fayetteville, Mr. Archy."

"Noooo, gahdammit. You go to Fayetteville. Ha-ha, never thought 'bout that, did you? You go to Fayetteville. Here, gwoan, take th' wagon. Go. Git. Scoot. Wake me when you get back. G'byyyeeee, Bennnnnn. Have a nice trrripppppp!"

THE GREEK TRAGEDY WAS STILL working.

"Oh, Ben . . . ooooooh, Ben, it's good to know you're back. It's so good. So good, so good. Here, lemme help you down from the wagon. Watch y'step. There. Everything go all right? Here, lemme help you up to the porch so's y'can sit down in y'rocker. . . . Ah, that's good. You look good sittin' there, Ben. Always liked you sittin' there. Put'cha foot up there, up there on th' banister. There. Feel better? Want a chaw of t'bacco? Some more snuff? Make you feel better. How 'bout some sassafras, you like that. You want some later. Okay, I'll see that'cha get it. . . . Listen, Ben, could y'do one lil' teeny-weeny thing for me b'fore you tell me th' good news? An' it is good news, ain't it? Listen, Ben, c-c-could you just sing a lil' bit for your ol' massa? Huh? Could you do that? Could you do just a lil' bit for me? Go 'head, Ben. Go 'head. Oh, an' Ben—soft. Sing it soft, like y'all used to do. Go 'head, Ben—soft for th' ol' plantation master. Real soft: . . . Go down hummm-hummm."

> *"Go down, Moses, 'Way down in Egyp'lan. . . .*
> *Tell ol' pharaoh . . ."*

"Good, Ben, good—easy now—easy, I like this part . . . listen . . . easy . . ."

> *"To let—my peeple gooooo. . . ."*

"An' I let'em go, didn' I, Ben?"

"Shore did, Mr. Archy. You let 'em go."

"Night, Ben."

"Night, Mr. Archy."

"Oh, Ben, b'fore I go . . . Ben, b'fore I go—could'ja—could'ja tell me 'bout m'lan'?'"

"Yessuh, Mr. Archy."

"Who owns, it Ben?"

"Moses."

"Ha, ha, ha. Y'still joshin' me, Ben. You're just an old tickler. C'mon, now be serious, nice n' quiet—while nobody ain't listen', Ben—tell me, say—say, Mr. Archy—an' say it quiet, whisper it to me, Ben—say, Mr. Archy, th' lan' is yourn. . . . Lemme hear you, Ben—in this ear; no—in this one—whisper it in this ear—tell me, say to me, say, Mr. Archy th' land—all of it—every inch—as far as the eye can see—whisper, tell me who's lan' it is. . . . Go 'head, Ben—soft . . . say it real, real soft—say—Mr. Archy, th' lan' belongs to y—"

"Moses."

"THAT WAS SOME MIGHTY GOOD eatin', Unca Benny," Moses said, winding up the meal and sending quick, satisfying pats on a protruding belly that reminded one of a tiny cantaloupe.

Ben smiled and tossed an after dinner wad of tobacco in his mouth. "Y'say that every night we gits a chance t'eat."

"Yeah, but you said t'night was special."

"Well, it is."

"Is it a special day for Mr. Archy, too?"

"In a way."

The boy thought about it, and persisted. "What makes it so special?"

"Ooooh, lotta things."

"Lotta things, like what?"

Hoping to avoid more questions, Ben got up and took the tins to the tub and harmlessly splashed about a thimbleful of water on them, wiped them, and moved to the shelf.

"Huh, Unca Benny—a lotta things, like what?"

"Can't we say just a lotta things, an' let it go at that?"

"Noooo. An' you allus said, if you wanna know somethin', jus' ask. I'm askin'."

"Ummhum. But there's a lotta things a little fella like you ain't s'pose to know."

"Like what?"

"See, there you go again."

"Then why'd you tell me to ask?"

"'Cause, y'spose t'know things."

"But how can I know things if you ain't answerin' no questions?"

"You ain't asked th' right ones yet."

"Okay, I got'a right one."

"Shoot."

"Tell me what you know."

Ben sagged. "Good heaven, boy, I don't know what I'm gonna do with you." And then he thought about it. "Course, I don't know what I'd do without you."

"Why?"

Ben looked at him, shaking his head. "Questions, questions, questions. C'mon, son. Bedtime."

After the initial resistance, the boy always found something intriguing about sliding under the quilt and entering another world. Every night, after undressing and slipping on a pair of undies that rivaled a dark cloud for color, he would back off for a running start and pounce on the bed and reacquaint himself with the burlap that served as both mattress and sheet.

There would be no prayers, appeal, tribute, or silent acknowledgment of a Superior Being. But had Sweet Elsie Pratt lived, there would have been, and the comforts of religion would have occupied both his days and nights. The big woman would have told him, and he would have understood, the unending mercy of God, the Father. She would have spoken of all His children, and of the big book—the book with pages she could not read but nevertheless understood through the inexplicable miracles of godly communication.

In her own eloquence she would have spoken of a creation so stupendous in magnificence that man would always stand in awe and would forever be unknowing of its fullness. She would have spoken of Adam and Eve, and of Cain and Abel, and of good and evil. She would have taken him back to the Garden of Eden and likened the actions of the serpent to that of the slaver. She would have spoken glowingly of Mary and Joseph, and of the Wise Men, and of days unknown to him— Christmas and Easter, events so monumental they would forever touch the hearts of all right-thinking people, and would forever change the course of history. From the Book of Genesis to Revelations—the beginning and the end, she would have recounted untold numbers of trials and tribulations; triumphs and defeats. She would have indelibly implanted on his young mind the great legends of the big book—from the forgivable wanderings of the Prodigal Son to the adventures of Shadrack, Meshack, and Abednego. She would have gone from the prophets Amos to Zephania, from the lands of Ararat to Zion, and to the seas. From the everlasting power and wisdom of the Ten Commandments to the outright dread of the Four Horsemen of the Apocalypse, and she would have spoken of these things in her own special way.

The big black woman with the roaring voice and glistening skin would have talked of the many tribes—the Assyrians, the Babylonians, the Canaanites, the Hittites, and of all the people, from the Jews to the Samaritans, she would have spoken of the Apostles, of Andrew, James, Jude, Peter, and Simon, and time and time again she would have retraced the steps of the favored Matthew, Mark, Luke, and John, and she would have constantly reminded him of his namesake, Moses, and what he was to the world—and what he could become.

It would have delighted him to no end, and he would have promised her that he would be as she wanted him to be. She would have talked on wisely and reverently, saying that there is pain in honor, and that it, as he, would not always be understood, but that if hurt, he was to continue, and be afraid of no man—for try as he will, the true power was not within him, but rather above him.

She would have said, be not afraid to turn the other cheek, and if harm was done to that cheek, be not afraid to cry, for the greatest of all men cried. Cry in pity, she would have said, and cry in forgiveness of the man that wronged him, and then cry again in toleration of the indignities. She would have said, dry your eyes—dry them in preparation, for the time was coming when they as a people would rise up and mightily smite those that had oppressed them.

Prepare, she would have said. Prepare, because even though they were the oppressed people, they were no less than anyone, and, in an unheralded way, they were the favored. They had been uprooted, stripped of hope, and been betrayed—and although they had not been nailed to the cross, they had been beaten, stoned, tarred, feathered, and denied—and without benefit of palms at their feet or wreaths on their heads, they had been lynched by the thousands and with God as a witness they would always suffer at the hands of a misguided breed of man. Though created in His image, they have violated His trust, and would forever be devoid of decency, blinded by the light of His texture, cursed by the notion of superiority, and unknowingly reduced to the level of a dunce.

BUT THERE WAS NO SWEET Elsie Pratt for the child Moses. There was only his uncle Benny, and so the typical good nights for the eager young mind centered on the next day's activity, which, of course, would change little. That was good, and it was comforting to have another glimpse of the uncle before meeting the people, places, and things that lived beneath the quilt. They were special. They enjoyed each other even when the southern summer nights sang with the heaviest of humidity, the cover would remain—and thus the friends of the world beneath.

Ben came in for the last-minute check and was immediately hit with the question: "Say, Unca Benny"—the boy frowned in thought, reassessing the day—"where's Mr. Archy gonna sleep t'night?"

"Ain't so much as where he's gonna sleep t'night that bother's me," Ben said, tucking him in. "It's where he's gonna sleep t'morra night."

"He can sleep in town?"

"Don't think Mr. J. D. an' them'll go along with that."

"Y'think he's gonna—"

"Awp—that's 'nuff questions. Too much on y'mind will make you have bad dreams."

"But I don't never have no bad dreams."

"That's 'cause you ain't got much on y'mind."

"Well, I'll shore be glad when I do git somethin'. I don't think it's so hot not havin' anythin' on y'mind."

"It'll come, son. It'll come."

Satisfied, the boy slipped way down. Ben lowered the lamp, knowing that the fuel wouldn't last much longer than ten to twenty minutes. He also knew the boy would have at least one more question.

He did. Buried under the cover, he probed: "Wha'cha think Mr. Archy got on his mind?"

"If I was him, I'd have you on my mind."

The head shot up: "Mr. Archy's thinkin' 'bout me?"

"Ummhum."

"*Really?*"

"He's got to be thinkin' about you, son."

The youngster smiled with an inner glow, thinking: Well, I'll be! Imagine that! Mr. Archy's *gotta* be thinkin' 'bout me!

"Hottt zigggiddy!"

Ben looked at the curled figure under the cover, thought about him, and prepared to leave the room.

"Unca Benny," came the voice from down under. "Did you really mean it when you said I was a Mist'r?"

"Ummhuh," Ben said generously and quietly. "An' you're the best Mist'r I ever did see."

No finer words could have ever been spoken. "Hotttzigggiddy! Just wait 'til m'friends hears 'bout this. Mr. Moses is a Mist'r! Whoooooweeee!"

Hootttzzzigggidy!

fourteen

AS IN THE CASE OF Mr. Archy—which was about the only thing they had in common—the old Red Springers never cared much for the advent of night. This was particularly true of Silas and his stoop-sitting bunch. They didn't care for darkness simply because of the age-old condition of not being able to see anything—and seeing was always a part of a true stoop-sitter's diet. Of course, and to repeat, there was not that much to see—even in the light of the midday sun all they were able to digest were the exact same sights they had been staring at for well over a half century.

Still, the old-timers felt the cheat of dark, and Silas, years back, had complained that McMillan, as a storekeep, should have lined the more strategic areas with lanterns—strategic meaning lining the entire Red Springs road in the hope something commentable would show up. Silas advanced the idea because he had heard that's what they did in big cities. McMillan politely rebuffed Silas's notion with the suggestion that he would do just as well by setting fire to the match that he used to unwax his ears and pick at his few remaining teeth. The offer, of course, led to another yearly round of arguments with Silas always threatening to burn down the store and take his business elsewhere. The fact that Red Springs had no other store didn't seem to trouble him, though even if there had been another store, any management worth his salt wouldn't have tolerated him or his paying record.

Silas was a nonpayer from 'way back. McMillan couldn't remember the day he had ever seen him with money—other than the time he cleaned out Cruddup. But the ever-talker was really no different from the rest of the old regs—none of them had anything, and in contradiction to circulated yarns, not all of them had been farmers or slavers, but they claimed it. It just wasn't true. Only Tonic, the quiet and suspected halfbreed, and Okra had been farmers in the group, and only the late-arrived canehobbler and storekeeper McMillan were actual slaveholders; the rest of them simply could not afford the luxury, and even if the market price in Fayetteville for slaves had slumped all the way down to three cents a body, Silas and J. D. and all the rest of them couldn't have purchased one under any circumstances. Individually and/or collectively, they couldn't have bought a slave if the rate of exchange had been the proverbial pot. They couldn't buy time, and yet, to listen to Silas, one would have assumed that he had had a whole plantation of bondaged humanity. Not to stretch the point, but Silas was poorer than a freed slave. Angling for a loan with one prospect the same afternoon slavery was over, he offered to put his house up for collateral. The ex-slave took one look, declined, and kept on running, fortunately. Silas never had legal title to the six logs and a piece of canvas anyway. But like J. D., he was never much of a homesteader, and only in the early days did they both enjoy back-to-back shacks that measured only a few feet longer than an outhouse.

Of the group, only Cruddup, the big oaf who died in the name of ignorance, had a place worthy of mention, and that was only because of an inheritance. But be damned if he didn't let the place burn to the ground one drunken summer night. In fairness to his memory, though, the occasion was not entirely his fault—thanks to the agile mind of the bony Mr. Silas Crookashank.

The incident occurred somewhat in the following manner:

Cruddup, the dumber one, came to Red Springs from the neighboring little hamlet of Lumberton. In Lumberton, word had reached him that his dear ol' "Granny Rapp of the Springs" was on her last legs, and since he was the sole survivor, it might be a fairly warm idea for him to come and give final aid and comfort to the kind old lady who melted and sighed even at the name of her "beebee in Lumm'tum." But when the big "beebee" came, he did not give comfort to the old lady; instead, he spent all of his time around the front of the store, trying to establish friendship with the irrepressible Silas. But Silas wouldn't give the stranger the time of day; couldn't stand him. Hated the big, dumb ox. Wouldn't even allow him around the pickle barrel. And so the outsider's days were spent dawdling around the outer edges of the stoop without anyone even bothering to learn his name. Finally, Granny received the call from the Great Beyond; but before leaving, her feeble old hands saw to it that the "beebee from Lumm'tum" was taken care of. The "beebee from Lumm'tum" was heir to the second largest place in Red Springs, and it was not too far from the storefront. That was a great convenience because Bobby Jo Buggs, another coot of questionable repute and even less intellect, had taken it upon himself to act as town crier in such matters. Bobby Jo's brain was as about as stable as a teacup on the Mississippi. One sunny morning, while fitting himself with a pilgrimlike hat, he got the bright idea that he would combine poetry with town crying—just what Red Springs needed. When someone became sick, he'd grab pencil and paper; if they were *really* sick, he'd start collecting data; if they were on their last legs, he'd start writing. If they recovered, he'd start cussin'. When Granny's great call came, though, he dutifully dusted off the hat, put on some leggings, grabbed a cowbell, and paraded to the storefront. On that low-over-hanging day he stood in front, mournfully intoning:

> *"Anothern's gone. . . .*
> *An' a house is pass'd on.*
> *Granny Rapp is He'ven boun';*
> *But her house r'mains on th' ground.*
> *Whose it is now is news to me—*
> *'Cause h'its in th' name*
> *—of a lil' beebee."*

While "beebee" Cruddup remained aloof over at his section of the stoop, the others were leaning forward in hopeful attentiveness, for the passing of property was *the* major event in Red Springs and at no time was a single word to be missed. Fading minds did strange things, and one never knew who left what to whom. The cowbell kept working.

"Gawddangit, Bobby Jo!" Silas fumed, voicing everyone's thoughts. "Can't you stand out yonder an' give me more infa'mation than that?"

Bobby Jo sang:

> *"Anothern's gone. . . . An' a house is pass'd on."*

"Gawddanggit, Bobby Jo! What'n th' blazes is you talkin' 'bout? A beebee! What'n hell's that? You see any dam'd beebee's 'round here?! You know of any beebee's 'round here? Who got th' pr'perty, y'ignant cuss!"

> *"Find th' beebee*
> *An' you will seeee*
> *Who is got—*
> *The prop-pit'teeee."*

"Bobby Jo Buggs! Y'gawdamn sot!"

"Anothern's gone.... An' a house ..."

Away went the town crier. But who—and what—was "th' lil' beebee?"

While others went off to ponder the unknown entity, Silas remained on the stoop, digging his toes in the pickles, and fighting hard for the answer. It was even more difficult because Cruddup, unmoved from his position at the far edge of the stoop, was there with his long, dragging face, and annoyingly hampered Silas's serious thinking. When Silas tried to drive him off, Cruddup brushed away a tear. "I'm leavin' anyhow. I'm goin' t'see my granny. I been here all this time an' I ain't even see'd her once."

"Well, hurrup," said Silas without giving it another thought. "B'fore she kicks th' bucket."

Cruddup stood and brushed away another tear. "I used t'be her lil' bay-beee."

"What?"

Cruddup went on to reveal the story, and by the time he had finished, Silas had his arms draped around the big man's neck and both his feet soaking in the pickle barrel.

Now they were the best of friends. "Good, good, buddies." Glue. Inseparable. It fell to Good Buddy Silas to protect Good, Good, Buddy Cruddup from the evils of others. Granny Rapp's house was a museum of antiquity. The word *mausoleum* would have worked as well, but in deference to Granny and her rat-packing, pipe-smoking ways, one favored the less heavier of the two. Her house, large by any standard, was one of the first built in Red Springs, and everything the workers left was still there. Sawed-off planks of lumber, discarded nails, tar, and so on had found a home in her pantry. She had a collection of art, passed on from a father who spent considerable time in Europe claiming that he was a collector while all the while being a mas-

ter at the slave trade. The Red Springers knew of Granny's
eccentricities—meaning she was apt to have anything, so
when Good Buddy Silas led Good, Good Buddy Cruddup
over to the place, he made sure they were dragging sacks
behind them. Needless to say, neither of them knew the
value of art; neither of them had ever seen art. Good Buddy
Silas looked at the collection and said Granny must have
been pretty handy with crayons, and they both started filling the sacks. Good Buddy Silas at one end, and Good,
Good Buddy Cruddup at the other. In the process, Good,
Good Buddy Cruddup asked what the plan of action was
going to be. Good Buddy Silas told him that it would be a
pretty good idea to take everything movable over to his
house, come back, and:

"Sell!"

"Good thinkin', Good Buddy."

"When we come back, Good, Good Buddy, *we* gonna
have a gran' openin'!"

"Good thinkin', Good Buddy. How we gonna do that?"

"Tell somebody, Good, Good Buddy."

"Good thinkin', Good Buddy—how we gonna do that?"

"If it's gonna be gran'—you gotta tell 'em gran', Good
Good Buddy."

"Good thinkin', Good Buddy. Wha'sit gonna take?"

"Whas that in y'right pocket?"

"Oh, jus' some money."

"Toss it in m'sack. Gotta take it home. Gotta inspect it."

"Anythin' else?"

"Whas that in y'left?"

"Oh, jus' some more money, Good Buddy. Gotta check
that too?"

"Might be fleas on it. Gotta air it out."

"Right, Good Buddy. Anythin' else?"

"Whas upstairs?"

"Jus' some jew-ry m'granny left. Need that?"

"Got to."

"Righ', Good Buddy. Anythin' else?"

"Whas that back there?"

"Jus' some more ol' jew'ry an' furnishin's."

"Toss 'm in m'sack. Th' bigger the pot, th' better th' tew."

"Righ', Good, Good Buddy."

"Whas that on them walls?"

"Jus' some more ol pit-turs m'Granny pick'd up when he went fo'rin."

"Toss 'em in. Th' bigger th' cob, th' better th' kernel."

"Righ', Good Buddy."

"Whas that hangin' up yonder?"

"Jus' some ol' light m'paw gave to m'granny, second me he went fo'rin."

"Th' bigger th' plate, the better th' belly."

"Righ', Good Buddy."

"Whas that on th' floor?"

"Jus some ol' rugs m'paw gave to m'granny when he went to Per'sha."

"Th' bigger th' pod, th' better th' pea."

"Righ', Good Buddy."

"Whas that back yonder?"

"Jus' th' kitchen."

"Th' bigger the—*hold it!*—thas where we can put th' till!"

"Good thinkin', Good, Good Buddy."

Good Buddy Silas was so enamored with the idea of having a still in the kitchen, he took the two sacks, pawned them off, got drunk, and returned to the house two days later, lugging two fun-size jugs under one arm and an apple-mouthed pig under the other. Tagging behind him, equally drunk, and carrying equipment for making the still was Good, Good Buddy Cruddup.

"What we gonna do with th' pig?"

"We gonna roast it."

"Well, we shore got th' backyard for it."

"Noooo," heaved Good Buddy Silas. "Th' proper way t
treat a pig is to treat it like it was a guest. Roast it where
ain't been roasted b'fore."

"An' where's that, Good Buddy?"

"In Granny Rapp's livin' room."

WITH THE APPLE-MOUTHED PIG in the fireplace, and the drie
curtains blowing in the gentle breeze, Good Buddy Sila
struck the match and ceremoniously held it up. "Let th
fires begin!"

The house burned for three hours and twelve minutes.

fifteen

FAYETTEVILLE, NORTH CAROLINA, THE ONETIME state capital (1789–1793), seat of Cumberland County, fifty miles south-southwest of Raleigh. Founded by the Scots, named for a Frenchman, and occupied by Sherman. Benefactress of the Cape Fear River; scented by magnolias, spotted with azaleas, and flavored by a mirage of exquisitely dappled sunrises.

Changed now, but exciting were the early days of the big streets. Under a roving carnivallike atmosphere, the curious mingled with the serious and the serious mixed with the shoppers and became lost behind gracefully frocked ladies with spreading hats and wandering parasols. Eager-eyed youngsters flitted around them and gathered innocently at the far end of the street, plotted their course, grinned mischievously, and hopped merrily alongside surreys, carriages, and carts that cluttered Hays, Gillespie, Green, and Person streets. At the big circular intersection they would skip across to the big-bannered Fayetteville Market House—site of where the action would take place. Quickly, they would post a lookout and duck around to the rear and steal sniggling glimpses of the chained and squatted merchandise. Confirmed, the children would skip off to find rocks and other items suitable for throwing. They would return and the fun would start.

Dallying music swelled from the park, and amid the bowing, scraping, and dainty amenities of the day strolled buyers, who, flushed with the sense of gentlemanly astuteness and newfound importance, bounced big cigars from their lips and hacked over exaggerated figures and counts.

But in those early days it was the auctioneer who was the man of the hour—he was the crowd pleaser, and on a particularly good day, he would prefer abandoning the traditional courthouse steps to conduct his art on a platform that ran in, around, and in front of the newer and more prestigious Market House, so that everyone could see him and the quality of the product that sweated and gleamed appreciatively under a posh noonday sun; and if necessary, and to insure an exceptionally good appearance, he would instruct the handlers to see that the slaves were partially exhausted (obedience) and oiled before coming out for display.

They would come out but neither the oil nor hoped-for submissiveness could mask the hurt. They were all there because of color. Some were leathered and mahogany, few were bronze, chestnut, and cinnamon. But most were chocolate-brown and black. Some were sheened in ink black, there was the sooty black, the velvet black, the midnight black; and some appeared with a dark so dismal dark that it could never be described. Some had been captured, some had surrendered, most had been duped. For some their native kings had sold them out. They had been seduced by liquor—intoxicated and bedazzled by the fact that one of their own could fetch as much as one hundred and fifteen gallons of rum. Others were there because they had been traded for cheap, out-of-use cotton goods, glass beads, old flintlocks that could never fire, and by defective guns

owder and useless cowrie shells. Others stood there be-
ause they had been prisoners of tribal wars. For some,
ack home was a time famine; others had been the subjects
f the out and out greed of their own village leaders.

All had not been saints. There were thieves, bandits,
lunderers, warriors, spear-makers, devil worshippers, er-
ant witch doctors, abusers, and all levels of the wicked and
efarious.

And there was the good; there was Africa's future.

But all who stood there now had been fettered in a coffle
nd dumped into barracoons to await the ships that would
ake them to the New Land. There were slaves who did not
vant to end life. They were not like the Ibidio and Efik, the
entle tribes from eastern Nigeria, who, while being canoed
) the ships and knowing they would never see their home-
ands again, would jump overboard in unison. They were
ot like the ferocious Coromantees who, after mutiny,
anged themselves in groups, twenty at a time; nor were
ey like the clean and fit Mandingoes of Senegambia, or
ke the Ashanti, the Ibo, the Fanti, and a host of other
ibes and deities who fought capture and enslavement to
eir deaths.

Setting sail and journeying to the New Land was called
e Middle Passage. With anchors aweigh, the slaveship
rews, themselves devastated by cholera, scurvy, dysentery,
nd other illnesses suffered on the way over—and sub-
cted to more during the months of waiting on the African
oast—the first day aboard ship was a beehive of activity.
he first order of business was to again make sure that the
uskets and fixed bayonets were secured. Then there was
e matter of chaining the slaves two by two. Next came the
dorous and skin-crawling chore of branding the slaves on
heir breasts with the big, fire-hot irons. After that, there
vas the chaining of the men below decks, and then came
e chaining of the women, and then the children. Last, and

on top, for easy access for the crew, would be the young women.

Some of them would arrive in the New Land not realizing they had been impregnated.

Overcrowding was a problem on the ships that crossed the Atlantic. America showed heart. The nation became concerned, and in 1788, a law of mercy was enacted restricting vessels of three hundred tonnage or more to limit the number of slaves to 450. The slaveship *Brookes* apparently didn't get the word. On one voyage she carried a cargo of over 600. When informed that the *Brookes* had violated the law and had landed with a shipment of over 600 slaves, the Lawmaker Breckenridge was succinct. "Good catch," he said.

He wasn't alone in his concern. Others expressed the same sentiment but were more thankful that the *Brookes,* as well as all the Middle Passage ships, hadn't ended up like the *Kentucky*. Mutiny was always feared in the slave trade and many did occur. But for the freedom seekers the price of failure was deadly. The slaveship *Kentucky* was a case in point. In 1844 she had put down an uprising and in short order the captain exacted swift and brutal punishment. The crew of thirty-five men and six officers hanged forty-six men and one woman. They were shot at, mutilated, "made sport of," all while hanging.

But the record for at sea barbarity was not held by the American slaveship *Kentucky*. That distinction belonged to the English. In September of 1781 the master of the *Zong* threw 136 slaves overboard. It was not done because of a mutiny. Captain Luke Collingwood did it to collect the insurance.

ABOARD THE *BROOKES* AND OTHER slave ships, with two and a half feet allowed for head room, the slaves were made to lie in the *spoon position,* naked, on hard boards, and with the left wrist and ankle shackle of one person, shackled to

he right wrist and ankle of another. From the mouth of the
iver Congo, the journey to the Americas was expected to
ast for six weeks, but it sometimes stretched into three
nonths, and very often when the ships reached port, any
umber of the cargo had been lost. "Disobedience,"
laimed many. Illness claimed more. Some were driven
nad by the conditions and by lying helplessly in the belly
of the ship and hearing nothing but the moaning lamenta-
ions of chained bodies, augmented by the constant rolling
nd pounding of the sea itself. Others, for no other reason
han being paralyzed by the loss of freedom, thought of sui-
ide. Those that sought to carry out the final hope found it
irtually impossible to do so because of the shackles and
nore often than not by the inability to even sit upright.
They were left with the lone act of self-starvation. When
he condition was noticed, and making certain that it was
ot a normal case of seasickness helped by ground corn,
nolasses, and rice, or other foods the blacks were not ac-
ustomed to, the crew would spring into immediate action.
Motivated by the fear of economic loss, they would first try
o beat the offenders into opening their mouths with the cat
o' nine tails. Failing in that, the crew would get a bucketful
of piping hot coals from the galley and push the recalcitrant
ead and lips either directly into the scorching bucket or on
ts side. Sometimes the purpose would be defeated entirely.
With the chains conducting heat, the hot coals would be
ried to the lips, or the cheeks would be cooked to the
ucket.

With no medicine aboard, all would be lost.

Along with the hot coal method, another system was
sed. It was called the *speculum oris*. That method required
orging a flattened metal device between the teeth to force
he mouth open, thus food could be funneled down the
hroat. A thumbscrew was used at the same time. It was to
livert the pain.

In the long run neither method proved successful and, as

matters ended up, if it didn't appear that the self-starving slave would have a change of attitude or that he was unlikely to last the journey, he, or she, was released from the shackles and removed from below deck. He was simply thrown overboard.

But the troubles aboard the ship were of no concern to the auctioneer. The slaves had made it to the New Land. From Angola to the little kraal on the other side of the Zambezi they came. And now they were in Fayetteville, North Carolina—chained and oiled and ready for sale in an English-inspired structure so unique that it stole the thunder of a courthouse and became the focal point of a city.

Built in 1832, replacing the old State House where forty-three years earlier the state of North Carolina ratified the Constitution of the United States and where, too, she chartered a university and generously ceded her western lands to form the state of Tennessee, the Market House was an architectural wonder. Flanked by two beautiful second-story white balconies, it was made of pink brick, laid in Flemish bond. The entranceways and windows were cathedrally arched and pink pillars elevated eyes to the second floor, where a large Boston-made Howard clock chimed at mealtimes and fell in line with a melodious bell that rang from the cupola.

Sometimes, on a slow day, there were not just all slaves on sale at the Market House:

REAL ESTATE AND NEGROES AND FURNITURE AT AUCTION—At the Market House on Thursday the 22nd inst. I shall sell at auction a house and lot situated on North Street known as the Market House and adjoining the lands of Mr. James Kyle; 42½ acres of the land 3½ miles north of the town of Fayetteville on the Raleigh Plank Road opposite Mr. C. P. Mallett's, adjoining W. B. Wright, Esq. One negro (sic) woman, 25 years of age and child three years old. A lot of furniture among which is one piano, one extention dining table, bedsteads, chairs, and so on, and one excellent milk cow.
                            —January 9, 1863.
                            John H. Cool, Auctioneer.

And sometimes there were still fewer:

NEGROES FOR SALE—I will expose to sale on Tuesday, the
10th day of November at the Market House in the town of
Fayetteville at 12 o'clock P.M. four negro slaves belonging to
the estate of the late James A. Byrne, a decree of the County
Court has been obtained at September term for the sale of said
slaves in order to effect a division.

—October 21, 1863.
J. T. Warden, Commissioner.

But on the good days at the Market House—the distribu-
tion days, they were called, the site bristled with activity,
but no one could do more than keep an eye on the auction-
er. He was a proud man. Usually well traveled, he considered himself a true artisan, a master of the trade. It was his
feeling that no one knew the market better than he, and he
was quick to leave the impression that no statistic avoided
his uncanny mind and eye. He could name dates, titles, and
places, and without being pressed, and no doubt generated
from his own imagination, he could recount tale after tale
of the white man's heroics in capture, and he would expertly lead an enraptured audience from the wilds of Africa
to the stormy ports of the Americas. The auctioneer was es-
sential to the South; and in some cases, he was the South,
and to his way of thinking, he was that galvanizing link between man and beast; he was au courant—transient light of
the Dark Continent. The auctioneer knew his map and he
knew his people. His favors were highly sought, and sometimes he would come into town and cases of whiskey and
stuffed envelopes would be at the waiting; and better still,
the telltale hankies and pungent perfume of the late-night
female callers would leave him with amply more than mere
good wishes.

At the start of the auction, particularly if it was held out
front and in view of the coy eyes of fanning belles, the glib
auctioneer would meander through the crowd, spilling

quick bon mots about slaves as a people, and the looks and ways of the savages that remained in the jungle. His dialogue and their habits would leave the audience laughing in enriched smugness. Banter would take the good sport back to the platform.

With everyone uplifted, he would call for the start of the parade. Quickly the handlers would race off, and in an instant the first line of bodies would be led from a barren warehouselike structure across the street to the beauty of the Market House—and there they would stand, frozen in place, tied, heads bowed, and spirit weak in surrender.

The master of the trade would not let dejection take hold. Almost like a lion tamer, but with the artistry of a badinaging salesman, he would lead the slaves around the platform and by the time he had completed the second circle, everyone was convinced that dejection and misery was but the better of obedience.

If the first group of slaves appeared strong and virile and had those big backs that could hump the fields and stir the soil with animallike stamina—and if they had that added touch of moping docility—the audience would applaud enthusiastically, a clear signal that it had been a good catch, and that the traders and the plains of Africa had not run dry. The applause also meant that any and all troublesome stateside slaves could now be dealt with properly and without endangering progress.

In the matter of the children clinging to their elders, or the old holding firm to the young, or in the case of entire families holding on to one another with such intensity that fingernails would gouge the skin and send droplets of blood slithering off fingertips, there was nothing—no sympathy, no commiseration or pity for the ones from the jungle. There was nothing, either, for those that red-eyed each other in the deep and merciful hope of staying together in a land with strange customs, which spewed a language they did not understand. There was nothing except the cold, hard

fact that the hope of one species did not affect the will of
the other, and all he, the latter, had to do was to simply
nod—and the auctioneer knew: Mr. Suchnsuch will take
that, or it, or them. Without that additional tilt of the head,
the auctioneer knew that Mr. Suchnsuch did not want them.
He will take *that*—and *that* alone, and obligingly, *that*
would be ushered aside—and whether it was man, woman,
or child, the threat of the backstage bullwhip hung high,
and anything the whip couldn't handle, the butt—or sometimes the muzzle—of the rifle would. The cold qualm of
guilt touched but a few in those days, and the North's be-
lated, self-righteous unwillingness to accept slavery for
what it was would be cleverly shot down by a new thing
called the American Colonization Society.

To be organized in Washington, D.C., by Robert Finley,
the Presbyterian minister from New Jersey, and encouraged
by President James Madison and Senator Henry Clay, and
other influential leaders, the society would create and provide a homeland for the free blacks. Land would be purchased in Africa. An African state of Maryland on Cape
Palmas would be founded, and the colony would become
Liberia.

In 1822 the dream came true; but the first group of settlers, totaling 114, was almost destroyed by disease. Other
organizations were to follow the society, but they, too,
would fail.

Mr. Archy, as well as others, didn't know this, and it is
doubted they would have cared. The abolitionists and insur-
rectionists never received serious Fayetteville talk. The
abolitionists, it was felt, didn't care any more for the cause
of blacks than anyone else, and all the flag-waving rhetoric
was nothing more than bloated talk and thinly veiled efforts
to cover their own guilt-ridden inadequacies, as their true
feelings didn't run any deeper than a duck walking on
water. "Take the downtrodden beast of a man," it was argued, "and put him in the comforts of the abolitionist's bed,

and then see who would want to banish what." The insur-rectionists felt, too, that the abolitionists were far too errant, disorganized, and insignificant to create harm, and even if not, the South had organizations that would eventually blast them back into obscurity.

Before the Civil War, along with the *Brookes,* there was another incident that created somewhat of a stir in Fay-etteville, and that was the case of the schooner *L'Amistad* wherein the slave hunters had captured a group of Sierra Leone natives and headed them for Spain. But four days out at sea, and led by their young chief, the natives arose, killed the ship's captain and cook, and forced the remaining whites to surrender. Cinque and his men had hoped to re-turn to Africa, but the vessel mistakenly ended up in New York's Long Island harbor, where they were promptly ar-rested and jailed. Because of international implications and the outright boldness of Cinque's act, an act that could have fired every slave in the nation into rebellious conduct, the slave owners became concerned and hoped that the United States would dispose of the matter quietly. But the case proved to be much too complicated. Several court cases en-sued, but thanks to John Quincy Adams, the former Presi-dent, who at a weakened and almost blind age of seventy-three, later argued the case before the Supreme Court, and who had previously introduced resolutions into the House of Representatives directing President Van Buren, a southern sympathizer, to report to Congress the authority by which the Africans were held, the United States admitted lack of jurisdiction. On March 9, 1841, a landmark decision was handed down: The Africans were il-legally held and therefore were not liable.

In November, Cinque and his band were returned to Africa. Accompanying them was a group of breast-beating, Bible-toting missionaries. They would show the Africans the proper way to live in the jungle.

Long before the *L'Armistad* incident, however—starting

with the period right after the turn of the century—gradual changes began to take place in Fayetteville. Some of the glitter of the slave trade became commonplace, and the artful auctioneer no longer enjoyed celebrated status. As with the carnival atmosphere, his star dimmed and eventually gave out, and, as it was said by some, so had the quality of the slaves—although it was not the slave quality that spelled the end of one of Fayetteville's better-known practices. Oddly enough, that distinction belonged to Mrs. McBride, Mr. Archy's imperious but dippy wife.

On her second visit to market, the first having led to the second marriage, she had stood and criticized the notion of applauding. "Are we sick?" she charged, startling everyone by doing the most unladylike act of speaking her mind. These people are from the jungle, and yet we're applauding them? I have never heard of such a thing, clapping for a man from the jungle! Nowhere—nowhere on the face of the earth is that done! It is preposterous! We are white people! *White* people! *The superior does not applaud the inferior!*" And just like that, she charged away, leaving mouths ajar.

Mildred McBride, nee Byrd, daughter of Carruth C., was an unconventional sort, so unconventional that her sanity had always been in doubt. It came into further question when days after the death of her first husband, Ollie Priminger, she married young Archibald McBride, at the time a handsome but poverty-stricken escapee from the back roads of Mt. Mitchell, high point of North Carolina's Appalachian Mountains.

Two things set up the marriage: her wealth and his designs.

Archy McBride, then a slender and sandy-haired Scot whose father had jumped ship, gotten lost, found a house, claimed squatters' rights, sent for his family, and lived a long life, was about thirteen years younger than his salty-faced wife. His job at the time was to prepare the slaves for delivery—and there the duty was supposed to end. But the wealthy lady from Red Springs caught his dollar-signed eye on that first-time visit; he delivered the slaves she had purchased after saying more than once she would no longer be a holder of slaves and that she would get rid of those left to her charge. She was there to receive the slaves and the young Scot.

Four days later, the honey-tongued Appalachian had acquired a wife and a plantation load of slaves.

sixteen

THE ROAD FROM RED SPRINGS to the city where it all began, and a city Archibald McBride hadn't seen in years, was hard and long and treated the plantation owner from Red Springs with telling disrespect. Insects, bumps, and lack of sleep united with the pitch-black night and tried to stop him, but it was those strong, reverberating words that pushed him on: "Go to Fayetteville, Mr. Archy. Go to Fayetteville."

Dawn came.

She lived up to her name. Majestically, as though a host of chariots should have heralded the approach, she came gowned in the dust of a spreading mist and slunk with the grace and intimacy of an unhurried seductress. Sure, coy, she slithered forward—slowly—and made it appear as if the universe would benefit from low-lined cushions of haze. Softly, like an enchantress, she toyed with the dew and sent her long, elegant fingers weaving through the stillness and set sight on the only thing that dared interrupt the calm. Without anger, though, she sighed, dipped her graciousness closer, and there caressed the head of the straight-eyed old man who loosely held the reins and directed the crunching

wagon on its course. It was a stubborn and cantankerous old
head, and though persuasively touched, it would not surrender completely. Though slowed, the wagon creaked on. Un-
worried, dawn swayed and jested with the foliage and then,
with something on her mind, she went to her breasts. She
stroked them for him. The mule was not the subject, but he
was the first to feel the effect. He stopped, and after a moment or two he yawned himself to sleep. Unwillingly, the
head aboard the wagon followed suit. It tilted back and over,
and for a time looked as if it would lead the body tumbling
down to the ground. Confoundingly, it struggled back and
fought to remain upright. Dawn was undaunted. She smiled,
and taking her own sweet time, she disrobed completely.
Like the seductress that she was, she slinked her everything
on top of him. And he was deep in the dungeons of sleep.
She looked at him, smiled, and rolled over. She waited for a
moment more, and then she arose, and without doing anything more, she pranced away.

The hot rays of noon, she knew, would not be so kind.

Dawn was right. Noon came resentfully and tried to singe
the man to a crisp. The sun had so badly beaten, baked, and
confused him that when he arrived in Fayetteville, his mind
was still in a state of siege. It was hours before full orientation
came—and the changes in Fayetteville were of no help.

The textile and lumber mills were still scattered about, but
there were no signs of the big, smoke-billowing silos that
reached for the skies as he had imagined. There were still
many cotton houses, but it was the tobacco houses that established prominence. Fayetteville was now a leader in industry,
and the unlimited stretch of new and revamped and strongly
odored buildings attested to the fact that it was the industry of
the future. Workers, wagons, and scales were everywhere,
and it was for certain that everyone was gearing up for the arrival of the new cigarette-making machinery.

It was said that the new invention could cut, sort, sift, roll,
recut, reroll, resort paper, print, and trim a whole cigarette

without being touched by human hands. Tobacco could even
be boxed and shipped to loading platforms without human
guidance.

The machines were not here yet, but they were due.

The new industry was not, however, the concern of the
troubled man from Red Springs. He had memories and he
would not allow himself to go through the center of the city.
It was not a wise decision. He had forgotten or was still too
disoriented to remember that the road he often took to get to
the now-old Market House was sprinkled with a group of old-
timers representing the low end of the city. Usually there
would be a dozen or so, but the ranks had thinned and today
there would be only a sextet who squarely reminded one of
the Red Springers. On this day there was Epps, Wills, Bud,
and Austin, and one other old head who never said anything
to anyone and stood leaning against a post staring longingly
at the nearby intersection as if trying to look the new tobacco
machine into being. The five or six old saws spent their days
idling up on the stoop and underneath a warehouse sign that
inappropriately announced WE BUYS AND SELLS
TUBACCA.

The warehouse was empty.

Wills, a stringbean of a man with a protruding belly, and a
Silas counterpart, had found enough energy to paint the sign,
and had never gotten over the artistry. He was always first to
arrive at the stoop and last to leave. Going or coming, he
would always acknowledge the great work with a beaming
wave of the hand. He even suggested covering it up at night.

"I like it," he said that day, and as he had said every day for
the past eight years. "Y'like it, Mr. Epps?"

Epps, the proprietor of the drab, bone-empty building, had
never liked the sign, had never commissioned it, and never
paid for it. His everyday response to Wills was to look up and
say: "High art."

Wills would beam even brighter. It was a magnificent compliment. What Wills did not know was that Epps was not re-

ally talking to him. The story goes that Epps, a man of short
sentences, was a rather surly but uncommunicative child and
never spoke to his father. His name was Arthur. Friends
called him Art for short. When the father died, Epps, realizing
the errors of his ways, promised himself that he would speak
to his father every day. Thus . . .

THE CONVERSATION AMONG THE MEN—and indeed the city of
Fayetteville—was always about the impending arrival of the
machines. Not a store, not a shop, not a place, not a person,
not a thing, could escape the daily talk.

The stoopites were typical, though they didn't have as
much to gain as in the case of many of the others. Needless to
say, they were not farm or land owners, nor were they the big
moneymen, but they did have a modest stake in what was to
be. Their conversations usually started about an hour after
sunrise and would conclude at dusk. Wills, since he was first
to arrive in order that he could check on his sign, would often
start by inquiring—as if anyone knew—what the condition of
the new machines would be, hinting and hoping they would
arrive unpainted. If they did, he wanted the franchise. If they
did not, he wanted the franchise. His argument was that
Fayetteville had its own color scheme, and no city northerner
should ever paint for the South. Bud would counter the argument by saying that the machines were coming because of industry, and the color didn't make a damned bit of difference.
Austin would follow by quite rightly pointing out that people
chewed tobacco, not paint. And then it would start. They
would argue for hours. The only time they would stop and
collectively come together was when they would see a person
of negro descent, usually strutting with jaunty independence,
crossing the street to the nearby meat market.

The blacks were generously friendly and could be counted
on to toss an eye up on the stoop, give a cheery wave along
with a musical "how-de-do," and keep on strutting. Somebody in the group could always be counted on to deliver an

unkind response. On this morning it was Bud—the one who said the color of the machines didn't make any difference.

"Don't be 'how'doin' me, y'thief."

That was typical. The man was not a thief. Bud didn't even know him.

"Why you want to call him a thief?"

"Had to call him somethin'."

"Why?" A question—or position—which would start another argument. There were mixed emotions about freed blacks in Fayetteville. The bounteous city with the bright future didn't know whether to encourage or discourage, whether to open arms or close doors, whether to move for or to stand against. The one thing it promised itself it would not do, it didn't. It did not stand still.

When Mr. Archy finally rolled in that morning, he caught the Fayettevillians by surprise. They hadn't seen him in years. They still wouldn't like him, and what had caused them to dislike him so much was that the poor Appalachian had changed radically after marriage—or to be more accurate, after coming into wealth. Jealousy no doubt played a large part of it, after all, the country widow, while painfully hurt in the looks department, was a prize catch—financially speaking. It was said Archy used underhanded tactics to get her and the slaves. In a sense he did. In the case of Mildred, the tactic was obvious, and was as old as sin. In the matter of the slaves, he was more inventive. Knowing that a slave sale depended on a slave's appearance, Archy, an ambitious and very fine groomer at the time, would go down to the pier at night, sneak aboard the anchored slave ship, go to the galley, and steal all the flour he could carry. He would then make a mixture and take it to the hole and dust the more virile and promising-looking slaves with the concoction. In the morning when they came down the gangplank, it would look as if they had a skin disease.

Young Archy didn't have to resort to chicanery. In being a pretty good groomer, he had an intuitive and uncanny knowledge of the slave physique, and, when he wanted to, he'd make it work for him. There were times when, working legitimately for the market, he'd use that knowledge to advise, give tips, and generally do things favoring the house. Often, in using that uncanny ability, he'd be at the gangplank before anybody else, sizing up the merchandise when they made those first few steps downward. Several times he was offered a job as a trader, but he declined, saying—doubtfully—that seasickness was a problem.

"WHAT TH' HELL BRINGS YOU back to Fayetteville, McBride?"

"An' in a wagon. Sure can't be lookin' for slaves?"

The man on the wagon thought it best to seek information elsewhere. But he didn't know where else to go, and he was in a hurry, and he was bone-aching tired. "Th' County House—where they keep all them records, where is it?"

They knew something was up. "Righ' next to that buildin' where we used to have th' auctions."

"Next to where you used to *control* th' auctions," said Austin.

He left without comment. But he didn't get far before turning to look over his shoulder—and sure enough, he could see two or three of them following.

His presence alone would provide enough gossip to last through winter.

The building Mr. Archy was looking for was a small but beautiful structure, winged in a deep parklike setting. Off to the left, and as though guarding the pure, natural wood of the door, was a somewhat imposing statue of Gen. Robert E. Lee. The pigeons hadn't been kind to the shoulders or face, but it was still an impressive piece of work. Looking north, and respectfully away from the general, was another monument—a big cement pedestal with rows of chains hanging down from a series of iron posts, a tribute, said the plaque, to the great days of slavery.

Inside, the building was exceptionally clean, and spotted

behind the big counter was an efficient, young, balding talker by the name of Warren. When he could get a word in, and when the clerk wasn't constantly interrupting about how exceptionally loving and seductive the early morning had been, and that he hoped the same would be true when the new machines arrived, Mr. Archy introduced himself, and after suffering another barrage from the clerk, explained what he was looking for. Warren talked himself through several logs and files but could not come up with the name. There was no "Archibald" McBride. McBrides, yes. But no "Archibald" McBride.

The plantation owner was concerned, but not overly fazed. Try "Mildred McBride."

The clerk did as suggested. Double checking, there was no "Mildred" listed. But the clerk quickly rectified the mistake: "No wonder. You said Red Springs. I'm looking in the Fayetteville files," he said, spinning to head upstairs. "Don't get many requests from that part of the country. S'matter of fact, don't think I ever had one from Red Springs."

Now there was no reason to worry. Mr. Archy's records were there—everything was in order. For a moment his mind wondered about the tobacco industry. Should he commit to it? He took a glimpse out of the window to see what the spying trio was up to. Epps and the sign painter were the culprits. They made little attempt to duck, and simply stayed across the street, staring.

Mr. Archy, as he had been throughout, was surprisingly calm. He withdrew from the window and his mind took a turn and made an involuntary trip back to the early days. Across the street, where the men stood, was where he first laid eyes on Mildred.

What an empty-headed, argumentative, suspicious, and spooky old woman she turned out to be, he thought. And that moaning and crying all night. Priminger, the first husband, had been in his grave for three solid years, but by moaning over scented candles Mildred, strange Mildred, had found a way to keep the memory alive, and daily, *daily,* she would find a way to have it intrude upon their lives. If she thought so much of his memory, why did she become Mrs. McBride so quickly? Why, in less than four days after they had met, were they married in Lumberton? She would never answer the question. Even with others she would always avoid questions relating to the marriage. Mr. Archy was inclined to believe that in the long run she married him because he knew how to handle slaves.

It was important for her to marry young Archibald McBride because she was a lonely woman in a huge house with nothing but slaves between her and total isolation. And *that* was terrifying. Most women alone—most white women—while excellent at putting up a good front, were deathly afraid of slaves. Slaves were too unreadable, sometimes too quiet—especially at night. Slaves were a bunch of ignoramuses, so crudely imbecilic that they were apt to do anything—anything in the world. And they would too. They would because they were from the jungle and the fragility and daintiness of whiteness could stir them to beastly heights. And as far as Miss Mildred was concerned, they even looked at their own women menacingly.

What if she said something out of the way to them? Suppose she had reprimanded one of them, night came, and she was alone—again. What was she to do? Whether there was one or a hundred and one, there was just something about a slave and that stinking, ebonized body that got to her—as it did with all the women of the South. What could a southern woman do?

And the nights—oh, those terrible, terrible, god-awful nights—nights when even the silent movement of the house-boy would send shivers up her spine; and that Ben—that new creature Priminger found. He was the worst. And what about that—that sickening moaning from the fieldhands—slave chants; singing, they said. They should be ashamed of themselves calling those gruesome sounds singing. It's too flesh-crawling. Why do they have to do that? And when Priminger died, the moaning was nonstop. Why? Priminger had been their captor. He was their *slave* master. Didn't they know that? Didn't they know better? Mourning the man who had virtually chained them up and brought them here? That was just about as stupid and asinine as the Fayetteville auction applause Priminger used to talk about. She would go to the auction and tell them exactly how she felt. Would she buy a slave? Under no circumstances. Slaves were too scary for a woman alone. And she'd get rid of the ones she had—that's what she would do. And then the nights would be restful. Silent.

Why is a house so silent after death? Why does a big house creak so much after a body's been laid out for viewing? Up North and in the larger cities they have funeral parlors for things like that. They don't have you sleeping in one room and the body stretched out in another—hanging around for three days and nights. How ghastly. Why is it that the dead don't take their all with them when they go? Don't they know how frightening it is for those who remain to hear them? They lay there, whispering your name when they're supposed to be gone, reappearing, ghostlike, inviting you to join them in some forsaken place you've never heard of. Don't they know that fear rides with the silence of night—for those who are alone? Why do memories have to hang on? Why do they taunt so? Why can't they be uprooted? Why can't they be plucked out? Why can't they go away? Why can't they shrivel up and die? It is ungodly to hang around and taunt the lonely. All living things must die, all from the soil must return to the soil—all, that is, except for the memory. And just why is memory more privileged than anything else? Because it's intangible? What kind of an excuse is that? Excuse me. Yes? Priminger? I'll be joining you shortly, dear. Archibald McBride can't be trusted.

"BOTH DEATH CERTIFICATES ARE IN order, and, let's see . . . hummm—double-checking the date of deed transfer . . . hummm-hummm—and signature . . . prior to death. . . . Oookayyy; and notary . . . out of Lumberton . . . Yep, it's all here. S'all in th' name of Priminger."

The prematurely balding little clerk had been standing there a full two minutes, talking. Talking to himself, as it turned out. Mr. Archy did not hear him, or so it seemed. It was as if his mind had taken leave at some point before the clerk returned from upstairs, struggling with ledgers, records, logs, maps, all while reading, quoting, and pointing. If Mr. Archy heard him and was aware of the documents and all that Warren was saying, he certainly didn't show it. His look contradicted everything one would have thought. He stood there, saying nothing. Even when the clerk tried to poke him into saying something, still he said nothing.

It could have been that he had already started a change, and that in thinking of Mildred and that bent state of mind, anything could have been possible. Perhaps not legal, but certainly problematic.

But what about the law? What about the legalities?

Mr. Archy did not grant it full significance at the time, but the very next day—after what he thought was a rather strange marriage ceremony—if it could have been called a ceremony in a house without witnesses and with a preacher who didn't use a Bible and who never once asked them to repeat a vow, but on the way back to Red Springs, Mildred brought up the subject of the property, marriage, and the law and pointed out with further untimeliness: "Always remember, Archibald McBride. One cannot dispose of property one doesn't own."

"One cannot dispose of property one doesn't own," he remembered thinking at the time. "One cannot dispose of property one doesn't own. What th' hell does that mean?"

He said nothing aloud at the time and never bothered to question it further.

*   *   *

AT THE COUNTER, WARREN, THE clerk, took it upon himself to reread certain information aloud. On the third reading, not getting a response from the previous two, he took it upon himself to reread the entry louder and slower. He was careful to fully enunciate every word. There was a delay, but eventually there was movement. When the man from Red Springs finally brought his eyes back to the counter and up to face the clerk, they couldn't stay there. It was like they had been coerced into going back down again to fulfill a promise the head had made, but was not sanctioned by the rest of the body. Again the eyes went down to scan the log that rested near the relatively small and dusty cardboard box. Knowing that it was not necessary to perform full duty, the eyes came back up to face the clerk again. Warren said something else, but there was no need. Mr. Archy was gone.

For the sake of brevity, Warren had repeated that the described property had to be located by address, as the property was not in the name of Archibald McBride or Mildred McBride. He had told the man from Red Springs—as he was later to repeat to the snooping two from across the street, and who were to subsequently get it wrong. "The property in question," Warren repeated, "had been owned by Mr. and Mrs. Ollie Priminger, both now deceased. Mr. Ollie Priminger preceded Mrs. Ollie Priminger in death. In the intervening period, however, and under notarized signature of mother and widow, said property had been kept in the Priminger name. It had been deeded to one Moses Priminger, heir and only son of Mr. and Mrs. Ollie Priminger."

The widow Priminger never remarried during that intervening period.

WHEN IT HIT, IT HIT hard. *Mr. and Mrs. Ollie Prim*—?—What kind of crazed—What'n th' hell! What kind of convoluted crap! Mr. and Mrs. Ollie—Priminger? Mildred McBride was Mrs. *Ollie Priminger?* An' Mrs. Ollie Priminger was a widow—and the widow Priminger never *what?* An' that little conscious-nagging sunovabitch was *who? Moses Prim-inger? Son* of Mr. and Mrs. Ollie Priminger? *Mother! Mother* and *widow?* Th' boy was the son of a man who's been dead for over twenty years, and couldn' even get it up when he was alive, was the father of *who? My* son? Archibald McBride's son? Th' hell you say! What gaw-dam'd gall! It's gawdamn insanity! Wicked! Is th' world done gone plum' crazy? What *is* this? How unbalanced could a human bein' get? If this ain't th' gawdamn joke of th' century, I'll get on my hands and knees and sop mule puke! It's insane! Madness! What kind of a sick, distorted, and evil mind could even *think* of something so gawdam p'verted? An' think she could get away with it? An' notary? What kind'a gawdam notary worth his salt would go along with such buffoonery? Th' whole thing was sick. Mildred McBride was sick; a lunatic, depraved. A gawdam'd sick, depraved lunatic!

Lunacy was not restricted to Mrs. McBride:

What are you going to do about the property now, Mr. Archy?

Sorry, couldn't hear you, sir.

Still couldn't hear you, sir. But moving on . . . Your son, you've just acknowledged him for the first time. Did you know that?

Do you realize you did that, sir?

Can't hear you, Mr. Archy. But you've acknowledged your son. What are you going to do about him?

Mr. Archy? Mr. Archy, did you want to say something about your son?

Mr.—Mr. Archy? Mr. Archy?

seventeen

THAT DAY—THAT—"MARRIAGE" TO the widow Priminger did come back again. It hung heavy. It would not have been excessive to use the words *almost comatose* in describing the condition of the man who had been on the other end of that "marriage." It was a mummified man who now sat aboard the wagon that slowly creaked past the pigeon-stained statues, the monuments, the slave-reminding icons, the stores, the stoop-sitters, and everything else Fayetteville had to offer. Later, on the long road home, he did not see the spot where he had encountered the passion of dawn. There would be no seduction this time. Even had there been an attempt, it would not have penetrated. The former plantation owner was too busy fighting for the return of another visitor: full sanity.

Owing to the impaired shape of the mule, his condition, and the hardness of the distance, they plodded along all that evening and all through the night. Mr. Archy did not set sight on Ben's place until late in the afternoon of the following day, and when the old shack did appear in the dark-ened foreground, he did something he had not done during the journey. He stopped the wagon. He stared out at the old place and lowered his head from the trancelike position. He came out of it but, still, it was as if all the pressures of the world had weighted his shoulders. He remained downward for an extremely long while and, finally, as if he could find no answers, he pulled his head up and wearily sighed. He stayed in that position. His eyes went back out to the place. Minutes more, and slowly, lightly, he tugged at the reins and the wagon chomped at the remaining distance. If full sanity was returning, he knew, it'd better hurry.

Ben knew that it was about time for Mr. Archy's return, and so he had positioned himself on the porch, and with Moses at his side, he waited. An hour later he was still in his rocker, motioning easily, dipping snuff, sipping sassafras tea, and staring out at the broad fields of corn that were before him.

The boy did not know the wagon was coming and celebrated another good day by downing the last few gulps of a concocted mash consisting of blackberries, mixed with strawberries, cantaloupe, watermelon, pears, peaches, plums, huckleberries, gooseberries, walnuts, peanuts, and pecans. Nicely sated, he reared back and comfortably arched seeds, pits, cores, shells, shucks, and hulls at the big red ants and the zooming green-backed flies.

The world was at peace.

When the wagon finally arrived to within earshot, the boy scrambled to his feet and started to bounce out with a greeting. Ben's tap on the knee kept him in place. Back down he went.

Slowly the wagon inched to a stop in front of the porch. There was an acquired silence, with neither of the two men looking directly at each other. Moments passed, and with Ben determined not to say anything, the man on the wagon looked at the boy, and then looked over at the vast acreage. He was vague and gaunt, and after a time sat there and tried to fish for words. But the words did not come easily, and when they did, unlike the ring of old, they were soft and with that oily mixture of humbleness struggling for strength.

"Got anything to eat, Ben?"

Ben sipped easily on the sassafras and said unheavily, "Oooh, I s'pect there's somethin' back there worthwhile chewin' on."

"I can make you summa what I just had, Mr. Archy," the boy volunteered.

It went unnoticed. He wanted to say nothing more. But the man was starving. "Think you could fix a little somethin' up for me, Ben?"

"I think you can rustle it up yourself."

Mr. Archy nodded understandingly and relapsed into silence. The boy's eyes darted from one to the other, not having the slightest idea as to what was going on. All he knew was that Mr. Archy had never looked worse and that his uncle Ben, on the other hand, had never rocked so freely in his presence.

And then he was truly stunned.

"How you doin', son?" the man on the wagon came back.

The word *son* had slipped out, but Mr. Archy did not want a retraction. For the boy, he'd just heard the other side of the universe. Heaven just called. His ears popped and there was wide-eyed joy. *"Me?"* And then he couldn't think at all.

Ben rescued him: "Well, tell 'im how you been."

"Oh, er—*fine*. I been jus' fine—suh."

Mr. Archy nodded quietly, and continued to look at him, thinking.

"Y'look tired," Ben said, bringing his attention away.

"I am, Ben. I am."

"How was things in Fayetteville?"

If Mr. Archy was at all ready to open up, the question did

much to push him back into an unhappy silence. Down went the head again. Mentally he went away again.

"Y'ain't feelin' good, Mr. Archy?" the boy asked as though wanting to help.

Mr. Archy said nothing, and as the boy waited for an answer, he moved close to the edge of the porch and started to say something else. Ben quieted him with a polite look.

Minutes later, and with his actions grounded down to the slowest of movements, Mr. Archy lifted the reins and prepared to leave.

The boy looked quickly at his uncle, who did nothing to try and stop him. If the uncle didn't he sure would. "Where you goin' Mr. Archy?"

"Home," he answered vacantly.

"But—but you ain't got no home. It burn't up."

As if on cue, Mr. Archy allowed the reins to slip from his hands. Finally, Ben stood and came down to the wagon.

"Better come on in an' get'cha somethin' to eat."

Mr. Archy was in no shape to refuse the offer, and responded to Ben's extended hand. Down he came, and Ben helped him inside. Moses, feeling better, trailed with dancing eyes.

Feebly, Mr. Archy was seated at the kitchen table. The boy quickly climbed up to the shelf, got a plate, hopped back down, and slid it in front of him. With the kettle already simmering, Ben took the plate and spooned it full of food.

"Y'in for some mighty good eatin', Mr. Archy," the boy said, crawling up in a chair and propping his elbows up on the table so that it could rest a head that was watching the visitor's every move.

With the plate in place and sight of the contents strongly contradicting what the boy had said, Mr. Archy cooled a polite forkful and bit down gingerly. It was most unappetizing, but he wouldn't let it show because he was too exhausted, hungry, and deflated.

"Howz it taste?" the boy asked eagerly.

Mr. Archy nodded affirmatively but weakly.

"Got 'nuff there, or you want some more?"

"No, this is fine, thank you."

"Plenty more where that came from, huh, Unca Benny?"
Ben nodded.

Moses persisted. "Want th' kettle?"

"No. No, thank you," Mr. Archy munched tenderly.
"This is fine."

"You can have th' whole kettle if y'want."

"Thank you. But this really will do me."

"Unca Benny learn't how t'cook when he was in th'
cav'ry. Was you ever in th' cav'ry, Mr. Archy?"

Ben knew the answer would be directed at him. And it
was.

"No," Mr. Archy said as though trying to penetrate
armor. "That's one'a th' pleasures I've missed in life. Fact,
I've never been off th' plantation."

From plate to lips to the Adam's apple, the boy excitedly
eyed Mr. Archy's every move. It was an extraordinary time
for him. He had never seen Mr. Archy eat before. He had
never seen him in the house. In fact, he had never seen Mr.
Archy do anything but sleep at the creek and wagon into
the yard. And that was no way to get to know someone.
"Bet'cha never thought you'd be eatin' this good, huh, Mr.
Archy?"

It was the most anemic of all head shakes.

"Why don'cha give 'im some cracklin' bread so's he can
sop his plate, Unca Benny?"

"S'all right," Mr. Archy courteously interjected. "I don't
care for anythin' else. But thank you anyway."

"Y'dont know what you're missin', Mr. Archy," said the
little salesman, "th' cracklin' bread soppin' th' plate is th'
best eatin' of all."

"Sounds wunnerful."

"Want some?"

"No, no, no. No—I'd better not."

"Well, you can get some if you want."

"Thank you, but—cr—" It became lost.

Moses waited for a moment and energetically popped: "Bet'cha I know somethin' you don't."

"Um?"

"I'm a Mister. Jus' like y'self."

"Nice," the man chewed thinly.

The boy was quiet for a second or two and then, with his eyes still planted on the movement of the food said, "Where y'gonna sleep t'night, Mr. Archy?"

"All righ', m'boy," Ben said, "that's enough questions— c'mon, out'cha go. Go play on the porch."

"Can I get m'hoe an' go down by the creek?"

"S'an even better idea."

" 'Bye, Mr. Archy."

"See y'later, son."

See, there was that word *son* again. He didn't know exactly what it meant, coming from Mr. Archy, but it sounded awfully, awfully good, and added to that he said, "see you later." Happily, he left them.

Outside on the porch, before getting his hoe, the boy took a moment to reassess matters. It was a breathless time, there were so many things happening. The world was spinning by at break-neck speed, and these two were responsible for it. He had to catch up. These two were not just ordinary people—they were the hubs of the universe and something told him that there was more than work to be done, there was a commitment to be made. A dedication to the notion that these two hubs deserved the best he could give them.

So, no, he would not race down to the creek, he would grab his hoe and walk. That way he could think. The two hubs deserved no less.

Ben sat at the table. Without rushing, businesslike, he tossed a lidful of snuff inside his jaw.

"Now, Archy," he said loosely, "lettus get down to brass tacks."

Mr. Archy looked up from his plate. "Didn' you forget somethin'?"

Ben looked around to see what was forgotten.

"*Mister* Archy," the plantation owner said, reminding him of his station in life.

"*Mister* Archy?" Ben toyed with the word. "Well, ain't gonna be no more of that 'Mista' stuff when th' boy ain't around."

"Oh?"

"An' when I do say it, I will be sayin' it for his benefit an' his benefit alone."

"Ummmhuh."

"Y'see, I don't want him to lose r'spect for you—jus' yet."

"I see," Mr. Archy said, suggesting that he was a step or two ahead of the black man that sat across the table. "Meanin' that if he was to lose r'spect for me, he'd lose it for you—bein's that I was always over you."

"You gettin' smarter, Archy."

"An' you ain't doin' too bad yourself," Mr. Archy said in a voice that differed from a compliment.

"Noooo, must say I ain't."

"An' it seems you ain't just started."

"Well, now, I have been sorta keepin' up with things—you know how 'tis."

"No, I don't, Ben. S'pose you tell me."

"We'll get to it."

Mr. Archy pushed the plate aside and picked at the debris that had lodged between his teeth. Ben picked up the can of snuff and offered it to the man.

Mr. Archy refused and tried to push the subject forward. "So what's next?"

"Y'gotta choice to make. An' it is *your* choice. Y'see, far be it for me to try an' 'pose my will on you—see, I ain't like some peoples I know—peoples that jus' forces other peoples to do things. Y'know what I mean?"

"Go on."

"Now, 'bout that choice. I was thinkin' that—well, you see, I been out in them fields all m'life—an' you, on th' other hand, you only been out there to—to—er, well, let's jus' say to—to visit. Now, for some reason or other, Archy, that jus' don't seem right."

"Oh, it don't?" Mr. Archy said easily.

"No. It don't."

"Well, then, why don't you tell me what is right."

"You know what's right, jus' as good n' well as I do."

"Can't you talk, Ben? After all, in y'new position, you gonna have to know how to do that. Y'gonna have to know how to deal with people. Y'gonna have to be able to state y'position, come to a point. What's y'point, Ben?"

"My point is simple, Mr. Archy—"

"Watch it, Ben—you just call'd me Mister." It was an easy reminder, the smooth work of the other hand at play with the born-to-be-inferior. Ben realized the mistake, hesitated for a bit, and then continued as though nothing had happened.

"Mr. Archy—"

"Yes, Mr. Ben?"

Ben hated—despised himself for making the same old dumb mistake. Mr. Archy smiled knowingly.

"It takes years, Ben."

"I don't give a good gahdam if it takes th' rest of m'life, I'm gonna do it!" he flared, and then realized for the first time in his life he had actually uttered a profane word. And again he felt terrible.

Mr. Archy looked at him and penetrated: "What are you tryin' to say, Ben?"

"I'm sayin'—not tryin' to say that, one: I'm gonna beat that Mister thing. It's gonna take me some time, but I'm gonna do it—an' two: I'm gonna see you out in them fields—*sweatin'*—like I been doin' all my life!"

Mr. Archy, still maintaining reserve: "An' then what?"

"I'll think of somethin', Mr. Archibald McBride. Th' ol' darkie will think of somethin'. An' you can sit there an' think y'self as high'n mighty as you want, but I will think of somethin'—an' no more will you ever get th' best of me—or th' boy."

"How've I been gettin' th' best of th' boy?"

"It's his lan'."

"I see," an unruffled Mr. Archy said, and then reared back in the weak-backed chair thoughtfully. "Lemme ask you somethin', Ben. If you knew th' boy own'd th' property, how come you didn't do nothin' about it before?"

"Mr. Silas an' them," Ben responded smartly. "Y'see it wouldn'a been healthy if they know'd a lil' colored boy owned anythin'—an' you could'a tied in with 'em. Now you can't."

"So, now," Mr. Archy said slowly, "you plannin' on takin' th' boy an' leavin'?"

"Oh, if I could'a done that, I'da done it a long time ago. You must'a didn' read all'a them papers, 'cause I know it say in 'em somewhere that the boy's gotta stay on th' property."

"An' why's that?"

"B'cause Miss Mildred wanted him to always be righ' where you could see 'im. Always in your eyesight. Sorta like a r'minder to your conscience we always thought you never had."

"We? Who's 'we?' An' who figgered all that out, Ben?"

"Miss Mildred," Ben said, conveniently over-looking the first part of the question.

"With whose help did you figger that?"

"Friend o'hers. In Lumberton."

"Th' same man who drove her to Fayetteville, I s'pose

th' same man who falsifi'd papers. My marriage. You're talkin' about that preacherman."

"Trouble is, Mr. Archy, he won't no preacher," Ben said knowledgeably. "He was a jackleg."

What Ben was trying to say—as the deed to the land was trying to indicate—was: "If they won't no real preacher, they won't no real marriage. An' if they won't no real marriage, Archibald McBride won't entitled to no real property."

Had Mr. Archy been normal, had he been able to think clearly rather than leave Fayetteville in a state of shock, he would have concluded that the above notion was ridiculous. But then to hear Ben give credence to the absurdity by saying the preacher was a jackleg was a horse of another color. Obviously it was something he should have thought of before, but he wasn't going to worry about it. He had no reason to. Bogus and sham marriages were nothing new in the Carolinas. They even sanctioned inbreeding. The courts had dealt with the issue; the courts had ruled on the issue. There was nothing else to be said.

Archibald McBride was on firm ground.

So convinced of his position was he—and of something else he had in mind—Mr. Archy did not devote undue time to the matter, and though it appeared that his seeming calm and upperhandedness had crumbled at the sound of the words, there was a resiliency about him. He was not the same; it was not the same old Mr. Archy who would fire off a barrage with or without sufficient cause. It was not that he was surrendering everything. But the feistiness was gone—the arrogance had waned. Oh, sure, he was still Ben's superior—always would be. But even that did not have the significance that it once did—it was not a fraction of what it had been the day before. Something else had replaced that complex mechanism that ticked the movements of Archibald McBride. It could have been argued that the trouble with the Red Springers—especially the killing, the

re, the destruction of the big house—Fayetteville—the id-
cy of even *going* to Fayetteville, let alone what had tran-
ired there, all or any one of those things should have sent
m under and, for sure, would have changed the balance of
y man's mechanism. But not Archibald McBride. And
w, best of all, full sanity was back.

Ben knew who he was dealing with, and he had to be
reful. He rose, went to the tub, and stayed in that area, re-
izing Mr. Archy hadn't said anything for a minute or so.
Now, like I said before, Archy," Ben said, studying him,
ain't th' kind that likes to be forcin' peoples inta things
ey don't want to do, so that brings you to a choice. If you
n't go this'a way," Ben said, pointing to the direction of
e fields, "then, you goes that'a way."

Patiently, slowly, Mr. Archy started unloading his posi-
on. "Now let me tell you one gawddam'd thing—"

"Ah, ah, ah," Ben freely admonished him. "Now, Archy,
want you to consider y'position. You is both homeless an'
iendless. An' that ain't good in this day an' age. An'
ssin' at me ain't gonna do you no good."

"Ben," Mr. Archy said advisedly, "If I had my rifle, I'd
ow a hole plum' through you."

"Ummhuh. An' then what?" Ben said, confidently com-
g back to the table and using the term he'd used before.

Mr. Archy did nothing. And though he looked at him
arshly, he still wasn't fired into action. And, as before,
hen he started to curse Ben—even when he made the
reat about the rifle—there was no real menace to his
ords.

"Y'kno somethin', Mr. Archy," Ben said, and not really
aring about employing the word *Mister*. "You gonna have
 start doin' a heap a'changin'. Things like that rifle talk
eps you in trouble."

It was obvious Mr. Archy's mind wasn't where he
anted it to be. He wanted to respond differently—but yet
e wanted to get something off his chest, something he had

wanted to say to the ex-slave earlier, and something he ha
been reminded of when he was in Fayetteville and saw th
Market House and all the things that brought back the day
of slavery. "Ben"—he seated himself and started off refle
tively—"you ask'd me why you stayed on my land. I sa
you stayed on b'cause you ain't got a pot to pee in. That
true, but that won't all. There's more to it than that. I bee
thinkin' about it. Thought 'bout it a lot. An' now, sitti
here, watchin' an' listenin' to you, I know a lil' bit mor
Lemme tell you what I've come up with; lemme tell yo
why you're still here. Out there you've got to fend for you
self. Y'all got what you wanted. Freedom. Th' master car
tell you nothin' no more. He can't tell you where to g
how to go, when to squat—nothin', cause you're free. Th
color'd man is *free*. Thank the Almighty for th' favor h
done. I've even thanked m'self! But then, on th' day I free
th' coloreds, I sent you out there to give 'em the wor
R'member? Y'know why I did it, Ben? I was inside feeli
sorry—feelin' sorry for who?—m'self or th' slaves? I dor
know. But I'll tell you what I said to m'self: I said yo
free'd 'em, Archy, but the first night of freedom—whe
they goin'? How they gonna get there? I said to m'self, te
'em don't go lookin' for th' northern white man that say h
fought for y'freedom. He's gonna tell you he's done all th
he's gonna do—'for y'freedom.' In his mind there's a sig
that says 'Niggers, go that-a-way'—go *away* from me. He
gonna say, 'Get away from me—an' *stay* away from me
Ben you're free, all right. You free, but you too dumb
read his mind and too blind to read the sign. Your slavery
over, but ain't nothin' gonna change. A hunnert years fro
today, *two* hunnert years from today, you still gonna be su
ferin' an' shufflin'. You might not be shufflin' as much, b
you gonna be sufferin' as much.

"Th' coloreds' biggest thing in life is not knowin' ho
deep the white man's dislike of you is. An' he's sma
enough to get you to do enough to dislike yourselves. No

when this slavery thing is completely done with, years from today, he's gonna give you a lot. Some coloreds might be livin' high on the hog one day, might even be invited to th' white man's home—might even share a drink or a cigar with 'im. But th' one thing he ain't never gonna give you— an' I'm gonna r'peat this, Ben, he will always—*always* think he knows more'n you. An' he ain't never, he ain't *ever* gonna give you 'spect. He can be twenty times dumber'n you, he ain't gonna give you the one thing that makes you equal: respect. An' like a fool, the color'd man ain't gonna do a gawdam'd thing about it—an' th' bad thing about that is the colored man's got th' advantage. He don't know it, an'll never use it.

"Now, there's somethin' else I want'd you to think about while enjoyin' your newfound freedom—an' I say this be- cause to be truly free, you've got to be truly *able:* You sick—your children need somethin' as simple as croatin' il, how you gonna read th' label? You free, but you hun- gry—fatback cost a quarter a slab, sorghum ten cents a bucket. Th' body need nurishin'. Go buy what you need. G'woan, dig in y'pocket, pay for it. Th' body needs sleep. Buy some burlap, some canvas. Get it! *Buy* some land, nails, tar, lumber; buy y'self a hammer, a saw, an ax; go ahead, *build* you someplace t'stay. Now, Ben, I know *you* can at least start on some'a th' things. A long time ago, and I don't know why she did it, but I saw Mildred give you a pocketful of money. How much was it, Ben? I'm sure you counted it a hunnert times. Show me how somebody from Africa is gonna function in this land of lib'rty. Tell th' mean, old ex-slave master, somebody hog-tied to ignorance and tradition, tell him; tell him how much you got. Do one simple thing for me—no, do it for *yourself,* go get th' money and *count* it! Add, multiply, or subtract! But *count!*"

Ben looked at him wordlessly.

"No, don't look at me like I'm crazy, Ben. Count. Like I

said, to be truly free, you got to be truly able. Countin' goe[s] a long way t'ward showin' what you got upstairs."

Ben withdrew his look and said nothing.

"You can do it, can't you, Ben? You're tellin' me ho[w] much you got goin'. Prove it. Count."

Ben still refused to do or say anything.

"C'mon, Ben! The price of wheat is risin'!"

Again Ben looked at him, still refusing.

"A simple little thing like countin' your money? C'mo[n] Ben!"

Ben finally surrendered. "I been too busy t'count."

"You're a liar! Count! One and one is *two!* Two an' on[e] is *what, Ben?*"

Once again the old black man lapsed into silence. He g[ot] up and moved away.

Mr. Archy was furious. He charged after him. "What i[s] one an' one, Ben? Two an' two? C'mon, count'cha money[!] The white man is gonna clean you out if you can't count[!] C'mon—add, Ben, add: One an' one is two, two an' one i[s] what? Go on from there, Ben! Can't do that? All righ[t] then, count: *One! Two! Three! Go on from there, Ben[!] Countin' is just th' start of it! If you ain't got it in you[r] head, you ain't got it nowhere!*"

"*All right! You made y'point! You done made y'point!* [I] can't read and I can't *count!* An' you *know* it! You know b'cause when th' slaves got t'gether an' did try'n learn [a] little somethin' you put a stop to it! You an' th' *law* put [a] stop to it! Now I can't read, an' I can't write! But that ain['t] got a damn'd thing to do with what's goin' on now."

"All righ', then, lemme get to that." Mr. Archy pos[i]tioned himself to say it: "Negro"—and it was the first tim[e] he had ever used the word. "I ain't no different than an[y] white man you'll ever see. I'll be dead an' in my grav[e] b'fore I let you or anybody like you take over my land."

"Then, Mr. Archy, you might as well get on out there an[d] start diggin', 'cause it's gone."

Mr. Archy started off slowly, and said as if addressing very black who ever lived, "Mr. Colored Man: If you can't o somethin' as simple as count, all the schemin' in th' orld ain't gonna do you no good."

Ben digested it and said "You wrong, Mr. Archy. Dead rong. I ain't been schemin'. I been thinkin'."

"You ain't capable of thinkin'! That's what I've been yin' to tell you all along! Colored man, you *ain't capable* f thinkin'!"

"I might not be able to think th' way *you* want me to hink, but I done 'nuff of it to put me in better stead than ou!"

"How?"

"Th' boy *owns* th' lan'."

"I wouldn't bet my life on that if I was you."

"I'd bet mine, yours, and his. I don't know what I haft'a o or how to make it more clear to you, but th' boy *owns* he land! An' he got it by *me thinkin'!*" Ben shot up from he table and fired again. "Me, Ben—*THINKIN'!* An' if I adn'a been thinkin', what would'a happen'd to 'im—even vithout th' lan'? What would'a happen'd to him if I hadn'a tayed on 'round here? What would you'd a'done with a lil' lack young'un you can't stand th' sight of? Huh? What vould'a happen'd to him? You would'a tarr'd an' feather'd im, that's what you would'a done! Tarr'd an' feather'd im! An' ask y'self this—who sav'd him? What would'a appen'd to 'im if I hadn'a been interest'd in what was oin' on? What would'a happen'd even if I hadn'a been tandin' there that night, waitin' for th' birth of somethin' hat *you* was r'sponsible for? That's how long I been hinkin', Mr. McBride! That's how long's it been!"

Ben had been excessive, as Mr. Archy would not have arred and feathered anyone. He would not have physically armed anyone.

Ben had scored heavily with the point. And Mr. Archy new it. He remained motionless for a long while. His mind made another involuntary trip back to that night—that nigh the results of which could not have been questioned.

Mr. Archy had been in Fayetteville for the week, but stil his body tensed hard, always as if he had been there tha night, always as if he could hear the screams, and always a if he could see the blood spewing from an uncoordinated uterus and an unwilling placenta that crooked themselves with a cord called the umbilicus and together refused to comply with the natural order of birth.

Louder grew the screams that night as the team swelled and used a blockinglike tactic that for a moment looked as though they would prevent any hope of life-bearing passage. And the screams grew louder still, screams from a young black slave-girl, swallowed in the newness of delivery, sweating, grunting, and pushing with a determination that only a mother would know. It was through her efforts and her efforts alone that defeated the conspiracy.

The moment came. There was a release. Down it came and so did the blood. But the blood would not stop.

The boy survived. But the mother would never know.

"Ben . . . Ben, you just said 'standin' there that night waitin' for th' birth . . .' " Mr. Archy had measured and reevaluated what Ben had said. It took a while longer, and then he asked: "Ben, you just said—" He lost it for a moment. He came back, lost it, and came back again: "You said *standin'* there *waitin'* when the boy was born, didn' you? An' that's been your story all along, ain't it? *Standin'* there *waitin'*."

Ben wouldn't answer because in firing off his delivery, he had slipped. He made a crucial admission, and he knew it. What he said was at definite odds with the original story, the story so often repeated when Mr. Archy would come into the yard with the troubled mind, reliving again and again:

"What a night that must have been."

"It was a rough one, Mr. Archy."

"_A goddamn plantation full'a slaves, an', Ben, you couldn't find one of 'em. An' when you got back from lookin' for help, it was too late._"

"_Too late, Mr. Archy._"

"_An' not a midwife in sight._"

"_Not a one._"

"_An' it rain'd that night?_"

"_Storm'd._"

"_That's why I hate storms to this day._"

"_Me too, Mr. Archy._"

"_If—if only you could'a found—what was that loud, fat one's name?_"

"_Elsie Pratt. But she won't here at th' time._"

"_If you could'a found somebody like her—somebody— anybody—somebody that could'a taken charge—somebody who knew 'bout birthin' . . . Charlotte wouldn'a . . . She'd still be here . . . She'd still be alive._"

"_She'd still be alive, Mr. Archy._"

"_An' you had to d'liver th' boy by yourself._"

"_By m'self._"

"_All alone._"

"_All alone, Mr. Archy._"

"_All alone. An' from a dead woman._"

"_Yassuh._"

"_Poor Charlotte._"

THE TROUBLED OLD WHITE MAN ran it through his mind twice more. Suddenly he came alive: "Ben, Ben, you couldn'a been _standin'_ there. You couldn'a been _standin'_ there when th' boy was born. You won't there. You said you went to the far slave-house to get one'a th' women folk who knew somethin' about birthin'. A midwife. You said you went to find somebody—anybody—an' when you came back, Charlotte was dead. _Alone_ an' dead. An' _then_ th' baby was deliver'd—by you. _All_ by yourself. Ain't that what you told me, Ben? Ain't that what you told me and Mildred? Ain't that what you told th' slaves? You told everybody—you won't there! Ain't that wha'cha said, Ben?"

Ben was trapped, and he knew it. He was silent. Drawn.

Mr. Archy charged from around the table. "Talk to me, Ben!"

Ben said nothing.

"Gawdammit, man. Talk to me!"

Still Ben would say nothing. By this time he had managed to sit, but there was an urge to move because Mr. Archy was standing directly over him, his body shaking with threat. *"Talk to me! What did you do to her. Ben? What on gawd's earth did you do?"*

Now the man with the hump on his back had to move. He rose, brushed Mr. Archy aside, and went and stood by the tub.

Mr. Archy started to charge after him, then stopped, lowered his voice, and pleaded, "Ben, for gawd's sake, please—please, tell me what you did."

Ben stood motionless by the sink.

"Tell me what happen'd. How did she die? How did she go, Ben? You can tell me somethin'."

The pleas fell on deaf ears. Ben stood there, still saying nothing, looking at nothing. The hump on his back was hurting.

More time, and Mr. Archy came to his own conclusion. Slowly he said, "You—you just let her die, didn' you? Didn' you do that, Ben?"

Still there was nothing from the man.

"Ben—didn' you *let* Charlotte die?"

Although Ben said nothing, Mr. Archy knew. He knew that his servant had let the young girl die.

Mr. Archy came closer. "But why, Ben? Why? Why'd you do it? Why?"

He would ask him several more times, varying the question, but Ben would say nothing. The white man came back to the table and buried his face in his hands for a moment.

He then got up, circled the kitchen again, and returned to
the table.

"You *let* her die—you just *let* her die. You let my
woman and that boy's mother die." The old white man simply could not come to terms with it. "You *let* Charlotte
die. . . . Do you have any idea what she must'a felt? What
she must'a been goin' through."

There was no way he was going to be able to get over it,
and the only thing he could think of doing was to go outside and walk around—which he did. But it was a failing
effort. He didn't rush, but when he finally came back inside, Ben still hadn't moved.

Mr. Archy sat. He wouldn't let go, and as though talking
to himself first, he sighed heavily. "All the years—all the
wasted years. . . . All the hurt. B'sides takin' her
life . . . Ben, do you have any idea how much of my life
you wasted?" He did not receive, nor was he expecting an
answer. He took more time, and went in a different direction: "You kill'd somebody. You kill'd one of your own.
Why?"

Even if Mr. Archy had continued looking at him directly,
Ben could not face the man, and, again, it did not appear as
if he were in search of an answer. For a moment longer he
stood there, hanging on the tub. Soberly, after that, he col-
lected himself and went out to the front porch. Mr. Archy
did not follow him.

It was a bad night to recall, that September night when
the boy was born. It had been ushered in by weeks of stiff
and solid Carolina rain, and the young girl was terrified at
being in the old unsteady place. Worse still, as she had told
Mr. Archy months before, she simply did not like being
around the old black man with the tilted head and a hump
on his back.

If slave Charlotte had remained in the big house, where
she normally was quartered, there is no doubt the outcome
would have been different. But Mrs. McBride had so

taunted her during the last days of pregnancy that she, at Mr. Archy's strongly worded suggestion, moved in with Ben. Ben, as he promised Mr. Archy, would take care of her. At the proper time it was said that there would be a midwife on hand even though Mr. Archy knew that there was apt to be trouble with some of the female slaves. This was so mainly because of Charlotte's saucy independence. As far as getting interim help, Ben had told Mr. Archy that owing to harvesting season, he had been rebuffed at every turn, but at the expected time, someone would be there to assist in the delivery. It bothered Mr. Archy that none of the slaves would come over before that time, but he was also aware of the demands of harvesting. Further complicating the matter was the fact that neither he nor Ben could do much more than gently nudge for assistance in fear of arousing added suspicions, particularly those of the now strangely subdued Mrs. McBride.

If anyone had reason to be suspicious of the pregnancy, it should have been Mildred McBride. Often when she and slave Charlotte were alone, the perky and uppity young miss would float all too freely around the big place, and, as though she were momentarily about to be crowned lady-in-residence, she would gaily chime about redoing this or restructuring that, and, in general, revamping the entire plantation. In her second favorite spot—the first, she inaccurately said, was the lovely little setting underneath the sprawling oaks in the front yard. But it was in the master bedroom, her true favorite, where she would coo and sigh and drop unsubtle little tidbits about the titillating prowess of the plantation owner—still later, even though it had been drilled into her head by Mr. Archy and meekly supported by Ben, that the escaped slave she had once taken up with was supposed to be the father, she further rippled waters by enrapturedly melodizing to the lady of the house. "M'baby's gonna have light skin, an' rich, straight hair—sump'um like Mr. Archy's."

Small wonder the other woman once again went to her preacherman friend in Lumberton. Revenge is mine, sayeth the Lord.

THE NIGHT OF BABY MOSES'S birth had been particularly rough on Charlotte. Thunder and lightning belted the skies, and the rain came through Ben's ceiling as though it had never seen a roof. Every inch of the old shack was soaked, and his plugging and patching efforts didn't do anything but postpone the inevitable. Already afraid, and rhythmically paining, and now panicking on the drenched cot, with sweat and rain blanketing her face, the young girl cried out in further pain, "Bennnn! Ben—h'its comin! H'its comin, Ben!" She had cried out earlier as well, but not with the same pain and urgency. Pain or not, urgency or not, Ben did nothing. Incredibly, he made no attempt to go and fetch help. Incredibly, he stood there—in total detachment, fumbling with an old patch rag.

Sporadic pain gave way to the short bursts, and the girl screamed her last series. It was only after she had pleaded and bloodied herself into unconsciousness that the old black man with a hump on his back finally made a move. But then, instead of helping her, or going for black help, he went to the big house—and there, carrying out what had been secretly prearranged, Mrs. McBride—Mildred—met him at the door. They talked in hushed tones, and she accompanied him back to the shack.

There she performed the delivery. She cleaned and wrapped the boy called Moses.

They did not look at—nor did they touch the young girl. A moment more, and Charlotte had no more blood to give.

eighteen

THE GENUINELY DISTRAUGHT MR. ARCHY did not stay in Ben's kitchen long, and when he left, he was still grim, still searching. At the edge of the porch he stood, staring out in thought. The two men did not look at each other, and though tired, Mr. Archy would not sit. Finally, with an unreadable commitment on his haggard face, he ambled off the porch and walked slowly down the path that led to the creek. He hoped the boy was there.

Moses was comfortable on the ground, legs cocked in the air, both hands serving as little pillows under a daydreaming head. The thinking period had been put on hold. With the hoe beside him, he was taking in the deep blue sky—another of his all-time-favorite activities. He loved the sky because one could lay on the ground and still paint a thousand and one pictures on the never-ending ceiling and still have room for more. And the clouds: ah, those great, great wonderful clouds. What a treat. Clouds were always Johnny-on-the-spot, always at the right place at the right time, adding that right touch. Even when they moved, they did so with a gentleness and solemnity that defied words—

and they were mindful enough not to erase the pictures.
The big puffy clouds were his favorites. They were dim-
pled, huggable, and they reminded him of giant, free-
formed marshmallows. Sometimes they made him hungry.
He imagined they were not quite as tasty as that little piece
of lightly fried licorice he had that time, but there could
have been a nice sponginess to them. Lately he had begun
to wonder if any of his friends had ever taken a plug out of
them. But that would not have been right, he thought, and
went on to wonder if any of his friends had ever ridden on
them; and, if so, what was it like? Were they as cushy and
soft as they looked? An' what made them move?—Ain't no
horses up there. Do they have fun?—Don't see 'em
laughin'. They ever get sad?—Never seen no tears. How'd
they get up there in the first place?—Ain't no stairs up
there. Did they have a mule?—Don't see no barn. An' how
can they just stay up there?—Ain't no string tied to 'em.
An' where do they sleep at night?—Ain't no beds up there.
Where they eat?—Don't see no tables. What happens when
it rains?—Ain't got no shelter. An' when it gets cold?
That's it. Clouds should have something to keep them
warm. Maybe a quilt. He had a spare. And if they didn't
need his quilt, he would try and reach them anyway—they
should get to know each other. But first he would check
with his friends beneath the covers.

   Maybe they would like to go along.

"'LO, SON."

   The boy rolled over without fully seeing the stooped figure. "Well, hi—oooops, Mr. Archy!" he said, finally realizing he was not talking to a dropped cloud, and
simultaneously starting to scramble to his feet so that he
could run.

   "No, don't get up," the man said. "Mind if I have a
seat?"

   "Y'mean you gonna sit on th' ground?"

"Why, of course. I don't see too many chairs 'round here."

"No," the boy said, seriously looking around. "Don't see none. But I'll run back to th' kitchen an' get'cha one."

"No, no." Mr. Archy smiled and tried to sit without showing undue strain.

It was a most difficult time for him and it was probable that he would not have survived had it not been for the boy's quizzical but innately bouncy spirit.

"Shore is a pretty sky, huh, Mr. Archy," the boy said with more than a wee bit of nervousness still hanging on.

"Ummhuh."

"S'got a lotta clouds hangin' from it. I like clouds. Clouds r'mind me of Sweet Elsie Pratt. Y'like clouds, Mr. Archy?"

"Love 'em."

"How far y'think they is?"

"Too far for an old-timer like me to tell."

"Y'really a old-timer, Mr. Archy?"

"Yep. An' at th' moment I feel every bit of it."

"Howz a old-timer feel?"

"Not too good."

"Is Unca Benny a old-timer too?"

Mr. Archy tossed something he wanted to say about the other man away, "In a way, I'spose he is. Might even be a little bit more." He then tossed a small lump of dirt in the water and watched it sink.

"You know somethin', Mr. Archy," said the boy, itching, but yet with the solemnity and pace of a confession, "I know y'been mad at me, but I don't mean to do y'creek no harm. I mean, I—I—I jus' come out here 'cause I like it. This is my f'vorite spot in th' whole wide world. I did do number one in it a couppla times, Suh, but never number two. An' th' water never did get salty."

"That's all right, son. You keep on comin', an' do in it wha'cha want."

"An' you ain't gonna get mad at me no more?"

Mr. Archy hunched his knees up and rolled a ball of dirt between his fingers. "From now on, th' creek is yours, son."

"Mine?"

"Umhum."

"Th' water in it is mine too?!"

"Can't have a creek without water."

"Oooh, Mr. Archy—this is jus' sooo nice. This is th' best thing I ever did get."

"I'm glad to do it."

"Is th' mud mine too?"

"Th' mud, th' water—everythin'."

The boy swelled: "Oooh, L-L-Lordy, Lordy." He jumped. "Hottttzzzigidy. Can I run an' tell somebody I got it?"

"Sure. But who you gonna tell?"

The boy thought about it for a second. Mr. Archy was being real, real nice but would he understand the friends beneath the covers? Anyway, they were secret pals. "Nobody," he said. There was a lowliness to it, and then he looked at it and bounced back: "This is sooooo nice."

"Listen, son," Mr. Archy said after the boy had settled a bit, and after deciding it was best to forge ahead. "D-d-do you think you could ever get along without your uncle Benny?"

"Ooooh, nooo, suh. Never in a million years," the boy said automatically and sincerely. And happily—and unable to keep his eyes off "his" water.

"S'pose . . . s'pose—I mean if he did somethin' bad. I mean real, real bad."

"He wouldn't do nothin' like that. Y'think th' water needs anythin'? Maybe sumthin' t'eat?"

"I'm not really sure. But I don't think so." With such firmness on Ben, Mr. Archy knew it wasn't going to work. Without looking up at him directly, he consumed more minutes and picked up with: "Your maw. You ever give any thought to who your maw was?"

"Unca Benny said I never had one."

"You had one. An' she was a good one, the best."

"You know'd her?"

"Yes. Yes, I did."

"Did'ja like her?"

"Mor'n that, son. . . . Far mor'n that."

"Why?"

"Why? B'cause they didn't make 'em any better." Mr. Archy thought about her for a moment more. "She had spirit. Heart. An' she was very smart, an' very special. You're a spittin' image of her."

"That time when Elsie Pratt come by, she was like a maw. Maybe a gran'maw. She told me to be good, an' always love th' Lord."

"T'was nice of her. Now, son—"

"Know where she went?"

"No, no, I don't." And he didn't. He didn't really know her. She had been just another number, a worker—and like so many of his numbers who disappeared without reason, he'd never given her much thought. But now that the subject came up—where did that loud thing go?

Mr. Archy never knew a body had burned in New Hope Church that night. Of course, he knew there was a fire. The church sat deep off the road—along that vast stretch between his place and Red Springs.

Mr. Archy had smelled the smoke, came out on to his porch, saw the smoke and the distant glow, concluded that it was nothing belonging to him, and never thought any more about it.

"Your paw. Did your uncle ever say anythin' about him?"

"Said I ain't never had one'a them either," the boy said, untroubled.

It was rough on the old man, but he continued on troubled waters: "If you had a chance to have a paw, a paw that was, well, s-s-sorta different—" His voice halted uncomfortably and the touchiness of the subject left him on more than unfirm grounds, for if the boy had answered in the affirmative, what would he have done?

The boy nonchalantly withdrew a foot from the water, and then thought: *It's my creek.* Back into the water went one foot, and into the mud went the other. "Y'aint mad, is you, Mr. Archy?"

"No, son. You jus' go on an' enjoy yourself."

The boy sought to do just that. Fully clothed, he jumped in and started paddling like a rowboat.

"Son—what if—? H-h-how would you take to havin'—to havin' a paw?"

"Don' really need one long's I got Unca Benny."

"Ah, but you'd have a paw—your own flesh'n blood. You'd have somebody that cares for you, somebody to teach you things, somebody to look out for you."

"But that's Unca Benny."

"Do you know what a future is?"

"No, suh."

"Well, that's what you gotta have. An' as smart as you is, you can have a great one. You ever hear of a thing called school?"

"No, suh."

"Y'ever hear of a somethin' call'd readin' an' writin'?"

"Yessuh."

"Would you like t'start learnin' how to read? How to write?"

"Ma'be t'start learnin' how t'read."

"Y'can start both of 'em."

"No, suh."

"Why not?"

"Lately I been thinkin' I don't wanna learn 'bout no writin'."

"Why not?"

The boy came out of the water briefly, spotted a worm, and slid back in.

"How come you don't wanna learn no writin'?"

"I'm color'd," he replied. "I ain't got nothin' to write about."

It was obvious the boy's delivery had hurt him. It was obvious Mr. Archy was hurt in other ways as well. The cynic, the hardened, or the unforgiving could have very well argued that he did not have the right to be hurt and they very well could have questioned his motives. They could have argued, too—with certain justification—that he had lived a virtual lifetime desensitized to the lives of the downtrodden, and that it was because of people like him that this boy felt unattached to a past and bereft of a history. The cynic, the hardened, or the unforgiving could have said that he sat there manufacturing a change *after* the harsh and crushing news from Fayetteville and now that he was without the big house, he had no choice but to change, and sit there in clumsy and suspicious acknowledgment of paternal-ship—*if* he had changed at all.

But, to be fair, the trio should have taken closer scrutiny of Archibald McBride, and surely of the man on the *way* to Fayetteville—*before* he received the ownership news—if at the time he was capable of receiving news at all. But beyond anything else, the trio should have acknowledged that the change did not occur solely because of the transfer of the property's deed. It could have been a part of it, but there were other considerations. One, and it should have been examined more closely, the man—or the man's conscience— had been ground to a pulp by the mere mentioning of the name Priminger in connection with the boy, and then further along, it had been picked up, reassaulted, hammered, and traumatized by the sheer gall, the absolute audacity of Mildred, a supposed wife, who, with the help of a jackleg idiot from Lumberton, executed a document, listing herself as mother.

And then there was that matter with Ben.

"Your maw," said the man, getting up. "She'd a'been proud of you." He came over and placed a fatherly arm around his son's shoulder. The boy was a little bit frightened, a little bit exhilarated. He didn't understand it, none of it, but, then again, there was a lot about Mr. Archy he never understood—to include him being at the creek, and then giving it to him. My, my, my, ain't life nice?

To which he said, "Would Sweet Elsie Pratt be proud of me too?"

"Yes. Yes, she would." Whoever Sweet Elsie was, she would have been awfully proud. And then he had one question before leaving. "Son, if you had one wish, any wish you wanted in the world, what would it be?"

"I'd have to ask th' Lord for it."

"What would you ask Him?"

"T'make you an' Unca Benny like each other." It had a achievable ring to it; the man would not forget it. Moses continued: "An' I'd like to have a dog." And then he added dismissively, "But I don't really need one. Unca Benny say they eat too much. Maybe a lil' piece of licorice. But Unca Benny say they all out o' that, an' they ain't gonna make no more. But mostly in th' whole wide world I'd jus' like for you an' Unca Benny t'like each other. I dream 'bout that."

Mr. Archy gave it serious thought. He wanted to say, if that's what it takes to make you happy, that's what *will* happen. An' if you want a dog, I'll get you a whole kennel of dogs. An' the licorice—well, maybe a sack full. But he didn't say it. It was in his heart. But he didn't say it. What he did say before heading back to the house was: "Thanks for savin' my life." He moved part way to the path, stopped, and turned. Off to his left, away from where the boy was enjoying the creek, was the other path that led to where the plantation had stood. Mr. Archy looked in that direction for a long time. Memories came back to him, but he wouldn't allow them to linger. He turned back to the boy and said, "Thanks for saving my life—twice."

The boy was at a momentary loss. He had forgotten all about the fire, and that second thanks? Whatever it was for it was nice to hear.

"Thanks for th' creek, Mr. Archy. I'm gonna take th' best care of it. An' if you ever need anythin', jus' holler."

Mr. Archy did something he hadn't done in years. He laughed pleasantly. He thought about it—and the plantation. He moved away, smiling.

In the water the boy did a half cartwheel. "Wait 'til m'friends under th' quilt hears about this!"

Mister Moses owns a creek! Mud an' all! Yeah, yeah, yeah.

IT WAS A SURE BUT strained darkness that enveloped the old place. A pensive and motionless Mr. Archy was sitting on the far side of the porch. The other chair, well away from him, was empty but shared the weak light that emanated from the lone bedroom window. There were moments of cricket-chirping quiet, and then, inside, Ben's silhouetted figure doused the light. The new owner of the creek slid excitedly under the liberally and permanently stained patched quilt, and the muffled voice was heard to say, "Say g'night to Mr. Archy. An' tell 'im I gonna take good care of our creek."

The thought did nothing for Ben, and he left the room without comment.

When he came out on the porch he did not acknowledge the other man's presence and moped over to the rocker as though he didn't have a care in the world. It was strictly a pretense because the man that was sitting to his far left, aside from a greatly eased conscience, was in enough trouble to last for quite a while. He knew, too, that something had to give. But the problem was that if he gave—even if he did something as unthinkable as getting out of Red

Springs forever—the situation still could be described only
as precarious—worse because there was no way on God's
earth that the Red Springs bunch would even come close to
tolerating the thought of all that acreage falling into black
hands.

Whether Mildred had a legal right to turn over the property was not the point. The legalities, he knew, could have
been contested on several counts—except one. And that
one could not have been easily dismissed. It was a major
issue and it surely deserved more thought.

In all accuracy, though, and as stunning and woefully
contrary as it might have sounded, on the way back from
Fayetteville, and further supported by his trip to the creek,
one of the thoughts that had seeped into his mind was that
he—Archibald McBride—should have been the one to
have given the land to the boy, and no one had the right to
usurp him of the privilege. He was old, time was running
out—what was he going to do with it? But no matter what
he thought, Mildred beat him to the punch. Mildred did it,
and Mildred was an idiot. Mildred was a long-gone dead-
and-buried idiot who had no right to do what she did. Earlier he thought he would fight the issue. That was one of his
positions, and whether that one came about because he was
tired, whether he felt life had already beaten him into sub-
mission, or whether, and certainly more likely, that one
consideration was aided by the seductive qualities of a
strange morning's dawn that had oozed inside of him and
brought back those never-to-be-forgotten bed-shaking, free
and wild and enraptured times known only to him and a
slave that could turn him upside down with the bat of an
eyelash, that was his position. Archibald McBride's position.

There was an addendum to the deed. The document, as
written, stipulated that the boy had to remain on the land,
where he would always be seen by Mr. Archy. But then, if
it had to be questioned, what if Mr. Archy were no longer

around? What if he died? The land reverted to the state. Additionally, the boy was not of legal age; there was no record of birth; and Ben, as his guardian, in fact, was not his legal kin, and even so, like most of the slave-reared fieldhands, he couldn't prove his own existence—legal or otherwise.

In the matter of Ben, surely the questions would come: Where were you born? When were you born? Parents? Where were they born? What were their names? Don't know. Don't know. Don't know. Don't know. All right, what is your name? Ben. Ben what? Ben nothing.

It was a dirty, rotten shame, that's what it was. Ben what? Here he was, an ancient, beaten-down, hump-backed black who knew absolutely nothing about himself or the world he lived in. The only thing he knew was that he was born somewhere, at some time, and at some place; born to do nothing but labor all of his natural life and to be burdened by a hump that pained him at night and grew worse with the passing years. He didn't even know the name of the hump. Worse, he didn't even know his own name. Ben. It wasn't anything like *Ben*. That was not what he was called when he was a child. Forget the niggers, darkies, coons, pickaninnies, and all the other things he had been called at one time or another, he had a name. A name of his own. When? Long time ago, that's when. Long before that knot he got from his mother started spreading and swallowed the neck and crooked the head to the side; before African-named maw know'd that African-named paw was sold and sailed quietly out of view down the Senegal River, leaving her to hold everything together. Long before he came over on the boat, and long before, too, he saw her in the same look-alike chains, being taken off the same look-alike boat.

From plantation to plantation the Mauritanian from Nouakchott went back then, and the name—and in some cases, the number—changed at every owner's whim. The

knot was growing too, and there were no more whims. The
deformed were unsightly and therefore not welcomed
around the plantations. Rather than be killed as sport, the
hunch became a wanderer and for a few years lived in isolation just outside of quiet little Shannon until found on a
hunt by the trader Ollie Priminger. Priminger liked him,
named him, and gave him a home. At first Mildred thought
it was an appalling idea, but relented somewhat when Priminger convinced her that he would be exceptionally obedient, and that because of his deformity, he was less likely to
be unruly.

The years were good to Ben. Eventually Oberoma, the
head fieldhand, died; the position and the shack were given
to the old hunchback. But the loneliness remained, and despite the privileged position and the house, the age-old
problem remained—companionship for the deformed. Ben
would have accepted anyone.

But there was one he wanted beyond all others.

"You wanted Charlotte for yourself, didn't you, Ben."

It was an honest half-statement/half-question, and it cut
through the silence and darkening night like an arrow.

"Yessuh," Ben said, reflectively low. "Yes, I did."

The other man was equally quiet in his questioning.
"Y'ever tell her how you felt?"

"Yessuh."

"When?"

"As late as th' night th' boy was bein' born—and as
early as th' day you brought her home. First time I see'd
her, I know'd it. Th' prettiest and most specialist thing I
ever did see." He added with a great deal of pain: "I'd
a'lived an' died for that young 'un."

"Did she know how you felt?"

"I tol't her every chance I could get."

"What'd she say?"

"When?"

"Th' last time you told her."

"Between the pain, she managed to laugh. Same as she did th' first time. Every time I tol't her, she done th' same—laugh. Always laughin'. Even when Miss Mildred tol't her for me, she jus' laugh'd."

"What did Mildred say?"

"She told her th' same thing I tol't her."

"What was that?"

"How I felt—an' that I would be good for her. But she tol't Miss Mildred that if she want'd a slave, she'd go back to that first one she had. Th' one you drove off."

"I didn' drive 'im off. He escaped."

"You drove 'im off, Mr. Archy. You an' Charlotte drove 'im off."

The statement would not be contested, mainly because Ben was right, and Mr. Archy, for the most part, couldn't remember. He probed gently. "Did Mildred ever say anythin' to you about me an' Charlotte?"

"Umhuh. She used to talk about it all th' time," Ben said quietly. "You used to think Miss Mildred was crazy, but she won't. An' she never would'a kilt herself if Charlotte hadn'a kept teasin' her 'bout what y'all was doin'. An' that night, well . . . that night, after she saw th' baby—" He broke it off, wanting to say that while the two of them did nothing to save the girl's life, they spared no effort in saving the boy's. He wished he knew how to say that Charlotte had constricted unmercifully, and had Mildred not been there, without question the boy would have died with the hemorrhaging mother. He thought about it again and, trying to get away from it, he concluded, "That whole night was jus'—jus' too unreal."

As far as Ben was concerned, the subject was dismissed. Again, never once weighing the gravity of his wrong.

Fortunately Mr. Archy never knew of the conspiracy, and fortunately he didn't have that to contend with. Still, it took a long while for him to speak again, and when he did, it was about Mildred. "Mildred never would'a understood what I had in my heart for Charlotte."

"How minny white wimmin would'a unda'stood, Mr. Archy? An' th' way you went 'bout it, she thought that it violated somethin'."

"What? Marriage?" Mr. Archy said, thinking back to the occasion and what they had talked about earlier. "I'm suppose'd to believe that there won't no gahdamn marriage. Ain't that's th' whole point of it? Th' gawdamn preacher was a jackleg." He could have also added, since the entire matter was clear to him now, that not only was the preacherman a jackleg, he was also a falsifying notary. This was a matter he was going to get to later, as well as what he intended to do about it. But the old man concluded his thoughts with what he thought was a touch of irony:

"So young Archibald McBride was tricked by an old woman and a jackleg preacherman."

"Umhuh," Ben said.

"A jackleg preacher an' suppos'd to be a notary. What a combination."

"Guess it didn' matter who he was. Th' lan' was hers. All hers. She could do with it what she want'd."

"I'm gonna tell you again, Ben. Don't be too sure about that."

Getting married in lowly Lumberton was not fashionable and Mr. Archy did loosely question it at the time. Mildred said that it was something she wanted to do, and that was that. Mr. Archy had always believed that she felt uncomfortable because he was much younger than she, and that the union was far too immediate after Priminger's death. He also quite rightly reasoned that he was an outsider and that he would not have been welcomed even if he hadn't latched on to the wealthy widow. And there was the problem of Priminger's reputation as well. The dead didn't simply die in Red Springs. Reputations hung on. And if he was wealthy—as Priminger certainly was, and had a reputation that stretched from Red Springs to Fayetteville—as Primingers' certainly had, they hung on with renewed life. So there was no need for the young Appalachian to have questioned anything. Mildred selected the time and the place, and it was the minister of her choice. The fact that he was bogus, to learn that the whole thing was based on fraud and deceit—well, that was something else.

Ben intruded on his thoughts. "She said that's why y'all got married in Lumberton."

"I went through the *pretense* b'cause I was a damn fool. I'da done better if I'd done like a slave—a broomstick marriage. Jump over a broom an' say you married."

"At least you had somethin'."

"What'd I have? Charlotte was th' love of my life."

It took forever to get it out, but he had to say it: "She was th' love of mine too."

There would be no comment from the other man.

Going back, maybe Charlotte was the one-sided love of the deformed one's life; but, by his own admission, he'd never even had a life. And that was why, contrary to what she had hoped, Sweet Elsie Pratt never would have been a love. She would have been a companion, a warming companion, and he wouldn't have been lonely anymore. And neither would Moses.

Silence came and stayed longer than both of them had wanted. It was up to Mr. Archy to take the lead. "Y'know somethin', Ben," he said in a spirit of truce. "Lookin' back, ain't nothin' been too pleasant in our lives. I mean, if y' think about it, we both should'a been hung. I also got a feelin' there's a whole lot more you ain't tellin' me. An' I got a feelin' it's somethin' I don't want to know. I don't want to know how a man who don't know about birthin' a baby can suddenly learn to cut th' cord and nurse a baby from a dyin' woman. I don't wanna know how he could do that alone—how he could do it on a night with so much rain pourin' that he could hardly keep th' kerosene lamp lit;

how he could come even close to doin' anything like that without help from somebody much smarter than he is. I just want you to know that I'm feelin' somethin' about th' whole thing can't be right. But I made up my mind I can't be figger'n on things like that. It's too big for me. An' too late. Somebody, though, is gonna have to take it up with a power higher than me."

Ben looked away sullenly. He did not comment.

"But gettin' back to what I started to say, I had no business doin' what I did, an' you shore as hell didn't have no right—or cause—to do what you did, an' what I think you did. Right now, th' sun's settin' pretty low in our lives. We ain't got many of 'em left. That means we gonna be takin' a trip soon—an' at th' end of that road there's a man that's gonna be sittin' there, an' we gonna have to face him. You know who he is, Ben?"

Ben said slowly, his mind elsewhere: "I do."

"We're gonna be facin' God, Ben. We're gonna have to face God, face-to-face. Wonder what we gonna say? What're you gonna say to Him, Ben?"

Ben said nothing.

"Say somethin', Ben."

Mr. Archy could have asked him a dozen more times, still he would have said nothing. Ben was amazing. Truly amazing. Here, Mr. Archy, in a most clear-cut fashion, all but told him that he knew there was complicity in Charlotte's death. He was generous enough to indicate he was not going to do anything about it, preferring to leave it in God's hands, and he spoke of his suspicions in the most conciliatory and accommodating way—but yet there was Ben, sitting there, swelling over something else Mr. Archy had said. He was not thinking of the gravity of the crime or the downright wrong of fostering someone's death; that didn't move him in the slightest.

Ben sat there aiming his thoughts on what he considered an irony: "This man's done changed," he thought, meaning

Mr. Archy. "At long last, this man is goin' to *say* something to God. Not *tell, say!* The white man don't *say* something to God. They *tell* God, just like they do with colored peoples. They *tell, yell, shout.* They *order*—cussin' an' haranguing: color'd man do this; color'd man do that—God *damn* this; God *damn* that. Orderin' color'ds—an' *tellin'* God whatever and whenever they wanted! An' God's done given 'em everythin' under th' sun. The color'ds, on the other hand, had nothing. They had absolutely *nothing*—and always *beggin'* God. Every Sunday—an' all through the week—mornin' and night, on their knees—*beggin'.* An' somewhere now, still doin' it! Still at it—beggin' and beseechin'. Not *tellin',* not *orderin'.* Beggin'. An' still ain't got nuttin'."

The old non churchgoer went on to think, with equal inappropriateness, that maybe, just maybe, that's why when he was first introduced to the idea of joining the rest of the slaves in attending New Hope, thought that it was a rotten idea. To begin with, the church was misnamed. There coloreds had no hope—new or old, and he saw no reason that they would even bother to have those bi-weekly "freedom" meetings. Freedom didn't mean free. The white man didn't chain a condition, he chained a color. Old Ben concluded his thoughts by mulling over that final night. The church should not have been burned to the ground. Elsie was in there—not *tellin',* not *orderin',* she went in there bein' color'd. She went in there *beggin'. Beggin'* and *besee-chin'.*

He was sorry about what had happened. And he was sorry, too, that the week before he had been seduced by the storekeep's kind words. Nice words from the man, an inquiry about the church, and a little piece of licorice.

The white man didn't *ask* God, he *told* Him. And he burned His house to the ground.

There was a body in His house—a plantation worker. And the plantation owner never even bothered to find out whose.

"You might as well start talkin', Ben, b'cause we gonna have to tell Him something. It's gonna be a long line, an' we gonna have to talk fast. An' we better know what we gonna say, an' better start gettin' ready now. We gotta chance to tell 'im that we didn't have time to let it grow, but we did plant th' seeds for somebody. We was tryin' to do good for somebody who d'serves it. We gotta chance to tell 'im we ain't expectin' to be let off th' hook, but simply at the end we at least tried to do a little good for somebody. We can do that good startin' now—through th' boy. Now, I know, as wrong as I think you've been in some things, you've done y'best for 'im. An' I know you ain't just started doin' it, an' you ain't just stay'd on because of what Mildred put in them papers. You stayed on b'cause you was hurtin' deep, down inside. You stay'd on b'cause your conscience was hurtin' you, ain't that right, Ben?"

Ben lowered his head, but said nothing.

"C'mon, now, Ben, it's time to start tellin' th' truth. Am I righ' or wrong? You stay'd because your conscience was hurtin', didn't you?"

"I don't know what to say, Mr. Archy."

"Well, then don't say nothin'. Sit there and do nothin'. An' then think about what choice you got if we don't get t'gether an' try an' do somethin' positive."

Ben surrendered. "I ain't gotta go that far. I really made a'mess of things."

"An y'conscience's been hurtin' you."

"Killin' me."

"An' mine's been hurtin' me too. But we can start doin' right for right's sake—not for forgiveness, but because it's right," Mr. Archy said truthfully. He slid to the edge of his chair. "Look, Ben, I found out that some new tobacco machines is due in Fayetteville. They expect 'em any day, now—an y'know, some things like that is gonna r'volutionize the entire South. Th' smart money is gonna gear up and gonna go with 'em. Ben, they gonna be right in a might big

way. Now, I'm askin' you to forget about the past. It's
gone. All of it. If we really want to do some good for th'
last few sunsets, let's do it for th' boy. We can build this
place up for 'im. We can build this place up for 'im so's he
can one day be one'a th' biggest suppliers in all'a North
Carolina—maybe the whole South. An' the best thing
about it is, plenty a'people can grow cotton, corn, soy-
beans, an' all'a that. But they can't do what we can do.
They can't produce th' quality of tobacco like we can.
Did'ja know that?"

Ben wouldn't say anything.

Mr. Archy got closer with the chair. "Man, think about
what I'm sayin'. We got somethin' special here. We got th'
land—an' we got a lil' boy who's got a mind that when he
grows up can compete with anybody's in the country. Ain't
nobody can touch 'im. Now, put two an' two t'gether. Th'
boy supplyin' th' machines. First, an' here's why them machines is gonna be so big: They gonna be able to make
chewin' tobacco, pipe tobacco, cigarettes, cigars; they
gonna be able to pound snuff faster'n anythin' known to
man. Smokin's here to stay, Ben. There'll always be somebody somewhere with some kinda tobacco hangin' in their
mouths. If they ain't chawin' it, they'll be smokin' it—all
over th' world. They might even put tobacco in medicine
one day—but tobacco is here to stay, and it spells one
thing, Ben. *One* thing. Power. Whoever controls the fields
in North Carolina controls the *power*. Now, I'm askin' you
to f'get the past—it's done with; over, gone.

"Now, I got news for you, Mildred, that Lumberton buf-
foon call'd a preacherman an' notary, and that clerk feller
in Fayetteville. That whole fabrication over th' land is so
stupid, it's downright laughable. This property could
never—*never* leave my hands unless I wanted it to.
Whether th' marriage to Mildred was legal or not, it's mine.
All of it. We lived t'gether as man an' wife. If you done it
for seven years, a small thing called common law makes it

legal. I lived with that woman for three or four times that amount. But, again, that's over. Th' land is in th' boy's name, an' it's gonna stay that way. Now, I wish I could'a given it to him in th' proper way, but proper or not, it's his. An' it's gonna stay his. An' we gonna work it for 'im. We gonna fix it up for 'im. If you d'cide you got somethin' better to do, then you go right ahead and do it. I know what I gotta do. And I'm gonna do it. An' whether I'm able or not I'm still gonna take these old bones a' mine an' go out there an' work the fields, an' if I ain't able to culta'vate but a foot of it, I'll still be able to say to my son, 'Here, here's wha'cha paw did for you.'"

Ben looked at him, "You'd do that for th' boy Mr. Archy?"

"I'm gonna do it for my son."

"You ownin' up to th' boy? You really is?"

"I'm ownin' up to my son," Mr. Archy reemphasized.

Ben grinned. "Lawdy, a'mercy," Ben said to himself. He looked at Mr. Archy again and saw the urgent truth working. He wanted more confirmation. "Y'serious, Mr. Archy?"

"Never been more serious in m'life."

"An' y'ain't jus' sayin' it?"

"Sayin' it for what? How many more sunrises do I have left? How many do you? Moses is got a lifetime a'head of him. An' that's who we're doin' it for."

Ben got up and circled the porch and shot an eye back to the unlit bedroom window. "An' you'd done already made up y'mind t'give th' land to th' boy."

"Every last inch of it. As God is my witness."

Ben's circle grew wider, and he was talking more to himself: "Lawd, Lawd, Lawd, to think that lil' color'd boy could *own* sumthin'."

Mr. Archy heard it. "He owns th' land. An' he *ain't* a Priminger. How'n hell can a dead man father a child? Th' boy is a McBride. He'll always *be* a McBride, an' th' way

is McBride is gonna fix them papers, ain't nobody on th'
ce of this earth is gonna be able to take th' land away."

Mr. Archy was convincing and Ben couldn't get over it.
Boy, that shore would be somethin'. Good God, that
ould be sumthin'." He came back up on the porch and
ied to temper himself. But he couldn't. "Mr. Archy, I
ink you done hit it."

"I know dang tootin' we done hit it, Ben."

Mr. Archy said, stressing the *we*.

More thought, and with his enthusiasm building again:
An' y'say th' place is gonna be built up for 'im?"

"Absolutely. Now, like I said, you ain't no saint, but it's
p to God and his mama to be th' judge. They up there.
Ve're down here. But to do what's got to be done down
ere, I need your help."

Ben rolled the words around in his mind and looked at
Ir. Archy, again seeing how serious the man was, and
iid: "Who's gonna do th' buildin'?"

"Me an' you."

"An' who's gonna work th' fields?"

"Me an' you. Side by side."

Ben knew that the man couldn't make it out in the fields.
Now, Mr. Archy, you know you can't—"

"Hold it, Ben. I can try. I can give it all I got. That's all
ly man can do. But we *ain't* gonna fail th' boy. We can
art. An' if an' when it gets too rough—"

"On you?"

"On me," Mr. Archy acknowledged. "We'll wagon in
ome folks from Fayetteville."

"Maybe out'a Lumberton or Charlotte—maybe out'a
ennert or Shannon, an' there's Raeford, an'a coupl'a more
f them lil' places in between."

"We'll stick with th' big stuff. But we gonna get it done.
ll we gotta do is get it fixed in our minds. Y'with me?"

Ben, by this time, had sat down and was standing again.

He sat again, pictured it in his mind, and unnecessari
asked, "When we gon' start?"

"Sooner than soon," Mr. Archy said.

Ben was now back standing and grinning again. Eve
though it was dark on the porch, it looked as if his few r
maining teeth had pushed stain and hardship aside
sparkle one last time. Feeling good, Mr. Archy extended
hand, "We gonna do it, Ben. We gonna do it. Teamwork
gonna do it."

Ben held on to his hand much too hard and then vigo
ously shook it. "You bet'cha we is, Mr. Archy. You bet'cl
we is."

In their exuberance they never saw the boy peeping fro
the bedroom. If ever there was about to be a happy mome
in a boy's life, this was about to be it. When he saw M
Archy extend for the handshake, he put his little hands ov
his mouth to breathlessly wait to see what the uncle wou
do. It was a moment of high tension for him, and when t'
uncle acknowledged the handshake in what amounted to
new and lasting friendship, and then gave it that somethi
extra, the boy didn't leap, he sprouted wings and levitate
back to the bed. Landing safely, he hesitated for but a fra
tion of a second, and then he pounced, and rolled, and wi
gled, and giggled, kicked his heels in the air, thought abo
the clouds, offered them some licorice, joined the cavalr
forgot about the dog, blew Sweet Elsie a kiss, promised
sweep the creek, slid under the covers, summoned the gan
put them on hold, came back up, hit the floor, spun arou
the room, looked for his horse, settled for a frog, an
slipped under the quilt again, and—*kerplunk*. The wor
was at peace.

nineteen

BEGAN AS ENVISIONED, AND in the long days that fol-
wed—which stretched into weeks, the trio labored under
series of bright and rotating suns. Ben did not keep his
rmal sunup-to-sundown hours because he knew that the
eer mugginess of August alone would have been too
ugh on the former plantation owner.

The old black man's concern was totally justified. Daily
r. Archy would be dressed in overalls and straw hat,
oking like—and moving with—the speed of a stationary
arecrow, and even at that he would be puffing like a train
trouble. Neither he, Ben, nor the boy was certain as to
w long he would last. The first order of business was
pposed to have been in the area of clearing the fields, but,
wing to Mr. Archy's condition, Ben changed the plans to
clude building on an addition and restructuring the tired
d place. Since it was easiest, Mr. Archy and the boy filled
e first few days wagoning in the lumber from Lumberton
hile Ben busied himself with the sawing, hammering, and
loading chores.

The questions and play had slowed from the boy because

he was in a modest state of dazzled shock. For the first tir
in his life he had seen something other than the grounds
home: He had seen the nation at work and play, nev
dreaming that it could be so huge and active. Why, Lur
berton (population 21) had more people in it than they h.
in the whole wide world. And Fayetteville was bigge
Lordy, Lord—Lord!

Mr. Archy promised Moses that he would take him to tl
big city, and he would have been more than happy to do
because, after all, it would spare him from another day
the fields. And, too, there would be the added bonus of l
cating a few bookstores—and possibly a school that wou
eventually be of benefit to the boy.

Moses had never been to Red Springs either, but had l
and Mr. Archy changed routes and passed through there
that particular September morning he would have fou
Silas, the cane hobbler, J. D., Shep, and one or two othe
already on the stoop, lazing to the early-morning sun.

Silas, without troubling himself to move, yawned insi
to McMillan, "Hurrup an' roll that other barrel ou'chee
Mac—I can't seem to rest right 'lessen I got m'foot prop
up on somethin'."

"Maybe," Shep said, "h'it's 'cause you got that the
foot people used to talk about."

"W'kinda foot is that?"

"Sidy folk's foot," said the cane hobbler. "H'it's g
one'a them hifalootin' names."

"A-letic," Shep said. "Comes from them there folks th
like to play them there games."

" 'A-letic,' " the cane hobbler confirmed, "S'it."

The barrel came out, and Silas, instead of getting up a
moving out of the way, pulled his legs up and lazily wait
for McMillan to place it in position. "I a-sumes—I said,
a-sumes we'll be gettin' some new pickles soon?"

McMillan went back into the store without comment.

Tonic asked the cane hobbler: "Why's ol' Mac all slick'd
up?"

"H'come you all slick'd up?" the cane hobbler hollered.

McMillan hollered back out, "Goin' to Fayetteville.
Gotta restock."

"An' while y'orderin' this time, Mac, don't forget my
raisins!" Silas hollered. "An' be good e'nuff to think of
m'feet. Bring m'back some'a them soft pickles." And there
was an afterthought: "Hey, Mac, see if they got some that
oats. I'd like to try standin' in this thing one'a these
days."

Although Tonic had used the term, *slick* was not quite
the way McMillan was dressed. But he did have on his
Sunday best, which took on the form of an unpressed dingy
off-white suit, capped by a crumpled fedora.

"Wanna take a ride in with me, J. D.?" He was outside
now, hollering from the back.

"Can't."

"Okra?"

"My feet's too tired."

"Doc?"

"Too much ridin' f'me. I'd be sorer'n a coon's can by th'
time we got back in th' mornin'," answered the cane-hob-
ler.

"Tonic?"

"Like to, but I don't trust your wheels."

McMillan didn't want him along anyway and only asked
him because he was standing in his face. He tossed a few
more empty sacks and jugs on the wagon, unhitched the
mule, and led him to the front.

"Think I'll take a ride in wit'cha," said Shep.

"Good. Me an' you always seem to light 'em up when
we get there."

"We th' talk of the cat house, all right. Hee, hee, hee.
So's I can really put on th' dog, maybe I should change
first."

"Into what?" inquired Silas. "It's agin' th' law to rid naked."

WHEN MCMILLAN AND SHEP ARRIVED in Fayetteville late tha day, Epps, Austin, Wills, and the other old-timer who neve said anything were engaged around a game of checkers McMillan always made it a point to stop by the warehouse first because it used to be a solid place to do business. I was the one-stop of Fayetteville. Epps sold everything— from snuff to syrup, pins to plows, thread to rope, and with out a doubt he could have still been in business had he no gotten caught by the glamour of the tobacco industry.

"How y'all been?" McMillan said, steering the wagor toward them.

"Can't kick."

"Need any sign paintin' out yonder?"

"Not'chet."

"Wanna be lookin' good for th' new machines."

"They here yet?"

"In a month or so."

"Keep me posted."

"Will do."

"Come to load up?"

"Umhum."

"Six munz done gone by that fast?"

"Longer. Year."

"I'll b'dammed."

"Time scoots."

"Shore do."

"Stayin' for a few?"

" 'Mornin'."

"Cattin'?"

"Got to."

" 'Njoy."

"Will do."

"Miss Middie's got a coupl'a new ones."

"Hee, hee, hee."

"Chesty."

"Ho, ho, ho."

"Leggy."

"Ha, ha, ha."

"Hairy."

"Likes it?"

"Lovzit."

"Haw, haw, haw; ho, ho, ho."

McMillan and Shep did enjoy a brief stay. But it was not vernight. Again they went to Middie's house of ill repute. s usual, they paid their money, selected two women, went) their individual rooms, laid there in vain, departed with xcuses, and spent part of the night in a saloon. But the ther part of the night would find the two on the road, peeding back to Red Springs like a bullet.

Epps and the sign painter had come into the saloon and, mid good drinking, had bragged to the two visitors how ey were getting set to sell tobacco products to some peo- le in Raleigh, the state's capital. McMillan and Shep didn't ally know that Raleigh was the state's capital, and trying ot to appear too dumb, they switched the subject to every- ody's favorite topic, Archibald McBride. Misinterpreting verything, the two were told that Archy had come to town nd went to the clerk's office to secure information about e new machines—and land values. No doubt he was up to mething.

"Must'a been," said the sign painter. "After he left, we ent in an' check'd. Warren told us he ain't got nothin' in is name anymore."

"Must'a done gone plum' loco," said Epps.

"H'gave some screw'd-up story 'bout him bein' Ollie riminger," continued the sign painter.

"Or th' son of 'em."

"Somethin' like that."

"Is you sayin'," McMillan digested, "Archibald McBrid«
was here tryin to tell th' clerk he was somebody else?"

"Not only that," said the sign painter, "but he don«
deeded all the property to his son. Whoever that is."

twenty

IF THE RIDE BACK FROM Fayetteville was blistering, one could have considered Mr. Archy's position. The man had never worked so hard and long in all of his natural life, and after the last wagon load, he was moving around like a punch-drunk fighter. Numbly, he would take a plank and do nothing but walk around in a circle. Out of pure sympathy for him, Ben thought it would be a good idea if they put the house-mending chores on hold and sought lesser work in the fields. It was not a good suggestion. Even there the rigors of labor got to him, and soon he was on his knees. Seeing him, Moses skipped out for bright assistance.

"H'ya doin', Mr. Archy?"

"Oh, fine," the man said as he quickly started patting the ground as though he had lost something.

"Wha'cha doin' down there?"

"Jus'—jus' lookin'."

"Wha'cha lookin' for?"

"Er . . . er—m'hammer."

"What would y'be doin' with a hammer ou'cheer in th' fields?"

"Oh, ha-ha-ha, never can tell wh'cha might have to nail up out here."

"Ain't tired, is you?"

"No," said the all-but-exhausted man. "Takes more'n this t'make this ol' workhorse tired."

"That's good," the boy said. " 'Cause Unca Benny says that since we runnin' a lil' bit b'hind, we gonna have to stay ou'cheer 'til it gets dark."

"What?" Mr. Archy shouted, and then caught himself and tried to disguise tragedy by easing into, "What I meant to say is, I'm glad that he feels that way. It gives me somethin' to look forward to."

"Me too," chimed the boy, and stood there waiting for the man to get up. Obviously they were not thinking the same thing.

The boy just stood there for a while. He wanted to offer assistance. But he wasn't sure it was wanted. Mr. Archy, conversely, wanted the boy to leave so that he could capture a few moments rest. For a while it was like a standoff, and when it appeared that the boy would outwait him, the man on the ground summoned the last of his energies, and then courageously but falsely said, "Well, time to get up. Back t'the grind. Nothin' like a good day's work, I allus say."

"I allus say th' same thing."

"Good, son. Good." It was said with a good-bye ring, but the boy didn't catch it. "Any chance y'uncle got a lil' somethin' for you to do?"

"I'll go see. But if you need anythin' else, just call me."

"Ha-ha-ha, I'll be sure'n do that," Mr. Archy said limply.

The boy smiled and darted away. Mr. Archy hung an eye on him, and when it looked as though the coast was clear, he started to go down again. Suddenly the boy stopped and turned and delivered a friendly wave. It was returned, and though lacking in spirit, it was enough to send the boy farther on his way, but not too far, as Mr. Archy was quick to learn when he tried to go down again. The boy stopped, turned, and waved again. Mr. Archy returned the wave, held for a moment, and down he went.

Ben saw Mr. Archy when he went down and mercifully signaled quittin' time. By the time Mr. Archy had struggled to his feet, the boy was on his way over to him again: "Whas' a'matter, Mr. Archy, don'cha wanna quit?"

The man was going around in circles.

"S'quittin' time, Mr. Archy," the boy said, grabbing his hand.

Mr. Archy still couldn't hear him.

"Mr. Archy! S'quittin' time!"

In slow registration, the head turned and reacted as if he were a witness to a slow but fading dream.

"C'mon, Mr. Archy," the boy said, now hand-holding him across the field. "Right this a'way."

At about the halfway point, Ben met them with the wagon, climbed down, and helped the man up.

"Y'kno somethin', Unca Benny, Mr. Archy didn't even want'a stop. He was gittin' ready to start all over again."

There was a small groan from the man collapsed in the back of the wagon. Somehow the groan contradicted everything the boy had said.

When the wagon pulled into the yard, Mr. Archy was assisted down and led onto the porch.

"Think you can make it now, Mr. Archy?" asked the boy, itching to take care of the mule.

"Oh, he'll be all righ' soon's I rustle up a lil' grub," Ben answered.

Mr. Archy opened an eye. "Er . . . maybe," he said, remembering Ben's habits in the kitchen. "Maybe I'd better skip eatin' t'night, Ben."

"Can't do that—good eatin' is th' onlyist thing that'll keep you alive out in the fields."

Mr. Archy smiled wanly, unable to make up his mind as

to which was worse: Ben's kitchen or Ben's fields. "Any chance of sumthin' simple, like ham an' eggs?"

"Aw, naw," Ben said. "You gotta have somethin' that's gonna stick to y'ribs."

IT WAS A STIFF MR. Archy that sat at the table later that evening, stiff because of the bevy of aches and pains, and stiffer still because he was not sure as to how he would avoid eating what Ben had prepared. The kitchen was small and stuffy, and this had been a particularly humid night, and Mr. Archy couldn't help but take note of the sweat that poured down from the dark forehead, slid down the chin, and continued on down into the cast-iron pot.

It might have been dandy for the boy, but the former plantation owner couldn't take another meal: "Got anythin' to drink, Ben?"

"Oh, I might have a lil' somethin'."

It was like manna from heaven: Thank gawd, Mr. Archy said to himself. "Lord," he said, coming alive, "I've found my supper."

Ben removed a pail down from the shelf, took out a burlap-wrapped package, opened it, and passed it under Mr. Archy's nose.

Mr. Archy took the bottle and chuckled. "Join me."

Ben slid a self-made tin cup on the table. It was filled to the brim. Grinning, he took a nice belt and significantly handed the cup back to Mr. Archy, who, without the slightest bit of hesitation, downed the remaining contents.

Ben cracked a broad smile, "You goin' be all right after all."

"Hell," said the renewed Mr. Archy, "that's what I been tryin' to tell you all along."

The boy came in and Ben helped him with the pail. Easing over to Mr. Archy, he cocked an eye on the bottle and cup.

"Tonic," said the man.

"Smells like mash t'me."

Mr. Archy looked over at Ben. "Smart lil' feller, ain't he?"

"Takes after his daddy," Ben said lightly.

Mr. Archy thought about the implicating response. For an instant his face went bland, and then it cracked in laughter.

Afterward, he pushed back in his chair and smoothed the cup in thought. There were inner questions, but time would provide the answers. The important thing was that there was hope, and so far, over the past weeks, they had gotten off to a very good start. The man with the plan did not delude himself into thinking that there would be no problems, and that the dark recesses of his mind would henceforth be stilled. No, he had not been entirely purged; no, he had not been entirely freed from the shackles of his own bondage— that was impossible, and the very fundamentals of life would constantly be urging and prodding and pulling him back to the old ways. But they would fail, and while he was not impenetrable, he was a man of strength; and while the call of the old ways might weaken him in the days and few years ahead, he was certain they would not subdue him. There was comfort in the knowledge that his had not been a further wreckage of life, but rather a start. And a good one it was, for all grievances were gone now, and that in itself was new. He thought about Charlotte and wondered what she would think. Here he was, sitting in Ben's kitchen, united with the man who had destroyed her. He then looked at the boy, and tried to be fair. Earlier Ben had asked where would the boy be without him; what would have happened had he not been around? They were good questions, very good questions. Mr. Archy did not have—rather, Mr. Archy did not want to think of—the answers.

The old white man sitting in the kitchen sipping on the refreshments shuddered a bit and thought of something else: If Ben was all that much of a wicked and sinister man, if his deeds were so evil and corrupt, and the boy, having nothing—*nothing*—or no other single living human being around to influence, to guide, to lead, to teach, to helm his eager young life, how could he have possibly grown to be as wonderful as he was? How could he be as pure? How could he be so unswerving in his devotion? And as deserving as he was, how could his mother—wherever she was—how could she look down from on high and allow this good and precious child to love this leathered old black puzzle so much? And then again, thought the father, God knows I've not been a saint either. How could he think so highly of me?

WHEN THE MEAL WAS OVER, the boy gave his stomach the usual pats and complimented the cook. "Y'did it agin, Unca Benny."

Mr. Archy, sitting at the other end of the table with the untouched plate politely off to the side, refilled his cup.

"Unca Benny did it agin, Mr. Archy."

"Done what, son?"

"Cook some mighty good eatin'."

"You sure you don't drink?"

Moses focused an eye on him, the untouched plate, his own, Ben's, and he still couldn't figure out what the man was talking about.

Ben smiled and slid back from the table. "S'bout that time, son."

"No playtime, Unca Benny?"

"Not as early as we's gotta get up in th' mornin'."

The boy looked at Mr. Archy. "You gonna get up early in th' mornin' too, Mr. Archy?"

"Son, I'll be up an' out'a here b'fore you even turn over good."

"Bet'cha won't."

"Bet'cha I will."

"No, y'wont."

"Okay, tell you what, b'fore we go to th' fields, let's see who beats who down to th' creek in th' mornin'."

"Y'gonna race me to th' creek?"

"I'm gonna *beat* y'down to it."

The boy was so excited, he started running in place. He couldn't wait. Ben started to usher him to the lone room, but Mr. Archy, in a more serious tone, told Ben to hold off.

"C'mere, y'cuddly lil' rascal. You know, you're one prince of a human bein'." He then made wide gestures with his arms: "Son," he began seriously, "all this is yours. Everythin'. Everythin' in here, everythin' out there—everythin' up to and beyond th' creek—yours."

"Whose?"

"Yours."

"Mine?" He didn't get the full significance, but it sounded good.

"Yours. An' one day you gonna make h'story with it. Y'gonna be sharin' your story with people, tellin' 'em about these days. Music's gonna be playin', you gonna be runnin' 'round the capitol there in Relaigh, you're gonna be all gussied up, sportin' a derby, lookin' like a lil' state gov'nor or somethin', drinkin' an' sharin' y'cognac, toppin' it off with champagne."

"Whas all'a that?"

"Champagne? Only th' finest drink th' world has ever known. You drink it on special occasions—for special people, r'served for kings, lords, and princes—an' anybody you think d'serves special treatment."

Ben didn't know what it was either, but led the boy in feeling good.

"But what's important—an' *who* is important is an' is always gonna be. *You.*"

"Me?"

"Right. An' for a while longer, y'uncle Benny an' me. We love you, son, an' we want you to have th' best. We want you to have all'a this, an' we want you to grow up an' be able to look back on these here days an' this here place with fondness and love, an' look back on us as two old men who saw th' light."

"An' so's you can keep this here place," Ben took a long swallow and joined in—"an' so's you can keeps it, you gonna be one'a th' first color'ds to ever learn to read 'n write."

"I is?"

"Yessuh. Mr. Archy's gonna see to that."

"An' when you're ready, we're gonna start thinkin' about the big schools, maybe in Raleigh. Maybe up north. Philadelphia, I say Philadelphia because it's the cradle of American history. It was even th' capitol sixty to seventy-five years ago. But I want you to go there. Learn. Go to great places like that. It's a mighty big world out there."

Ben said, "An' one day, after you seen it, I want you to do somethin' for me I always want'd. Now, I can't read one, but I always want'd somebody to write to me. Always want'd somethin' with my name on it. I don't care if it's a letter, or note, or just a plain piece'a paper sayin' 'h'lo, unc'l Ben,' I want it. I don't care how or when I get it as long's I get it. An' I want it from you. An' I don't care where I'm at, see that I get it. An' if you got it in you at all, write what's in your heart. A good story is allus carr'd in th' heart. But if you can't do that, drop me a note. I'd love it just as much. Do that for your unc'l Benny. Thas' all I want."

The boy, like Ben, was looking ever so serious.

"An' when you write to him, mention me."

The boy vigorously nodded his head to both of them.

"An' for yourself, I want you t'learn your hist'ry. Learn ev'body's hist'ry, but 'specially yours. Tell you why," Ben said, importantly remembering good counseling: "A black man without hist'ry is like a bird without wings—walkin' when they ought'a be flyin'. Y'undastans? Walkin' when they ought'a be flyin'. Don't you be in that po'sition. An' son, please—*please* don't grow up t'be like me—"

"Or me either," Mr. Archy interrupted.

"You won't undastan's it now, but one day you will. An' while you learnin', don't question God, listen. An' always, *always* try to be right in whatever you do. An' if you do that, you'll never never know th' thing that d'stroys a man inside out: a bad conscience. Both me an' y'uncle Benny suffers from that."

"We ain't been as good as we shudda, son," Ben added. "But we ain't been as bad as we could'a. An' we is truly, truly sorry for all our wrongs."

Again, not understanding the philosophy, the boy nodded his head in vigorous agreement.

"But, now, listen to me, son, 'cause this is just as 'mportant: North Carolina has got somethin' to offer th' world. We want you t'have somethin' to offer North Carolina. This is God's country. You ain't gonna find nothin' no better," the old son of a Scot said, continuing to show that he had more than an awareness of God and, for the first time acknowledging that he loved the land. It caused the boy to feel even better. It was all so wonderful, all so real and true. "What we been doin' 'round here," Mr. Archy continued, "is tryin' t'start buildin' this place up—for you. An' when we done, an' we got the whole place lookin' like we want it to look, you know who th' boss man is gonna be—y-o-u."

But neither Ben nor the boy could spell.

Mr. Archy quickly picked up: "See, that's why y'have to have learnin'"—Y-o-u spells *you! You* is gonna be boss man."

"Meeeeeeeee? Boss man?"

"You. Boss man."

"Boss Man Moses."

Already dizzy with the onslaught of information and promises made, the boy was swept away.

"But, now, son," Ben stepped in advisedly, "when you

grows up—in fact, you don't even have to grows up—all you got to do is be who you is, an' you gonna have enemies. An' them enemies can be poison."

"Rotten," added Mr. Archy.

"Don' even call 'em by their names—just call 'em 'thems.' An' them *thems* can put a hurtin' on you. Watch 'em like a hawk. Keep y'eyes on 'em."

"They're terrible people. They're like weeds. Like th' weeds in th' fields out there, cuttin' an' chokin' everythin' off—not lettin' th' good stuff grow. They ain't got no purpose in life, an' God Himself can't seem to stomp 'em out."

"Can't even burn 'em out," Ben added.

"But we countin' on you to never let 'em best you." Mr. Archy continued. "Even if you have to take 'em to heart an' kill 'em with kindness, don't let 'em pull you under. *Find* a way t'deal with 'em. There's always mor'n one way to skin a rat."

"An' rats is what they is."

"An' when you finish'd dealin' with 'em, look 'em in th' eye, an' let 'em know th' boss man did it."

"Don' let 'em take nothin' 'way from you, Boss Man. Don'cha ever let a weed do it."

"Use y'mind, son. Th' mind. Always use y'mind. Be clever. Very, very clever. That's what any McBride will do."

The boy didn't quite get the full implication. But in his own way he promised himself right then and there, he would always use the mind to serve them well.

Ben clarified: "You one'a them."

"I'm a McBride?"

"You're *the* McBride," Mr. Archy said. "An' if I'd had any sense about it at th' time, your mother would'a been a McBride." But the boy was too centered on the great news.

He swallowed again. "I'm a McBride? With two names?"

"With two names."

"I'm Moses McBride?"

And before the question could be answered, he was gone, too dizzy and breathless to continue. He simply couldn't take any more.

In his room, unlike the last time, when the friendship had been cemented between the two men, he didn't use birdlike power to get into the room. He spun, airylike. He didn't pounce on the bed, he melted—and with the slowness of syrup in winter, he oozed under the quilt. Lord, Lord, Lord, he was the happiest, the most gladdened, the most joyous, the most tickled somebody in the whole wide world.

The boy had reason to be at his height. He was living beyond a dream. He was a McBride; he had two names; he was a boss man; he was cuddly; he was a prince; he owned land; he had a creek; he was going to learn how to read and write; he would one day learn history, go places, drink champagne, and dress like the governor—whatever that was. But the benefits of living went on and on. And everything—*everything*—every single solitary thing in life was because of Uncle Benny and now Mr. Archy—*buddies*. And they were right there, in the kitchen, *talking,* talking to each other. Ben and Mr. Archy there, touchable, talking, *giving*—giving everything they had to him—giving him a universe, and all they wanted in return was for him to grow and make a contribution, to use the mind, to be wary of the weeds of life, and write them a note.

Good God Almighty.

There was a man beyond the clouds. There had to be. Oh, how he wished he knew how to thank Him.

BACK IN THE KITCHEN, NEITHER of the two men were overly wrought with pain. Mr. Archy had been liberal in his drinking, and Ben was coming on strong. The situation, and what they had said to the new boss man, had them feeling even better about themselves, and Mr. Archy said, hoisting the cup, "I think this calls for a small c'lebration."

They touched cups, and threw their heads all the way back—and the heads did not return upright until the last drops had been drained. They chatted a bit more, and Ben unsteadily arose from the table.

"Arch, m'boy, we might as well keep it rollin'."

"Y'mean, y'got some more?"

Ben nodded and weaved over to the shelf and pulled down another pail and showed the man two more bottles.

Mr. Archy grinned: "An' all th' while I thought you was over here sufferin'."

Ben unwrapped the corn shucks from around the bottles and said, "An' all th' while I thought you was over there 'njoyin' y'self."

Mr. Archy slid the cup aside and went straight for a bottle. "Y'ever know a lonely man to 'njoy himself?"

"I never know'd a lonely man."

"You knew me."

"Let's drink to th' lonely!"

They found about eight different things to toast.

Time passed and the solid drinking continued. Both men were reeling in that good and high state of mind, and when one dozed off or absented himself from the conversation, the other would find a way to bring him back.

"Ben, m'boy. I wouldn' mind a lil' cognac."

"An' cone-ee-yakee is, Mr. Archy?"

"A lil' sumthin' t'keep th' heart pumpin'."

"I'll have to put that one on m'list," Ben said as he stood by the shelf, peering up and getting ready to invade his private peach jars. "Cone-ee-yakee."

"S'good stuff, Ben."

"Bet it is, suh, but I'm fresh out. Anythin' else that a man like me would have handy?"

"On all great occasions we should have some'a that champagne I was talkin' 'bout. Y'aint liv'd 'til you had it."

"Gonna have t'put that one on order too," Ben said, and

then came up with what he thought was a sensational idea: "Arch, let's change bottles!"

"Great idea, Ben," Mr. Archy said to the notion that would take two and one half minutes to complete.

When that was done, Mr. Archy said: "I got one, Ben."

"Wha-wha-what?"

"Let's change seats!"

That mummified ritual took four and three quarter minutes to complete, and then they were stuck. Finally Mr. Archy discovered that they hadn't been talking for a while.

"What's on y'mind, Ben?"

"Nuttin'," Ben said, and reminded himself that he hadn't touched the bottle in over thirty seconds. He got it and took a swig: "But I'm gonna tell y'somethin', Arch—now, I know y'think I gave in t'you pretty easy. But I'm tellin' you, it shore was worth it, 'cause to see you out in them fields is one of the prettiest sights I ever done seen in my life."

"Yep," hiccuped the man nobly. "An' it's all b'cause of th' boy."

"Your son."

"My son." There was pride in the way he said it.

Ben took another drink and made an effort to continue the serious talk. "Y'know, somethin', Arch, th' one thing I always want'd to know? Somethin' that I allus used to sit out yonder an' think 'bout all th' time. Th' day didn' go by when I didn' think 'bout it."

"Wha'zit?"

"Howz it feel _t'think_ you can own somebody, to _think_ you can own another human bein'? Jus' to say th' words alone: 'I own somebody.' Kno' what I mean?"

Mr. Archy took a drink. "Want th' truth?"

"Amen."

"Ben, you'll notice two things I never had here. I never had an overseer. An' I never had a constable—or a slave-whipper as most folks call it—"

"But you had slaves, Mr. Archy."

"That's true, Ben," Mr. Archy said reflectively.

"At first, to be able t'say you own somebody is a pretty good feelin' an' anybody that owned one an' say different is lyin'. Pure an' simple lyin'. Which is why just about every race on th' planet has had slaves. Ownin' anythin'— controllin' anythin' a'peals to man's basic—a man's *natural* instincts of always wantin' to be superior—when, in truth, man ain't. What we is is full of fear. I ain't talkin' 'bout bein' fearful that you don't look like me, that'cha don't talk like me, that you ain't got th' white man's learnin's—yet—an' notice I said 'yet.' "

"I heard ya," Ben said, taking a drink.

Mr. Archy poured another one. "I'm talkin' about fear of th' truth; fearin' that you really is equal after all, fearin' that if God is a just God, our day of reckonin' is comin'. Y'see, we all jus' comin' an' goin'. That's all life is— comin' an' goin'. We ain't mountains or oceans. We jus' passin' through. We're jus' here changin' clothes—bein' sized up. But we'll be back after we find out God is serious. R'member this, Ben: Th' world don't stop when the white man dies. Next time 'round, I might be you." He laughed. "Treat me good, Ben. Treat me damn good."

"There you go agin"—Ben laughed with him—"forcin' me into makin' some hard choices."

They enjoyed another good laugh. Mr. Archy tried to squeeze another drink from one of the already-empty jugs. Ben tried doing the same with the other jug. Getting nothing, he went outside and came back grinning with three more containers, explaining that they were wet and cold because he kept them tied to a rope that stretched to the bottom of the well. Mr. Archy congratulated him on his inventiveness, weaved up, and hugged him like a long lost child.

"Ben, you're my kind'a man."

"Glad t'be of service," Ben said, unpopping a cork and filling the two cups.

Mr. Archy took a healthy belt. "Y'know th' worse thing that ever happen'd to me, Ben?" Before Ben could answer, he said, "Mildred. Gads, how I hated that woman. I'm gonna let you in on a lil' secret. When th' clerk fella in Fayetteville told me what all she done about th' property, an' listed herself as Mrs. Priminger, I got mad as hell. Then I thought about it again. When it hit me I never was legally married to her, halfway back to your place here, I swear I felt like dancin'."

Ben burst out laughing.

"I tell y'Ben, on th' way back here, you couldn't tell it, an' nobody'll ever know, but there was a point when I felt like climbin' out'a that wagon an' doin' a jig right in the middle o'th' road! You ain't got no idea how bad it was bein' marr'd to that woman."

Ben settled down and took an easy drink. "Ooooh, now, Mr. Archy, in th' right light, Miss Mildred—she won't so bad."

"She was the worst, Ben. Th' absolute worst."

"No, she won't."

There was something in the way he said it. He kind of sung it—offhanded like. With the true meaning somewhat submerged, he allowed the weight of it to settle on Mr. Archy. He then gave the man a look, followed by a sheepishly guilty smile.

It took a while, but the former plantation owner got the full meaning. "Why, Bennnnn," he spurted. "Ben—Ben, you ol' houndawg! You sunov—C'mon, now? What?"

Ben tried to hide his face behind a jug.

"You an' Mildred?"

"The boy got th' property, don' he?" Ben said.

Again the sheepish look had returned to the hunched black man. Mr. Archy met it with an astonished smile, and then like a slow-building wave, he began to chuckle, and then cackle, and that grew into an infectious roar. Ben started laughing again, and soon the two men were laughing so loud and hard that it carried into the boy's room and brought him tiptoeing back into the kitchen. Limp, and holding his stomach with one hand, Ben struggled for control and tried to wave him back to the room. Mr. Archy tried to lend assistance, but he was laughing so hard that tears filled his eyes. He couldn't remain upright—which started the boy laughing. He stood in the doorway laughing and giggling as though having witnessed one of the world's great jokes. Finally, Ben was able to wave him off, but the boy couldn't stop laughing, and when he got back to his room and slid under the covers, the bed vibrated like the movement of two piglets in a sack. He giggled himself to sleep.

With both men slobbering and slurping drinks between bursts, Mr. Archy, unable to speak, convulsed with an accusing index finger. Ben riotously pounded laughter into the table. No longer able to sit, Mr. Archy rolled out of the chair.

"Ben—Ben—Ben," he gasped. "Ben—y-y-you—y-y-you're just an old fox." He exploded all over again.

"An' that lil' change y'said she gave me? That didn' hurt either."

Mr. Archy roared. "You an' Mildred—" He coughed. "The two of you—hotttdammm! That *really* must've been a sight to see!" He kicked his feet up hysterically. "That *had* to be a sight!"

"Sights." The man with the hump on his back said, stressing the plural.

Mr. Archy whooped louder than ever and Ben, roaring right with him, came tumbling to the floor. Mr. Archy grabbed his aching stomach and kicked.

"Ben," he pumped. "If I could'a seen it, I'da given you th' whole plantation!"

"Mr. Archy—" said a side-splitting Ben.

"Huh?"

"She tried to."

And no two men ever laughed harder.

twenty-one

IT HAD BEEN A SPECTACULARLY beautiful morning, long on a southern morning mist that lifted gently and came forth with nothing but promise. Peace and airiness were everywhere except in front of the store. McMillan had brought the wagon to a skidding dust-building stop, and had sent Shep to round up the regulars. Before daybreak, they were holding court. For some reason, Silas was just now arriving. On the approach, he was scolding the air. "McMillan, whut'n th' name of chicken droppin's is you doin' sendin' that fool to wake me up this time'a mornin? I ain't even fried my watermelon yet!"

"Will ya hush, Silas," demanded J. D. "Mac an' Shep was tryin' t'git back here last night to tell us somethin'—"

"But th' wheel bust'd."

"Told'ja," Tonic said.

"That ain't 'mportant!" shouted the cane hobbler. "G'woan, tell 'im what Arch's done done."

"Mac's learn't Archy's done turn't all'a that prop'tee over to that black young'un a'his," volunteered the cane hobbler.

"What!" Silas yelled.

"An' then tried to pr'tend he was Priminger!"

"Tried to pr'tend he was *who?*"

"Priminger! An' turn't all'a th' prop-tee over to th' black young'un."

"He done *what?*"

"I still say that ain't like Archibald McBride," said Okra, and was backed by Tonic.

"Archy done done what?" Silas persisted.

"Tell you what," Shep said convincingly, "it might not be like him, but if you don't believe he ain't done gone inta Fayetteville and tried to pull a fast one, Mac'll let'cha have th' wagon so's you can go to Fayetteville an' check for y'self!"

"Archy done gone an' done what?"

"Now, I'm tellin' you what we know, Doc."

"Archy done gone an' done what?" Silas said, still overdoing it as they talked around him.

"Jay, all'a that land out there is now in th' hands of th' lil' black young'un."

"Archibald McBride done done what?"

"Silas, gawdammit!" J. D. shouted.

"Archibald McBride done gone an' done what?"

"Gawdammit, Silas, shut up so's I can think!"

Silas started to blast the air again, but decided to go and have breakfast at the pickle barrel.

"An' th' county clerk back there can ver'fies ev'rything we tellin' you," McMillan continued.

"Turn't it over to a color'd out'a spite. Pure spite," said the cane hobbler. "S'like when he freed 'em!"

"He's tryin' t'trick us," J. D. said. "He's plannin' on gettin' even with us."

"An' he knows it's gon' be a fight to th' finish."

"S'what me an' Shep thought," agreed McMillan. "He's prob'bly been layin' up in th' hunch's place, jus' waitin' for the right time."

"They ain't gonna be no righ' time!" Silas hollered, still digging in the barrel. "An' I a-sumes, said I a-*sumes* we ain't gonna let him trick us out'a whas ours! Hey, McMillan! Mac—"

"But th' lan' ain't ours," said Tonic, reasonably cutting in.

"So what!" Silas bellowed, and turned to McMillan: "An', Mac, I asumes, I said, I a-*sumes* you got m'raisins an' pickles in y'pocket?"

The cane hobbler overrode the response and said, "Th' shack's th' onlyest thing's left out there. Let's git rid of it."

"Let's burn it."

"But what if th' boy's in there?" Okra asked.

"I *said* let's burn it. Burn it an' Archy's gone for good."

"An' so's th' nigs," Silas finalized. "Mac, did'ja hear me? Th' barrel's empty, so I a-*sumes*, I said, I a-*sumes* you got somethin' in y'pockets?"

"Silas," J. D. screamed, "gawdammit, we got work to do!" He then started ordering. "Let's start movin'! Mac, empty th' wagon, an' y'all go inside an' get everythin' that can burn. An' get plenty a'rags."

"Them you wearin' will do nicely," Silas called to McMillan, and at the same time munched on a pickle.

"Let's hurrup!" emphasized the cane hobbler to anybody who would listen.

Quickly moving about, McMillan, Shep, Okra, and Tonic unloaded the wagon. The cane hobbler directed two more late arrivals to the rear of the store for the kerosene drum. Silas climbed aboard the wagon and directed the action from there while J. D. went inside and returned with an armload of jugs and bottles.

When the big kerosene drum was finally rolled to the wagon, J. D. ordered everyone to muscle it aboard.

Silas busied himself with the jug and bottle count so that

he wouldn't be available for the barrel effort. "Got any more jugs in there, Mac?"

"B'hind th' counter."

"Gettum. An' this time *don't* f' get th' matches."

"An'," said Silas, "some spare pickles."

twenty-two

FOR THE BOY IT HAD been an exhilarating though somewhat sleepless night, and the morning, as it had done in Red Springs, came with exceptional beauty. Brilliant, fresh, and pure.

The joy of living slanted through the window. Moses was still in bed, alert with happy thoughts racing through his mind. All the nights and mornings would be good now, but this one was especially good, for last night the bond between his two had been sealed forever. Nothing in the world could have matched that save for the reappearance of Sweet Elsie Pratt. It was odd that he thought of her that morning. Usually it was at night, but even then, the memory of the large woman had been fading, and the fading had been aided and abetted by his uncle's continued refusal to say anything about the night she went away. She was gone, and nothing further was said.

When he thought about Sweet Elsie that morning, he was touched by a slight foreboding chill, and that had never happened before. He had experienced a void and a hollowness shortly after she walked out the door that night, but it was not quite the same as this—and it wasn't doubled. This was, and, worse still, it was intense—magnified.

The boy's mind did him a favor by calling for a change, and then suddenly he remembered he had promised Mr. Archy that he would beat him down to the creek. Quickly, he scrambled out of bed to begin dressing, keeping an ear cocked for voices. He heard none: a sure sign of a losing effort, he thought. He had to hurry. Grabbing at the same clothing and string that held his trousers up for almost as long as he could remember, he was told by the angle of the sun that he didn't have time to put them on. Worse, he still didn't hear anything. No voices. Normally Uncle Benny would be in the kitchen, rumbling around, and if it was one of those extremely rare occasions when he had time to cook, the aroma would sweep the house. But this morning nothing. No sound. Nothing. There was a strong odor, a *very* strong odor that waved in and about, but maybe the mule had made a deposit; maybe Mr. Archy had found a pig and brought it into the kitchen—whatever, it meant that they were up. They were up and gone. Mr. Archy had beat him to the creek.

The boy sailed out the front door with the heart of his slitted moon improperly peeking through dark and dangerously thinned underwear.

No time for his horse, he hit the corn rows running. He had gotten quite a few yards under his feet, and then he stopped—cold. Something told him to go back. Go back to the house.

He went back, and tiptoed into the kitchen. There spelled the end of the race, for lying head-down in soggy little puddles of mash and puke was the man who was going to beat him to the creek. And right beside him, face-up and under the table, was the start-early man—and they both were unconscious. The boy was not disappointed, and, in fact, felt downright good about it because they looked so peaceful.

And he was not going to disturb them. If anyone deserved a good rest, Uncle Benny and Mr. Archy did.

Moses remained in the doorway, smiling for a long while. His eyes drifted over the kitchen's almost cyclonic condition, where the jars, cups, bottles, newfound jugs, pails, half-eaten food, and overturned chairs mixed with regurgitated and salivated puddles and made the entire room one big mess. Without question, they had had a rollicking good time, and according to the evidence, nothing fizzled until the crack of dawn. But it was over, and he couldn't leave without some cleaning effort—and, too, the stench was too strong.

Tiptoeing around them, he would occasionally drop an item or two, freeze in place, and check for a reaction. There would, of course, be none, because as zonked, hard-nosed, and mummified as they were, they couldn't have been aroused by a hurricane. But the boy didn't know this, and the task was done with utmost care.

It was not one of the best cleaning jobs, but it served the purpose, and after he had finished he thoughtfully capped it by washing their mucus-smeared faces and comforting the heavy heads with two quilts from his room. All done, he would go down to the creek and wait. But before leaving, he checked them over again. To his way of thinking, they were as peaceful as two peas in a pod.

He rechecked the kitchen again, and something told him to look the whole house over again. He did. This was home. He came back to the kitchen for a last look. "Tol'ja I'd beat you down to th' creek," he said to Mr. Archy. And to his uncle he said, "Bye, Unca Benny."

Moses did not run: He did not hurry through the fields, for once. He more or less sauntered along, absently pulling a weed through his teeth. For some inexplicable reason, he wouldn't even take his horse—he was without the hoe, and he showed no signs of missing it when he arrived at the creek. And there, too, he was different. He did not feel the

urge to make his usual morning deposit; he was not jaunty;
he tossed no pebbles, looked for no worms; and he did not
paint a picture on the big blue ceiling. Without looking or
thinking about anything in particular, he slumped to the
ground as if in answer to a strange sensation that nibbled
from within, as if he had been tuned to the echo of an
ozonic void. He couldn't understand it; he couldn't explain
it. But there was something. It was as if that very same
something had reached beyond all matter and hung him in
this—this airy and pressureless suspension, like an omen
saying that the world was to become soundless, and all that
touched would no longer feel; and that all things would be
stripped of color and form; and that all the senses would
become as sand on the desert, there but changing, there but
shifting to the trumpet of an unseen wind, there but devoid
of life and reason. The feeling was upon him that the sensation of fullness and spirit were moving on, and that soon all
things here and now would belong to another place in time.
And that was not good.

Sweet Elsie Pratt came to his mind again. Before he
curled up to go to sleep at the creek, he wondered where
she went.

MCMILLAN WAS BLISTERING THE HORSE'S flank, and the
wagon was biting the dust as it had never bitten it before.
There were seven of them on the move. The man with the
cane was standing, but holding firm to the seat. Okra and
Tonic were busy tearing strips of cloth and passing them
back to J. D. and Silas, who continued to jam them into the
bottles and jars. Decorating the rear tailgate and serving as
scout was Shep.

Ben's place would be no problem, they had agreed. He
and the boy were sure to be in the fields, even though they
were going to burn the place whether the boy was in it or
not. Whatever, the mindless and arrogant Archibald
McBride wouldn't be there, he would not lower himself to

e anywhere near the shack or around the black couple, and
would therefore be wandering off to points unknown. And
it was good that the shack was small, old, and dry. It would
burn in minutes and the Red Springers would be back at the
store before the smoke had cleared—and if anybody
wanted to do anything, let them. They would be waiting.

They continued to work as they rode, so that by the time
they had reached the yard's perimeter, everything was
ready. With two of them bracing the lip of the drum over
the rear of the wagon, the cane hobbler took command of
filling the remaining containers.

The wagon then thundered all the way into the yard, and
with the last strips already in place, McMillan passed the
matches back to the cane hobbler, who in turn fashioned a
torch and fired up the missiles.

J. D. was the first to heave his, and it landed with telling
accuracy. The bedroom window splintered, and in an instant the room lit up. The wagon angrily encircled the
house, and in rapid succession other missiles flew from the
wagon. On the far turn, the big drum rolled off and the mo-
mentum carried it to the barn. Grabbing a projectile and
cocking his free arm, the cane hobbler ordered McMillan
on a homeward course, and then said, "If this don't run th'
ol' buzzard off, I don't know what will." The arm came
forward, heaving a high throw back at the piles of hay. The
wagon sped off.

"Somethin' tells me we done seen th' last of Mr.
Archibald McBride," Silas said.

THE TWO BODIES WERE STILL motionless on the floor, and the
searing smoke was coming on strong.

The wagon had barely cleared the yard when the flames
from the cane hobbler's toss crackled for the hay. There
was an explosion, and seconds later it was followed by a
burst that almost rocked the earth. Joined by the contents
from the drum, the flames shot from the barn, ate the mule,

and reached out for the house. Like a giant octopus,
moved. With terrible ferocity, remnants of the big dru
shot from the barn and powered for the shack. The smo
mushroomed up and traces of residue carried all the way
the creek.

Already awakened and terrified by the explosion, the b
was on his feet, scanning the skies. And then in horrifyir
confirmation, the smoke came.

With all of his might he ran, saying over and over, "N
No. No." But the closer he got to the old place, the mo
the smoke swept ominously along and clung in and out
the tall, soldierlike cornstalks, whose leaves slapped ar
slashed at him as though he were the enemy. He could n
be slowed. Bleeding from the tiny but numerous cuts, ar
already running as fast as his legs could carry, he tried
go even faster. But it wasn't in him. His small heart wa
beating at an unsteady pace, and his breathing sounded
though he were on the verge of collapse; still, he called f
more. Now he was able to see the house, and it was beyor
hope, having already signaled the end.

Madly—wild-eyed, he tried to call out; he tried to yel
scream. He wanted to holler: *"Hold on Unca Benny. I'*
comin! Please, Mr. Archy, hold on, I'm comin', y'all. Don
go. I'm gonna save you. Please, please, please, don't go—
Unca Bennnnnny! Hold on—wait for me! I can save you!
can save youuuu! Hold onnnnn! Please, please, pleas
y'all!"

In rapid succession he tried to call the Lord and the
Sweet Elsie Pratt. But there was no sound in his voice, ar
his tear ducts were dry.

When he got to the edge of the yard, the heat blasted o
wickedly and would let him go no farther.

Time and time again, this now man-child tried to fig
his way closer to anything that wouldn't stop him, but eac
time the heat conspired with the smoke and dared him fo
ward. Frantically, he came back to the edge of the yard ar

ipped at the cornstalks for protection, but the big, stub-
orn weeds only slowed him and further bloodied his
ands. He tried clawing and digging at the dirt, but that
ouldn't do. In a fit, he circled wide for the side of the
ouse, and even though there was no entrance, he tried for
ie charge; but the oppression was just as strong, and the
lames shot out as if to say the rear wouldn't even tolerate
is presence.

But it was not a sane mind the holocaust was dealing
vith. In a frenzy he shot for the back door. There the fire
vas as vicious as fire could get. The main body of the
hed had already caved in, and the stacks of new timber
ad fallen near the door and was burning beyond control.
rom a distance he zeroed in on the door. It was much
oo late. Their life-preserving juices had long since been
ooked, and the bodies inside were charred beyond
ecognition. He wouldn't be stopped. He summoned his
verything and raced for the door. The heat roared up like
monster and slapped him to the ground, and then whiffs
f smoke came from his clothes. Still, he would not re-
eat.

Water, he remembered—the water in the well. Again
alling on reserves, he crawled out of immediate danger.
irst, he would straddle the pump, slide down the mash-
earing rope that led to the bottom of the well, submerge
imself—and then nothing on earth would stop him from
limbing back up and bursting through the door to save his
ncle and Mr. Archy.

When he got to the well, all did not go as planned. There
vas a loud, crashing sound. He looked back, and the sides
f the house had given way, as if to prove a point, down
ame the roof.

It was all over.

Now he cried.

The voice of the big black woman with the glistening
kin came back again.

This time she said:

> *"Cry in pity, and in forgiveness*
> *of those who have wronged you,*
> *and then cry again in toleration of*
> *the indignity; when you have cried*
> *your last tear, dry your eyes—dry*
> *them in preparation, for the time*
> *will be upon you, when you are*
> *to bring down those that wronged*
> *you and poisoned your way. . . ."*

And so ended the long, long story that began with th
sun shining bright on the outskirts of a lonely little tow
told by a youngster whose voice seemed to have aged wit
the telling.

One would have thought the ending would have ca
some sort of a pall over the old store, some sort of chill th
rode with the damp rain that seeped through the aged woo
and trickled on down and through the bags of rice, whea
flour, and sugar, and then angled off and snaked to the lef
soaking the barley and various bags of oats, but failed
penetrate the feet of the cognac-sogged bodies that sat son
nolently weaving around a potbelly stove that showed n
mercy and even less heat.

For the storyteller the story ended without rancor, wit
out bitterness, without any show of outward emotion.

For the old-timers—the Red Springers—the story ende
without undue concern.

There was a quiet, and after a minute or so, a new lea
was heard. It was magnified in the quiet and swung eve
heavier as the raindrops crawled along an up-top piece
tin and piggy-backed nosily down the chimney and found
new home under the stove. Though the cognac had n
reached him as much as it had reached the others, the stor

keeper McMillan broke the spell by somberly rising to feed the dying fire.

Although the fire was at its lowest ebb, the young story-teller's look was riveted on the dying embers that could be seen through the stove's cracked door. McMillan believed the embers mirrored in the youngster's eyes. Both Shep, who had dozed intermittently, and McMillan, who had not dozed at all, noticed that he was rocking hypnotically slow in the tilted chair, and his face was almost frozen in a catalepticlike mask. McMillan nodded for Shep to nudge J. D., but neither he nor J. D. was any too coherent, and the gesture went unheeded. Still eyeing the youngster, McMillan closed the stove door slowly. There was no change in the youngster. McMillan opened the door again, then slammed it shut. The youngster twitched a little, and then, as if coming back, the chair came forward. McMillan continued to eye him, but said nothing.

Both J. D. and Silas had drifted off early, but they, too, came back by the slamming of the door. Silas looked around and immediately set his fingers in search of another bottle. While he looked around the base of the chair, J. D. took another drink and was close to nodding off again.

The youngster tilted his chair back, clasped his hands behind his head, and looked at them.

"Well, gents," he said, his voice a bit froggy and raspy but without malice and with surprising casualness, "I s'pose that's it. That's your story."

McMillan, still not sitting, said in careful confrontation, "Is it?"

"Every word, every act, every deed." The youngster looked up, locking his eyes with the man who was standing across from him.

"I don't think it is."

"Why not?"

"I think you left out sumpthin'?"

"No, I was all-inclusive, sir," the youngster said withou
fear.

McMillan took his time and pushed with a deep and uncomfortable threat in his voice. " 'Ceptin' you forgot to tel
us you was th' boy."

The youngster was unnerved. "Couldn't have been, sir
As I said in the beginning, I'm eleven. Today the boy in
question would have to be seventeen."

This silenced the storekeep. He was still suspicious, and
he would remain suspicious. The youngster knew this, and
decided he would have to maintain a certain alertness. He
felt relatively good though. Once again he had taken splen-
did advantage of a brutish man's ignorance and gave life to
what was to become an adage that would last through the
years: *all coloreds look alike.*

*He was seventeen. He was of mixed parentage, and they
never knew the difference.*

J. D., though drowsed and already heavy with drink, ran
his index finger around the top of the bottle and pressed i
to his lips again. "Now," he said, slowly returning the bottle to his lap. "Let's us do some talkin'—let's us—"

"Wade-a-minnit, J," said a light-headed Silas, "b'fore
you do that—lemme ask 'im somethin'."

"What happened to the man with the cane?" the youngster interjected before Silas could get started.

"Died a'piece back," Silas answered unconsciously.

"An' Okra, and Tonic?"

"Dead. All of 'em gone."

"And you're the only ones left?"

"S'right," said McMillan. "But you tol't th' story. You
should know that."

The youngster responded quietly: "I told what I knew."

"Anythin' else?"

"They won't as good as they should'a. But they won't as
bad as they could'a. And they did see the light."

McMillan didn't like the sound of it.

"Listen here," Silas said, getting back on track and simultaneously reaching out for J. D.'s bottle. "If that story was true—an' I ain't sayin' it is—but if th' story is real, wha'chew think about it?"

Silas, at that point, didn't really care what the youngster thought, and even though he had asked the question, his dewy attention yawned elsewhere.

"Yeah," supported Shep, "wha'cha think 'bout it?"

"If it is not true," said the youngster conversationally, and with a nice change of diction, "you men are not the historians I said you were, and as such you deserve nothing—you are not the men I had hoped you'd be. If, on the other hand, it is true, you are all historians, and as such you deserve the best I have to offer."

"An' what is that?"

"What is th' best you got to offer?"

"Well," the youngster said despite showing many more signs of an oncoming cold, and maintaining enviable calm. "Right now, as small and as humble as it may sound, it takes on the form of champagne." He expected more.

"I heard'a that," said a delayed Shep, standing and fighting off sleep, and then deciding to move off to the back of the store to relieve himself in the hole next to the basket of onions.

"What is champagne, Shep?" J. D. called after him.

Squatting, Shep was stuck for an answer.

"What is that stuff you talkin' 'bout, boy?" McMillan asked suspiciously.

"Only th' finest wine the world has ever known."

"Gitit," J. D. ordered.

"Then I take it you are all historians?"

No response for a long while. And then McMillan said very slowly, "you tryin' to say we guilty of somethin'?"

The youngster looked him in the eye, and was equally slow. "Historians are fiery keepers of history." They stared at one another.

J. D. broke the icy silence. "Gwon. Y'been sittin' here runnin' off at th' mouth all this time—gwon out there an' get th' stuff."

The youngster was surprisingly firm. "I shall not move until I am assured you are who I think you are."

Silas reached down for another drink, and then, realizing his bottle had been empty for over an hour, leaned over for Shep's remaining drops: "I do d'clare."

"That's fine, sir. But the question is, do you declare yourself a historian?"

"Y'gawddang righ', I am."

"And the rest of you?"

"Jus' gwoan an' get th' stuff, boy," J. D. said, agreeing.

The youngster arose, wiped his nose again, and went to the door with the same vacant smile.

Silas turned and cocked an eye on him. "An' if y'get ou yonder an' d'cide to run, we'll get'cha b'hind one way or 'nother."

The youngster smiled more vacantly. "Sir, there is no place for me to run to." He stopped. "I'm like a bird without wings . . . walkin' when I should be flyin'."

The trio looked at one another in slobbering puzzlement There was something about the statement—and him—tha had that odd ring to it, and the accompanying look was about as confounding as they had ever seen. Perhaps, if it had not been for the sweet flow of alcohol, it would have been further discussed—surely there was something behind it. But it passed, and instead, they yawned and scratched and waited—all but McMillan.

The skeptical Mr. McMillan's doubts about the young ster had been growing throughout the story, and there were times when he wanted to put an end to it, but in deference to the other three he elected to say nothing. He had planned to challenge the youngster on several key issues after the story was over, but having always been contradicted, in sulted, and brow-beaten—mainly by Silas—he decided to wait until the others had finished their questions or, at least, until Silas had slipped into sleep. And then he would come with his clinchers, and he would prove that he was not the dunce they always made him out to be.

"See what he's up to, Mac," J. D. said sleepily.

McMillan took a drink, tiptoed to the window, and shaded his eyes with a hand.

"Can't see nothin'."

"That is why, Mr. McMillan," Silas said dryly, as if explaining the change of seasons to a child, "you should go *out*side."

McMillan did not greet the suggestion with any enthusiasm because he, as they all knew, had an intense fear of the dark, and the exit of the weird young black person did nothing to ease his mind. Had the storekeep gone out at that particular moment, however, he would not have immediately seen the youngster unless he had been nervy enough to test the dark at the rear of the store—which he wasn't about to do. The youngster had slipped to the back, confirming that the mule was there, and had come back around to the side of the store because there was that urgent matter with another sack.

Silas should not have been concerned. There was no question, the youngster would be returning.

After a grunting and straining effort, Shep had returned to the semicircle and was still fidgeting with his suspenders. Silas was just about to unload on him, when the youngster came back inside.

"Where you been?" McMillan demanded, beating Silas to the punch.

"Whas'n the sack?" Silas shot out.

"Patience, gentlemen. Patience," said the renewed young man as he hesitated at the door and then came back to the circle.

Silas eyed the sack: "I could'a went out yonder an' got that lil' soda-water lookin' thing m'self."

"But, ah," said the youngster, coughing slightly and un-tying the clanking package. "Could you have delivered the contents?"

The oldsters looked at one another with a soggy and baf-fled look. Before they could comment, the youngster had looked up at them and again produced that vacant smile. His hands were moving much faster than before, and every-thing he did seemed unnecessarily deliberate, and as though it had been practiced. When the sack was fully unwrapped, he motioned for Silas to inspect the contents.

Silas leaned over and was delighted. "Wheeeooo, S'nuff drinkin' for a month'a Mundays. Tuesdays too."

The youngster then removed the bottles, nicely wrapped in rubber, and passed them around. "On behalf of those who have seen the light."

"Tol'ja. This lil' nig's gonna kill us with kindness."

"What is it?" J. D. said, light-headed, but leaning over to see.

"As I promised, sir: champagne. Reserved for special oc-casions, an' presented to the doers of deeds. Lords and princes of history."

"How come they wrapp'd in rubber?"

"Th' storm, sir. The contents had to be protected at all costs."

"Th' way you soundin' an' coughin', y'shudda protected y'self," Silas commented.

"I'll be fine, sir. As long as I last 'til morning."

"Why 'til morning? An' how come these bottles ain't seal'd?" inquired McMillan.

"Dammit, McMillan," Silas said doggedly. "Y'always moanin' 'bout somethin'! Wha'cha want for nothin'?"

"Y'kno, Mac's righ'. That there stuff is s'pose to be—"

"Well, y'all go 'head an' argue 'bout it, I'm gon' on an' drink mine," Silas said, overriding both Shep and McMillan.

"Ah," said the youngster. "We must do it together."

"I was gettin' sorta suspicious," Shep said, taking a cue from McMillan, "you sittin' here not drinkin."

"I had to tell the story with a clear mind. And, too, my age, sir."

"You older'n than this here stuff, ain'che?" Silas tee-hee'd.

The youngster sneezed. "Yessir."

The youngster dug in the pack and came out with a bottle.

McMillan became even more suspicious. "Whas in that bottle?"

The youngster held it up for inspection: "Champagne. Same as yours. And the others."

"I don't think so," McMillan retorted apprehensively.

The youngster hesitated for an instant, and then offered his bottle to Shep.

"I got m'own," said Shep innocently.

The youngster held the bottle up and then dipped it down to his lips, and then as if to allay suspicion, he offered the bottle to McMillan. McMillan took the bottle, held on to it for a moment, and then took a sampling.

"Same taste, huh?" said the youngster.

"McMillan, you done took a drink out'a that an' he done had his runny-nosed lips on it!" Silas burped.

McMillan gave the youngster a look—another suspicious look—and returned the bottle.

"Now, then, gentlemen, shall we?" the youngster said, fully extending his arm for a collective touch.

Silas was first. He waited for J. D.

"And you, sir?"

"I'm gettin' like McMillan. Somethin' ain't right," J. D. said.

"Aw, c'moan, J.; have a lil'," said Silas, passing him a second bottle. "We gon' take all th' stuff an' kick 'em out soon's we have this one."

J. D. accepted the second bottle and held out a weary arm: "An' be quick."

Silas hotly demanded: "Now, will you two please tell me wha'chew waitin' on?"

"I'm like J. D. I don't—"

"Y'ignant cuss, don'cha see where J. D.'s arm is?"

Silas then got two more bottles, unwrapped the rubber from around them, thumped them into the individual chests, got out, and yanked both of their arms out.

"My," said the youngster.

" 'My,' my rear end," said the impatient Silas. "Gwoan wit'cha toast so's we can toss y'tail outta here b'fore you have us all snifflin' an' coughin'."

The youngster extended his arm. "The importance of the visit rests not with the visitor but rather on the morrow. Let it not be said I have not taken you all to heart. Historians all! Flyin' when they ought'a be walkin'!"

"Don't know wha'cha sayin', boy, but sound's good t'me," Silas said.

The bottles clanked. They all drank. The youngster smacked his lips and cast a sly eye on them, and then he said to the wordless McMillan—and not so much in the form of a question, "Isn't it interesting how all fires ain't the same. In other words, how you can burn an' not be on fire, and how you can feel fire but don't see no flames."

The storekeep didn't get it. He didn't get it. And he didn't like it.

"Mighty fancy-tastin' stuff." J. D. brightened after another sampling.

"Mac, you ought'a order some. Say, lil' coony," Silas said, sneaking another swig. "Where'd you say y'got this from?"

"Sirs," said the youngster, tilting his chair forward to cut short the amenities. "Your cuddly lil' visitor would like to answer all you questions, but unfortunately his welcome has worn thin."

"An' so is my patience," said Silas.

The youngster smiled to himself and pocketed his note-book, his tiny dictionary, and snub-nosed pencil. "Too bad we didn't have no music," he said.

"Wha'chew doin'?"

"It's called repocketing the tools of the trade."

"How come you didn' do no writin'?"

"A good story is carried in the heart. Always."

"Wheeoo-hoo," blurted out the contradictory Silas. "Tol'ja th' nigs gotta lotta smarts."

"An' now I think it's high time th' nig gets outta here," J. D. said.

"I couldn't agree with you more," said the youngster.

"Well, then, get to steppin'."

"A question before I go—"

"Whas that lil' coony?"

The youngster moved to the door, turned, and looked at them individually. Many moments were spent before he said anything; it was as if he were hoping they had one more thing to say to him, something that he could carry with him, something that would last. For an additional moment he looked almost apologetic, and then he formed a question that would relieve him—and possibly free them.

"Gentlemen, on the story"—his voice, suppressing a cough, dropped with a penetrating sincerity—"if—if—if you had it to do all over again, would you do the same? Would you repeat history?"

"In a pair of quicks."

The one voice said it for all. The youngster lowered his head and thought about it. He thought, too, about the precious fluid that now lubricated their throats. He thanked them and walked closer to the door. He thought about the word he had thought about so often, and when he was on his way there: *deserving*. And then he said: "Gentlemen, earlier I used the word *deserving*. I want to be right. I want to be absolutely certain. You *would* create history all over

again? There is no question about it? I mean, in the story—
you were not as good as you could'a, and far worse than
you should'a. People died. Loves were lost. A life was ruined. The good was never allowed to grow. And that doesn't
concern you in the least?"

"Not in the slightest. An' you heard us th' first time."

"An' there is *no* question about it? You're sure? You'd
really burn down the—"

"How minny times do we haf'ta answer th' question?
We done tol't you what we'd do. An' if'n you don't get
outta here—an' get outta here quick, we might get started
sooner than you think."

"In other words, we might be forced inta doin' it agin."

"An' not be settin' no fires. Might even use that rope we
got out back—if'n you understan's what I mean," Silas
said.

The youngster placed a hand on the doorknob. "I understand you—fully. And I hope you understand me, as well—
and why I did what I did."

They drowsily looked at one another. "What'd you do?
Hey, git back here!"

J. D. echoed Silas: "Git back here. We ain't finished!"

"You finished," the youngster said quietly, and then
opened the door with equal quiet. "You finished. Boss man
said all y'all finished."

"An' wha's *that* s'posed to mean?"

"It means: You burnin'. Boss man said all y'all burnin'."

They turned to look. But it was too late. The youngster
had already stepped out into the drab, rain-swept chill. Outside, he stood in front of the door—the door that looked as
if it showed the pains of a hundred rusted nails and lost
himself in thought and no longer was there a fire down
below.

For some reason or another, the old-timers did not really
believe the strange young man with the odd manner and
strange dress had left them for good. Perhaps it was be-

cause he had departed without bedazzlement or the expected finality, or perhaps it was because of the vacancy he created. Whatever, Silas comforted himself in the chair and stretched a yawn.

"Boy—I said it b'fore, I'll say it agin—th' nig's crazy."

J. D. slumped. "See what he's up to, Mac."

And then they fell quiet. Soon sleep would come.

McMillan did not go to the window as requested by the head-nodding J. D. Instead, he reknitted his brow on the bottle, knowing something was wrong. He couldn't put a finger on it, but somehow, somewhere, something was definitely wrong, and damn-damn-damn if he could figure it out. He sent another look at the door, as if it held the secret. Nothing. He got up and thoughtfully circled the store, and still he could not come up with an answer. Returning to his seat around the stove, he picked up a bottle and quietly ran his index finger over and around the top. Aged eyesight had him straining to see the tiny white substance. He had seen it before—but where? Uneasy now, he looked at the bottle again and picked up another one for comparison. It was the same as his, powder and all.

Quietly, he got up again and inspected the other bottles. They were all the same—all except for the one used by the youngster. The words spun around in his mind again: "You finished. Boss man said . . ."

With the apron serving as a filter, the storekeep took a tiny sip.

Silas opened a slow eye: "Why'ya drinkin' out th' coonie's bottle, Mac?"

Saying nothing, McMillan nervously eased the bottle back down and sat. Now he was growing as anesthetized as the others, but the little beads that glistened on his forehead contradicted the feeling.

Eyes closed, Shep tossed out, "Wonda who he was?"

"I wonda *what* he was."

"Dunno," a sleep-ridden Silas added, "but he sure could

talk—yakity-yak-yak-yak. An' that's one thing I can't stand is a talker."

"An' talk'd jus' a lil' too much, if you ask me. An' notice how he chang'd?" J. D. said, starting to snore.

"I knows they all look alike, but he look'd a mite older'n 'leven. Don't cha think, Mac?"

"He smell'd a lil' younger. Wha'cha think, Mac?"

But the storekeep was in no mood to respond. The beads were growing larger on his forehead. His whole body had become clammy and sticky, and now the first tinge of heated pain swept through the insides. Was it his imagination—or was it something else. Some of the words hit him again: *"History . . . See the light . . . Came from Charlotte . . . Bird without wings . . . Told what I knew . . . All fires ain't the same—burn an' not be on fire—feel fire, don't see no flames . . . Not as good as you could'a, far worse than you should'a . . . Boss man said . . ."* They went on and on.

Thinking hard, the storekeep recalled that the youngster had strategically dropped the words in. He didn't just *say* them—he *delivered* them. Thinking back, it was like they had been rehearsed or something. Planned. It was like everything he did was calculated—done for effect, and the words, all the words had been connected to a theme, as if he had been trying to tell them something. Certainly there was a story. But, thought the bigger and more corpulent man of the group, there was a story within the story. Now something troubled him even more, something that had slipped by all of them. He said: "Loves were lost."

Whose loves?

The long-ago boy came to mind. Not that anyone cared, but the thrown-away assumption was that everyone had been destroyed by the fire. And then there was that matter with age. But this boy simply knew *too* much—too much to have just innocently drifted into the store. Where was he from? He said Charlotte. He said he worked on the governor's staff. In Charlotte? Workin' in Charlotte on the governor's staff? In the saloon that night in Fayetteville, Epps said the capital of North Carolina was in Raleigh. And he said he was how old? 'Leven. His job was what? Workin' in the tobacco-processin' plant. What th'hell does that mean? Nothin'. There ain't no such thing. Pure razzle-dazzle, meaning nothin'. What was that black gal's name again? Charlotte. An' it took him *nine* months to come from Charlotte? An' when he first came in, he said somethin' about music—voices; he wanted *"sump'um kinda nostalgic."* Archy used to make the slaves sing to him. What was that song? *"Go Down—"* And what was *his* name?

Trembling hard now, the storekeeper arose and went to the counter, and stood there for a moment. *"Finished . . . Fire . . . Burnin'."* He came back to the stove, sat, got up, and then circled the room. He sat again, and in a moment sent a freed hand crawling under the apron and to the stomach. The pain was growing now. Slowly he arose and went to the counter. He stood for a moment, and then went behind it.

Shep, fading fast, said, "Wha'cha lookin' for, Mac?"

Silas, fading faster, said, "Pr'bly tryin' to see if he's got any of this 'ported stuff in somma them ol' tins. Tee-hee."

"Gawd, I'm sleepy," J. D. said, "An' I'm b'ginnin' to feel a lil' heat on m'insides."

"Same . . ." Silas said.

"Burnin' an' bustin'," J. D. said.

"Bustin' an' burnin'," said Shep.

"Need sumpthin' t'cool me down," J. D. said, trying to come back to life.

"Need me one for th' road. Jus' one mo' lil' squeeze. Mac—pass me—pass me that—that—that—," Silas said, drifting away.

A moment, and Shep was gone, having said, "Don't know what 'tis, but my insides . . . m'insides . . ."

Silas came back to life for a sleep-induced " 'S burnin'. . . . burnin' real hot . . . need a lil' somethin' to put out th' fire . . ."

J. D. joined him. "An' I'm beginning t'feel a lil' stiff."

And fittingly, Silas had the last word: "Yew tew?"

Behind the counter, the impregnated silence of suspicion was thrown asunder by the search of frantic hands that scoured the shelves. Sandwiched between the rusted old cans, on the lower shelf, were the baking-powder-like boxes.

The words would not go away: *"You finished. Boss man said, all y'all finished. You burnin'. Boss man said, all y'all burning. You finished, Boss . . ."*

Trembling and sweating more now, the storekeeper's hand inched down and slowly removed one of the boxes.

"You finished. Boss man said, all y'all finished."

The eyes were fearful—afraid to look. Something commanded them, saying they had to look. Again the refrain—louder.

"You finished. Boss man said, all y'all finished."

Slowly, very slowly, the eyes focused in on the picture on the label: a skull and crossbones with bold lettering that chillingly denoted the contents—contents that he had so often used in poisoning the big rats that often dominated the store.

"You finished; you burnin'. You burnin'; you finished; you burnin'. . . . Boss man said . . ." The words were now pounding—out of sequence—but pounding all the same, louder and louder, echoing and reverberating: *"Boss man . . ."*

Slowly, clumsily, the box was opened.

"You finished. Boss man said all y'all burnin'.

Breathing spastically, the storekeep sent a sweating, trembling hand to pinch an ever so tiny amount of the substance. In rapid succession came the words: *"You finished. Boss man said all y'all finished. You burnin', boss man*

said all y'all burnin'. You finished. Boss man said . . ."
And then slowly, distantlike, as if summoned by the beyond, the words trailed away.

Only the storekeep's broken and halted breathing was left to cut the silence. Up to a shaky and dried-out tongue went the substance.

Moments, and then it came: "Oh! Oooooohhh! Ooooh, m-m-y-g-g-awddd! M-m-myygoddd! L-L-Lord, Jeeezusss!"

"What th' hell is it now, McMillan?"

McMillan would have liked to've responded. But he couldn't. The vocal cords constricted and the free flow of air was no more. He struggled. He was partially successful. He wanted desperately to say it louder, but he was able only to gasp—lowly at first. The second time he was a bit louder. The storekeep said, "We been—we been—we been p-p- poisoned."

The dead and dying heard him.

They never screamed louder.

twenty-three

IT WAS HOURS LATER. IN the store, as far as the youngster was concerned, everything that was supposed to happen had happened. He did not grade himself, he did not think about the story. He thought only of the results. It had been a long time in coming; it was an achievement—insufficient for the moment but an achievement nonetheless.

He did not get far. He was on the back stoop of the store, alone in the dark.

Night had descended on Red Springs and the old store with such a deadening finality that it seemed as if the whole of North Carolina had never seen the light of day. It seemed that the entire state was in some sort of deep, dark repose, as if she had never existed. It was as if 1729's royal colony never knew she was favored by mild winters, magnificent springs, posh summers, and autumns so noble and resplendent that they defied description. It was as if she, the young country's twelfth state, didn't know she could boast of dogwoods, great timberlands, sky-reaching hills—flatlands without end, and valleys as deep and as wondrous as any nature could provide; as if the state that had come so far was unaware of a mighty ocean that touched her borders, spawned rivers, and gave rise to a thousand lakes, that as far back as ten thousand years ago the state that had come so far had been the land of untold tribes of Indians who roamed until the white man came and gifted him with disease and enslavement, that she did not understand her soil was so rich and varied in agriculture that she came forth with the largest melons all the way down to the smallest of nuts and berries, that she produced the blackest of dirt and the whitest of sand, that she ranged with buffalo, whitetail deer, beavers, eagles, and all manner of beast, fish, and fowl; it was as if she were unknowing of tradition and history, that she played host to Columbus, and was there for DeSoto's journey, Raleigh's settlers, and opened her arms to Lafayette; or that in the new world—the first colony—she was home to the first child born, that she survived the French, Spanish, English, and Scots, that she faced a war between the states, showed allegiance to her neighbors, seceded from the Union, lost more men than any of her neighbors, came back, and gave the nation a president.

It is probable that the youngster thought of all of these things that night.

Often, over the years, when he found his mind receding back into a darkened and overly troubled past, he would seek refuge in history. If not North Carolina history, history of some sort—most of which was learned on his own, having been discouraged in the schools of Raleigh, Fayetteville, and Charlotte—cities he had heard of in his childhood. Raleigh had a special importance, he thought, in recalling Mr. Archy's words. The governor was there, and it was the state's capital, the seat of power. Raleigh, though, was not to be as Mr. Archy had said. The boy never saw the governor and the seat of power did not include all people, and the few blacks that did have a modicum of influence with the schools did not hurry to his aid. Beyond an unwillingness to talk about his past, and a seeming show of instability, he was told that he was too white to attend black schools and too black to attend white schools. The latter situation was not totally unexpected, owing to the poor but kindly couple in Rennert who had found him starving and mindlessly wandering those years ago. The couple that had nursed him back to good health and with whom he stayed on and off. They knew nothing of his past other than he was hurt and was the obvious offspring of mixed parentage. It mattered not to them. They loved him. They had love to give. Because of who they were, they were sensitive to the ways of the South, and, as he grew, they tried to brace him for the consequences of not being a "purebred." What they did not know was that had he been fully mindful of himself he would not have chosen to be purebred; he would not have chosen to be either this or that. He would have remembered the tenets of his past, and he would have been simply a boy with promise.

But the youngster was not mindful.

In the initial stages, and although they had problems of their own, the loving couple had hopes that the boy would grow and become theirs even though in their heart of hearts they knew they would not have been his choice. He was incapable of loving—of giving, of belonging. He was unattached. He was a silent and withdrawn child, and for a time they thought he was retarded. He was not at all playful, had no exuberance, and showed no youthful interest in anything. Satisfaction eluded him at every turn. He would pick at his food, avoid daylight, tremble at the sight of fire, and walk away at the sound of a person humming. Always he would want to be alone. Sometimes he would sit for hours, saying nothing, doing nothing, and showing signs of thinking nothing. Often, and it would be of no use to question him, he would disappear for days, and when he grew older, it stretched into weeks, then months, and eventually he left them for good. It was hurtful, but not totally unexpected. The signs were there. Even in the shortest of conversations his mind drifted, and he was back looking unrooted and restless. They knew he had to go, and that he was going soon. They knew all too well that whatever it was that dogged and churned and ate at him would never free him.

Still, with the boy's last disappearance, dangerously premature for a youngster of his age, and surely for a boy whose mind rendered him useless through the day and kicked and gnawed at him all through the night—still they were left to worry and wonder, and lastly hope that someday the torment would be somewhat eased, and that all the gifts and special qualities that undoubtedly lay deep inside him would come to the fore, and that he would eventually belong, and that he would find his rightful place in life rather than be the lost, wandering soul he appeared to be.

The couple did take full refuge in one thing though. They did not know where it came from, nor did they have a chance to question him. But unlike anyone they had ever seen—unlike anyone they were ever likely to encounter in life—he *knew* the Bible. The revelation came when they asked him about his name that last night. Incredibly, he walked them through the entire Book of Genesis. He did it quietly and without effort. But by morning he was gone. And quite tragically if, along the way, someone had asked him the race, creed, or nationality of the poor but blessed couple that had nursed and nourished and prolonged his life, he would not have known. He did not remember them.

After many false starts in Raleigh, and many more there in Fayetteville, and then back and forth to Charlotte, the youngster disappeared again, having remained in circulation only long enough to fully carry out the start of another promise—the one having to do with the bird without wings. Two years later he surfaced again—in a Philadelphia library. Books and libraries had become a way of life. His only way of life. He remained in the historic city for over a year and then he disappeared again.

*   *   *

TIME SPENT IN PHILADELPHIA ADDED greatly to the youngster's knowledge of black history. At any given moment he could talk about the first black that landed on these shores, the things invented and created by blacks, the wars they fought, the troubles they overcame. He could go back and recount all sorts of influences, from the biblical to the sub-Saharan, and still astound with his knowledge of black contributions to modern-day society. He did not limit himself. He thirsted after the enemies of blacks, studying their history with a particular avidity—from *The Night Riders* to *The Knights of The White Chameleons;* from the dreaded White League all the way down to an insecure little band of troublemakers called the KKK—but then, at every turn it seemed as if he would stop and silently knit his mind with the two questions that would never leave him: *why and how?* The two questions would not leap out at him; they would not yell or shout or come with a voraciousness or vindictiveness; rather, they would come with a calm and a certain kind of reserved solemnity. The precocious young mind would then steal back and land on a quote he had read somewhere, something having to do with "man's inhumanity to man." The mind would steal back a little bit further: Why does one man have power over another, it would quietly ask; how is it that he is able to rob; why can he render life meaningless—to cause the days to be so barren and vacant, to make an entire universe empty and forsaken? *How and why?*

There would be no answers to these themes because the mind, in the attempt to crawl back even further, would become lost in confusion. There were times when his mind shirked its duties and became a maze. Shaking visibly, back to the books he would go, restudying Nat Turner's life, the works of Fredrick Douglass, the cause of the thirteen whites and five blacks who lost their lives following the radical John Brown in his raid on Harpers' Ferry. The wonderful and courageous liberator Harriet Tubman should

have been his natural favorite. Almost in looks and in
deeds, she was the reincarnation of the only great lady in
his life. Oddly, he would not linger on the memory. Brazil,
second only to the United States in holding slaves, was
studied. He moved on to Garrison's *Liberator,* and reread
the minutes of the abolitionist's convention at the anthe-
nium in Nantucket. Still unsated, he lost himself in the
Emancipation Proclamation and then in Lincoln's attitude
toward war and the troubled president's reluctance toward
ending slavery. The 1857 Supreme Court's decision deny-
ing Dred Scott the rights of the common man caught his
eye, but then, so did 1870's fifteenth Amendment to the
Constitution, granting the right to vote to all people. The
election of blacks to Congress held a modicum of interest,
as did the rising tide of getting the blacks out of Washington, but his concentration was fading and the two questions
allied with a long-ago plan, and together they pushed their
way forward and established unmoving dominance. He
knew, at last, that in all his travels and all his learnings,
nothing would erase a memory—nothing would change the
call.

It was this that brought the young man back to North
Carolina. It was this that brought him back to Red Springs.

Now it was midnight. The rain had stopped, but the Red
Springs air was still heavy with moisture. His suit, which
had not completely dried in the store, was back with that
wet heaviness. The frail young man was coughing more
and more, and it seemed that the dampness had penetrated
his skin and pained his ribs to such an extent that it slowed
movement. He was tired, very tired. In truth, he was lethar-
gic. He could not remember the last time he had slept. He
could not remember even being in a bed; he could not remember eating. He could not remember a number of things,
but he remembered his Red Springs past. He was there, and
save for the end, that was all he wanted.

Seconds later, he was coughing again. He needed

warmth. Silas, although he did not know what he was talking about at the time, had said something earlier about pneumonia. It registered with the youngster, but then—as now—he fought hard against the implications and, in that direction, would not permit his mind to think about anything but the immediate, or anything else that could possibly deter him from the completion of a task that was all too long in coming.

Hours later he was still on the stoop and he was even colder. He was not feeling well. The stove inside, although it was dying, too, could have provided relief, but he would not give it a second thought, nor would he give a second thought to the old-timers that had—and still—surrounded it. He had heard their final screams earlier, and, as now, he did nothing but lay there, unmoving, curled against the cold on the back step of the old store, eyes open, holding on to the envelope and shivering in the dark. Their mule was there, and next to the mule was the rope, enough rope to fashion a pulley that would enable him to retrieve the packs that went down with the mule, Tess. He had neglected to thank the old-timers for the mule and rope and wondered if his two would have approved. He started coughing again. Not a good sign for anyone who had to go underwater again. A minimum of three times, he thought, grossly underestimating the difficulty of the task. But no matter how difficult, no matter how many times, no matter how deep the pain, he would not be stopped.

He lay curled on the stoop in the one position for hours more. Breathing became difficult.

The pitch-black darkness reminded him of where his mind had been for the better part of his young life. Trying to fall asleep on the hard stoop reminded him of the boxcars and freight trains he had hitched going to and coming from historic Philadelphia. But here on the wet back stoop, here was a major difference. There was no rumble, no rocking or creaking, no forlorn cry of the whistle, no belch-

ing of the big smokestacks, and no fear of being caught and
thrown off the rumbling iron horse by the railroad men o
space-hungry hoboes. Here there was only a Red Spring
silence, amplified by the dead inside.

Unable to rest mind or body, he got up.

He would locate the bend in the dark.

Finding the bend where he had left the three bulky and
almost unmanageable packs in the dead of night was no
easy task, but he did it. Daybreak found the youngster stil
hard at work. It was backbreaking. He thought about slav
ery. Theirs was backbreaking. Theirs were without reason
He had reason, and that reason—that goal, that objective
that can't-go-on-living-without-aim—pushed him al
through the night. He stopped for nothing, and the obstinat
packs embedded in the thick mud below, along with an un
cooperative rope tied to an equally uncooperative old mul
that slipped, slid, and hawed on the muddied bank, mad
the chore all the worse. It was an effort that would hav
stopped the average man. But the youngster struggled, and
sheer determination prevailed—one by one, they fought
One by one they surrendered. Wet, tired, coughing, and
paining even more now, he did not stop to get a moment'
rest. He did not stop to feel good about the accomplish
ments, nor did he make the slightest attempt to dry himself
Feverishly, he continued to work. When the last pack wa
secured to the mule, he picked up the envelope and "gee
hawed" the animal back in the direction of Red Springs.

Forty minutes later, mud-drudging and slowed by th
sheer weight of the packs, the determined young man le
the recalcitrant mule on. Later, and still without stopping
they veered off the main road and set sight on the long roa
that should have brought back a thousand memories. It wa
the road that led to where the plantation had stood, and, at
distance, to the right, across a smaller road, was where th
shack had stood.

The youngster's eyes would go in neither direction. It i

unknown what he thought when he passed the area, but he did hesitate for a moment. Midway through the tall, lifeless weeds where he was clearing a path, he made a full stop. He looked up at the sky. The clouds were not the same.

Soon they were at the creek. It was not as far away—it was not as big and wondrous as he remembered. The water did not rush to points unknown, and it did not glisten and sparkle and wink with the goodness of a friend passing by. Still it was good to be there. He was educated now—worldly, clever. He was still a child but grown. The best of childhood memories came back. Good and warm and wonderful memories they were. He did not want to do it, but he allowed himself to think of how much the creek had changed.

That little bit of heaven that he knew so well as a child now trickled listlessly and slimed under dark, cold clouds. Instead of a course that gracefully turned and flowed on, hard rocks crooked a path, rose up, and claimed predominance. No longer was this the place where even the mud was soft and gentle and would ooze through the toes and tickle the imagination. There were no pebbles, there were only rocks, and even they were ringed by hard-walled stems of bamboo and other wild, tall-growing plant life that dotted along and swept up the bemired banks and stood like angered sentries. Away from them, thick clumps of berry bushes, weeds, and thickets mapped traversing courses and blotted out all traces of the past. Except for the insects, fowl, and rodents, and the slow-moving wind, it looked as if it had been stilled into oblivion. But it was fitting that he was there, fitting that even though Tess could not be there, the burdensome packs had been carried by their mule.

With a thud the three heavy packs slid from the animal's back and hit the ground. Reverently, he unwrapped them and labored them into position. When it was over, he stood for a long while, never once permitting his eyes to wander in the directions of where either house had stood. Somberly the eyes remained on the job at hand, and while working, he remembered all the joys he had known there. But most of all he remembered his uncle Ben, and Mr. Archy, and the all-too-brief moments with a woman called Sweet Elsie Pratt.

Though the tuxedo was again soggy-wet and muddied, it did not seem out of place. He was no longer circus-looking. There was a quiet dignity around him. When he finished, although weakened by fever, he knelt down and removed his derby. He placed it across his heart and closed his eyes in silent prayer. He remained kneeling for a moment, and then he reached inside his jacket pocket and carefully placed the envelope down—and just a little to the right he placed a Bible.

He stood again. He smiled warmly.

The deed's done, the moment over, it was time to leave Red Springs, North Carolina, never to return.

He was coughing heavier.

He waved farewell to the stones. He did not look back.

The envelope contained his writing. It read:

Dear Uncle Benny,

I am writing to tell you that I met with them. I told them a tale that was dear long ago. I told them about you, about us. I spoke to them, too, about freedom and purity, innocence lost, promises unfulfilled. But mostly, Uncle Benny, I told them about a time and a place where once there were row upon row of sky-nodding corn; where once one raced the fields and chased the winds—and embraced all the joys of living; where once the clouds, like the roads to the imagination, were free and clean and pillowy—and all the coming days of my yesteryears were to be filled with hope, magic, and promise. Those days were never to be, Uncle Benny. We were all shortened. But the wickedness of a cruel and heartless people could not take away everything. They could not take away that which I will always remember, nor could they dim the memory of three people I will always love, always cherish. Bye, sir.

And goodbye to you, Mr. Archy. And thank you, sir. Thank you. . . .

Oh, and, Archy? I hope you forgive me if I say over the years I've been too disturbed to use all of my mind. But, sir, there was a special occasion. I gussied up, and I think I was clever. I did my best—at least I tried to. And I know I've made a contribution to North Carolina. The Red Springs weeds are all gone now. And they were killed with kindness.

Bye, Sweet Elsie Pratt, I did not know you well. But I knew you enough to love you. Rest well.

All of you, rest well, I will see you soon.

The letter was center base of the three newly placed headstones that even before he left were being enshrouded by a chilled morning mist that took its time rising up and over an embankment where once there was a creek.

And so on a morning that had not quite decided whether to sparkle with brilliance or bestow its grayness, the boy pushed up a dampened collar and moved on. His movements were slow. Very slow.

He did not have the mule.

He was all alone.